The World's Classics

CCCCIX
THE TRUMPET
IN THE DUST

THE TRUMPET
IN THE DUST

By

CONSTANCE HOLME

The World's Classics

Geoffrey Cumberlege
OXFORD UNIVERSITY PRESS
London New York Toronto

'The Trumpet in the Dust' was first published in 1921. It was first included in 'The World's Classics' in 1933, and was reprinted in 1934, 1935, 1936, 1944 and 1949.

SET IN GREAT BRITAIN AT THE UNIVERSITY PRESS, OXFORD
AND PRINTED BY PAGE BROS. (NORWICH) LTD.

To

LORD HENRY BENTINCK
THIS WEED
FROM
AN UNCULTIVATED GARDEN

CONTENTS

I WAS on my way to the temple with my evening offerings,
Seeking for the heaven of rest after the day's dusty toil;
Hoping my hurts would be healed and stains in my
    garment washed white,
When I found thy trumpet lying in the dust.

Has it not been the time for me to light my lamp?
Has my evening not come to bring me sleep?
O, thou blood-red rose, where have my poppies faded?
I was certain my wanderings were over and my debts all
    paid
When suddenly I came upon thy trumpet lying in the dust.

    .   .   .   .   .   .

From thee I had asked peace only to find shame.
Now I stand before thee—help me to don my armour!
Let hard blows of trouble strike fire into my life.
Let my heart beat in pain—beating the drum of thy victory.
My hands shall be utterly emptied to take up thy trumpet.

The Trumpet—RABINDRANATH TAGORE.

PART I

REWARD OF BATTLE

CHAPTER I

Mrs. Clapham got up on that fine September morning like some king of the East going forth to Bethlehem. She awoke with a heady sense of excitement and power; not wearily, and with a dulled brain, as she so often did now that she was beginning to grow old, but with vivid perceptions and a throbbing heart. First of all, opening her eyes on the sunny square of her little window, she was conscious of actual enrichment, as if the sunshine itself were a tangible personal gift. To the pleasure of this was added the happy anticipation of something not yet quite within reach, thrilling her nerves as they had not been thrilled for years. Then, as the thought of what the day might possibly bring flashed upon her in full force, she warmed from head to foot in a passion of exultation, wonder, and grateful joy.

She started up presently to peer at the little clock by the bedside, and then remembered that she had no engagement, and sank back happily. Had not the Vicar's wife called, only the evening before, to inform her that she would not want her to-day? Mrs. Clapham chuckled as she lay in bed, telling herself that if Mrs. Wrench did not have her to-day, in all probability she would never have her again at all.

Mrs. Wrench, she remembered now, had been called to London to her daughter's wedding, one of those nowadays weddings which could only be called catching a bird on the wing—snapping up a sailor when he was a few days in port, or a soldier when the War Office happened to take its eye off him for a couple of minutes. The actual war was over, of course, but the war weddings still continued. In Mrs.

Clapham's young days weddings were things which took years to come to their full conclusion, slowly ripening to their end like mellowing cheeses or maturing port. The weddings of these days seemed to her like hastily-tossed pancakes by comparison; half-cooked efforts which had only a poor choice at the best between the frying-pan and the fire.

She was pleased for Miss Marigold, however, that she had succeeded in catching her bird at last. It was just as well not to waste any time, seeing how long she had been about it. Why, she was the same age as Mrs. Clapham's daughter Tibbie, who had been married these last eight years, and a widow for going on two! Mrs. Clapham experienced the conscious superiority of the mother whose daughter has long since been disposed of, in no matter what unfortunate circumstances. She had always been perfectly convinced that the Vicar's wife was jealous because Tibbie had got off first, and had even rallied her about it in her jolly, good-tempered fashion. Now, however, Miss Marigold had suddenly seen her way towards making things even, and Mrs. Wrench had rushed off in a fluster to see her do it.

Looking in, the evening before, in order to deliver her message, she had been so full of the impending change in Miss Marigold's life that she had quite forgotten the impending change in Mrs. Clapham's. Seated in the arm-chair that had been made by the long-departed Jonty Clapham, she had talked excitedly of her daughter in the Government office, who would be snatched out of it, pen in hand, so to speak, to be married to a bridegroom who, metaphorically, would still have one foot on his ship. She had also wept a little in the way that women and mothers have, and Mrs. Clapham, whose own tears over a daughter's bridal had been shed so many superior years before, had consoled her with words of sympathy and wisdom, and her well-known kindly laugh. Presently, Mrs.

Wrench had dried her tears and begun to tell her about her daughter's frocks, and Mrs. Clapham, whose Tibbie happened to be a dressmaker by profession, was able to shine a second time as a qualified judge. But never once during the conversation had she as much as hinted at her own bright hope which was so near its wonderful fulfilment. She had just allowed Mrs. Wrench to babble happily on, and kept her own thoughts hugged to herself where they lay so snug and warm.

Not even when Mrs. Wrench had risen at last to go had she referred to any possible alteration in her own affairs. She had merely sent her love and respects to the bride, and the bride's mother had promised to come and tell her about the wedding. 'And of course next week as usual, please!' she had said as she hurried away, and the charwoman had said neither yea nor nay, but had merely dropped her old-fashioned curtsey. It was no use reminding the Vicar's wife that, by the time next week came round, things might have become anything but 'usual'. There was always the possibility, too, that it might be unlucky, with the whole entrancing affair still hanging breathlessly in the balance. So she had let her go away without even dropping a hint of her personal prospects, and it was only after the door was shut that she had allowed herself to smile. Then she had begun to chuckle and chuckle, and sat down and chuckled, and stood up and chuckled, and sat down again and chuckled and chuckled and chuckled *and* chuckled. . . .

She chuckled afresh now as she lay thinking, and then reflected that it might possibly be as unlucky as singing too early, and therefore desisted. It occurred to her also that she might be tempting Providence by lying in bed, behaving, as it were, as if the decree which would set her free to lie in bed had actually been spoken; and, sitting up in a flurry, she threw off the bed-clothes and began to dress. It was more than

probable that she would have as much bed as anybody could want, in the near future. She who had
always been an exceptionally early riser need not
grudge an exhibition of the accomplishment on this
possibly last day.

The boards creaked under her feet as she stirred
about the cottage bedroom, moving cleverly in the
limited space and under the sloping ceiling. She had
always been a big woman, coming of big, upstanding
stock, and now at sixty-five she was stout as well. To
all outward appearance, though, she was strong and
sound, and it was only lately that her comely pink face
had begun its network of fine lines. Always as neat as
a new pin, to-day she took greater pains than usual
over dressing, giving an extra polish to her healthy skin
and an extra shine to her white hair. The day which
was bringing her so much—as she serenely hoped—
could not be encountered in any other spirit. She
looked at herself in the glass when she had finished,
and was glad to see that she stood her age so well. Her
hands alone troubled her—those toil-worn, charwoman's hands which spoke so clearly of her profession. Not that she was ashamed of her work—on the
contrary, she was proud—but in that moment of
personal satisfaction she was ashamed of her hands.

She turned away at last, and creaked across the
boards to the stairs, full of that pleasant consciousness
of sound health and of coming good. She forgot that
lately she had begun to feel old, that she had had
doubts about her heart, and that the knee which she
had damaged years ago on Mrs. Fletcher's stairs was
often too painful to let her sleep. She forgot that there
had been a day—not so long ago, either—when she
had suddenly found herself coming home thoroughly
tired out, not only in body, but in mind. The spirit
had gone clean out of her for the time being. She had
wondered, indeed, whether she would ever be able to
persuade herself to enter other people's houses again,

so utterly weary was she of their unvarying routine, their anything but unvarying servants, their dull furniture and their duller meals. She had even felt a spasm of real hatred for the houses themselves, which, no matter how often or how thoroughly she scrubbed them from roof to floor, were always waiting for her to come and scrub them again.

That unexpected break-down of hers had lasted at least twenty-four hours. The following morning she had actually refused to go to Mrs. Hogg, whose dwelling at any time was never one of those that she liked best. She had sent back word at the last minute—an unforgivable crime in her scrupulous code—and had sat indoors all day brooding and doing nothing. Towards evening she had had a vision of herself as a helpless old woman, and then she had broken down and wept; but next day her courage had come surging back, and next week as usual she had gone to Mrs. Hogg. Her work was as good as ever it had been, and outsiders had seen no difference. Nevertheless, there *was* a difference, as she knew very well. That day had marked the point at which she had begun definitely to grow old. From that day she realised that she had been scarred by the battle of life, and that before very long she must seek some haven to be healed.

This morning, however, sadness and doubt were gone from her mind as if they had never been. She went downstairs briskly, carrying the little clock, and set to work at her usual tasks with the zest of a young lass. Her knee did not pain her when she knelt to light the kitchen fire; her heart did not trouble her when she filled the bucket at the pump. She moved from one room to another as lightly as in the days when she had been a well-known local dancer, steady and untiring on her feet. She had never felt stronger or more fit for her life's work than on the morning of the day which was to see her bid that work farewell.

The very day itself seemed to know that something

uncommon was afoot, drawing by slow degrees to some poised and perfect hour. It was one of those days which are at the same time sharply etched and yet soft in tone, with their vivid colours as smooth as if seen through water or in a glass. In the village street, where the pillars of smoke were not yet set on their stacks, the low cottage-rows had clear black shadows under their eaves, and clear black edges along their roofs. The flag-staff on the church-tower was like a needle poised in a steady hand, and the tower itself was not so much built as flung by a brush on the gilded air. Below the dropping, curving street and the painted church the river was shedding its sheath of steel, ready for drawing on the faint-coloured robe that it would wear during the day. And always the hills to the west were growing in beauty with bracken and bent, the warm tones of turning trees, the fine sharp blue of stone, and the heather that seemed to keep all day long the colours of sunrise over the sea.

But in Mrs. Clapham's heart this morning there was so much beauty already that she scarcely heeded the extra loveliness of the outside world. She was glad, of course, that it was going to be fine, because life altogether was easier when it was fine. She was glad that the sun greeted her when she came down, splashing about the little kitchen that was always so greedy of its light, catching at it in the morning before it was well in the sky, and through the scullery door at the back snatching the last beam from the fading west. She opened the scullery door now, not only for a sight of the Michaelmas daisies bunched in the garden beyond, but because of the extra space it seemed to afford the exultation in her heart. As she went to and fro, her eyes drew to them as to flowers set upon some altar of thanksgiving, and the glow in her heart deepened as she passed through the warm sun. But the beauty of the day seemed only a natural background for the miracle that was coming. She trusted it contentedly, just as she was trusting other things in life. It was not one of those days of exquisite promise which languished and faded before it was noon. The perfect day was perfect and reliable all through, just as the perfect happenings of life went steadily to their appointed end. . . .

She thought of Miss Marigold again while she forced herself to eat her breakfast, difficult as she found it to sit still because of the tremor in her nerves. The Vicar's daughter would make a handsome bride, she said to herself, though no power on earth could make her a young one. She would look clever and nice and rather fine, but not the sweet little bundle of youth that Tibbie had looked. But then Tibbie had always had the pull in the matter of looks, even although Miss Marigold might be supposed to have scored in the matter of brains. Even that point, however, so Mrs. Clapham considered, was open to dispute. Tibbie, rosy and laughing and fair, and looking as though she hadn't a care in the world, had been clever enough in her own way. It was real shrewdness of character which had led her to choose for a husband the tamest youth in the place, whom everybody knew now to have been a hero in disguise. And she was so clever with her fingers that each one of them was worth at least the whole of another person's hand. Young as she was, she had been the village dressmaker *par excellence* before she married Stephen Catterall, and Mrs. Clapham's memories of Tibbie's youth were always shot through by the colours in which she had worked. Her bright head, gleaming about the cottage, had always a background of coloured cottons and silks. Mrs. Clapham's own best gown, still 'best' after years of wearing, had been also of Tibbie's making. Her heart leaped and her nerves thrilled as she told herself that, if things happened as she expected, she would crown the occasion by appearing in it to-day. . . .

Tibbie had even made gowns for Miss Marigold and

Mrs. Wrench, and she had actually been commissioned to make a frock for Miss Marigold's trousseau. That had been part of the information proceeding so copiously from the Vicar's wife, the evening before.

'It's a pale blue *crêpe de chine*, Mrs. Clapham,' Mrs. Wrench had said, 'and Marigold writes that she's quite delighted with it. Tibbie was always so dainty in everything she did, and Marigold wanted a frock from her for the sake of old times. It's the sort of frock that would have suited Tibbie herself, from the description. I remember she always looked pretty in pale blue.'

Mrs. Clapham had remembered it, too, throwing a glance at the photograph of the young widow, framed on a shelf near. The sober colours of life were Tibbie's wear now; not the delicate shades of youth making ready to be a bride. Yet the face looking out of the picture was neither bitter nor sad; thinner, perhaps, and deepened in shadow and meaning, but laughing and valiant as of old. Tibbie's husband had gone down in the War, together with many another lad whom Mrs. Clapham had first seen as a much bewrapped bundle in his mother's arms; but Tibbie's spirit had not gone down with him. By that time she had made for herself a nice little dressmaking business in Whalley, where she had lived since her marriage, and when Stephen was dead she continued to carry it on. Mrs. Clapham, of course, had wanted her to come home, but Tibbie and her two children were very comfortable in their little house, and there were the clients to think of, as well as other reasons. She, on her side, had wanted her mother to join her in Whalley, but Mrs. Clapham, too, had had her reasons for staying where fortune had happened to place her. She thought of those reasons now as she finished her breakfast—and chuckled; and took her last drink of tea and chuckled and chuckled and chuckled *and* chuckled. . . .

It was strange how full her mind was this morning of Tibbie and Tibbie's doings; not that the girl and her children were ever far from the old woman's thoughts. Probably it was Miss Marigold's wedding that was making her think of her own lass, and of the way life fuses and separates and alters and breaks. With what mixed smiles and tears must Tibbie have fashioned that gown for the Vicar's daughter, feeling a hundred years older in experience, although born on the same day! She knew something of Tibbie's feelings as she sewed at the blue gown, because Mrs. Wrench had told her that she had written a letter.

'Such a nice letter it was, Mrs. Clapham! Marigold was so pleased. But Tibbie always had such nice ways . . . you brought her up so well. She said she hoped Marigold would have better luck than hers, though she couldn't have a better happiness while it had lasted. . . . As a matter of fact, she ran the *crêpe de chine* rather late, though she didn't say why. Marigold was really getting rather anxious about it, but in the end it turned up all right.'

'Nay, Tibbie'd never fail nobody,' Mrs. Clapham had said, though rather absently, wishing herself alone so that she might sit and chuckle over the happiness that was coming.

'Nor you, either!' (Thank goodness she was getting to her feet at last!) 'I've never known you send me back word yet, and I don't think you ever will.' (Incredible as it seemed, she was out of the door and in the road.) 'Very well, then, good night; and I'll expect you as usual next week!'

Yes, it must be Miss Marigold's wedding that was making her think of the absent Tibbie, thinking so vividly that instead of absent she was very much present. In the little room where the sun kept pushing its way she seemed almost there in the flesh, catching and reflecting the light with her shimmering scissors and silks. The children, too, seemed unaccountably near, so that she felt as if at any moment she might hear their gentle if chattering voices and their sober if pattering feet. Their postcard photographs were on the shelf with that of their mother, seven-year-old Libby and five-year-old Stevie—stiff, grave, patient little people, who looked as if they couldn't possibly belong to laughing Tibbie. Those who noticed the difference said that they looked as though they had been born protesting against the sorrows of a great war, but those who had known their father and their father's mother said something else. It was from Stephen Catterall that they inherited their pale, haunted faces and their mournful dark eyes. When Stephen was killed, they said in Whalley that he had always looked as though the hand of death was never far from his tragic face, but those who had known him as a child knew it was never a little thing like death that had made Stephen afraid. . . .

Mrs. Clapham had once been to Whalley to pay her daughter a visit, and once Tibbie and the children had come to Mrs. Clapham, but on neither side had the visit been repeated. One had her charing to think of, and the other her sewing, and both had their other supremely important reasons. . . . But the result of the separation was that Mrs. Clapham knew very little about Tibbie's children, except what she was able to learn from Tibbie's letters. She was fond of them as far as she did know them, and of course proud, but she was always a little puzzled about them, a little uneasy. They were so very unlike what Tibbie had been, or Tibbie's uncles and aunts; so very unlike what Mrs. Clapham had been herself. But there was no reason to worry about them or their mother, as she knew, seeing that they were comfortably off, and had plenty of neighbours and friends. If it had not been for that, she could never have felt this satisfaction in the change which, other individuals being willing, she was shortly proposing to make. She would have been afraid that, as soon as the home was broken up, Tibbie and Co. might possibly want to come back. But there was no chance of such a thing as long as certain circumstances existed; Tibbie would never come. She fretted for her mother sometimes, just as her mother fretted for her, but, as long as a certain person remained alive, Tibbie would never come.

In all the history of mankind there could never have been anybody more free than Mrs. Clapham to take what her heart desired, and just at the moment when it was most accessible to her reach. All the ties and burdens of life seemed to fall away from her as she sat waiting there, looking for the news that was certain to come, with the happy expectancy of a trustful child. It was only when things were *meant* that they fell out so perfectly at the right time, flowing naturally to their end as the day flows into night. It was only then that they were accomplished without hitch or jar (unless you chose to consider Martha Jane a sort of jar). Everybody's hand seemed to stretch out to give you your wish when it came at the right time, and this seemed in every respect the perfectly right time. It had come, too, when she was old and weary enough really to appreciate it, and yet not too old and weary to care. She could say to herself that she had fought an honourable battle with life, and was now at liberty to seek her ease. She could say to herself with pride and as often as she liked that she had won her almshouse on Hermitage Hill.

Even by the fields the almshouses were at least a mile away from her little cottage, but in Mrs. Clapham's mind they showed as clearly as in a picture hung on the wall. Grey, gabled, flower-gardened, they topped the steep hill that ran up out of the village on the great north road, challenging by their perfection the notice of the passer-by. From them you looked down over grassy slopes to the roofs of the village, the long shape of the Hall against its wooded hill, and farther across still to the mystery of the sea. Unscamped and well-built in every inch, they were growing more aristocratic and mellow with every year that passed. The change to them from the uneven-floored, crooked-walled cottage in which Mrs. Clapham had lived so long would be, when it came, like the change to a king's palace. To have a roof of her own, with nothing to pay for it, nothing to fear, would make her feel little less of a property-owner than his lordship himself. Moving up to that high place from the huddled and crouching street would be like soaring on strong wings into the open spaces of the sky.

All through her working life she had hoped that she might be allowed to end her days in one of the alms-houses on Hermitage Hill. Especially she had wanted the house with the double view, the one that faced alike the humanity of the road and the miracle of the sea. Over and over again she had seen it fall vacant, and pass into fresh hands, but she had never attempted to ask for it until now. Never until now had she considered that she had a right to apply. She was the true type of worker, hardy, honest, and proud, and both her pride and her sense of honour had kept her from taking her rest before it was due. But she had always hoped that fate and the governors would see fit to make her this particular gift when at last she had really earned it; and not only had she hoped—she had also believed. She had always felt certain that, sooner or later, the house of her dreams would come her way. She had seen it as the natural apex of her mounting years, clear as a temple set on a hill. All her life it had cheered her and urged her on, standing alike to her as a symbol and the concrete object of her desire.

She had had her anxious moments, of course—moments when she had been hard put to it not to apply before it was time. Terrible qualms had seized upon her whenever a new tenant had taken possession of the corner house, terrible fears that she might outlive her in the comfort and peace. She had resisted temptation, however, in spite of her fears, and now she was being repaid. Most of the tenants had died obligingly quite soon, so that she had learned to believe that they would continue to die when she really needed it. And Mrs. Phipps *had* died, poor soul, thoughtfully and uncomplainingly, just at the time when Mrs. Clapham was beginning to fail. That, together with the fact that she had known and liked Mrs. Phipps, made the whole thing seem more than ever as if it was 'meant'. She would not have cared to follow just anybody in the corner house, but she was quite contented to follow Mrs. Phipps.

Yet she had not made up her mind all at once, even after Mrs. Phipps had so tactfully made room. Even then she had gone into the matter very carefully, testing her motives and her strength, and making sure, above all, that she was loosing no natural ties. But her final conclusion had been that the moment had actually come; and so, weeping even while she rejoiced, and trembling while she believed, she had sent in her name to the committee with a fine certainty of success.

There was not a soul in the place but would speak well of her, she knew; everybody, that is, whose testimony really counted. Hers was, in fact, that peculiar position which perhaps only the poor can ever achieve, dependent as it is upon character alone. Then, too, the very man who had built the almshouses had promised her one of them long ago. He was a rich Lancashire brewer, with a gruff manner and a generous heart, and Ann Clapham had been a servant in his Westmorland shooting-box before she married. 'Jones,' he had said to her one day—(she was Ann Atkinson just then, but he called the whole of his household 'Jones')—'if ever you want one of those houses of mine, you're to be sure to have it. I'll be dead then, of course . . . can't live for ever . . . but there'll be a committee. No d—d good, probably, but it's the best I can do. Tell 'em from me, Jones, that you're to have a house; and tell 'em from me, Jones, that you're a d—d good sort. . . .'

And now, after all these years, 'Jones' had at last repeated the millionaire brewer's words, and so realistically that nobody who had known the old man could refuse to believe them. Not but what she had earned the house right enough on her own merits, as she did not need telling; still, it was all to the good to be backed by old Mr. T. There were other candidates, however, so that a meeting had to be called, though she was assured time and again that it would only be formal. But when she came to her final canvassing for votes, she found that at least one of the other applicants had been in before her. Times had changed even in that remote little village, and it was not everybody now who remembered old Mr. T. Nevertheless, it had been a decided shock to her to find that her most important opponent was Martha Jane Fell.

Martha Jane was a neighbour of Mrs. Clapham's, living just up the street, and Mrs. Clapham knew all about her. Younger than her rival by a good many years, Martha Jane had been very pretty as a girl, and even now had a decided 'way' with her. It was a 'way', at least, that always went down with the men, and in pursuance of this particular piece of good fortune she had canvassed the men on the committee first. Mrs. Clapham could not help feeling it a distinct outrage that her most dangerous obstacle should take the form of this peculiarly worthless woman. Her own value seemed somehow to be lessened by it, her own virtue maligned. But then men, she remarked to herself scornfully, were always like wax in the hands of a woman like that. One of her own sex would have had her doubts any day about Martha Jane Fell.

The decisive meeting had been held the day before in the school, and Mrs. Clapham, scrubbing and scouring at Mrs. Helme's, had found it a terrible business to keep her mind on her task. More than once she had found herself on the verge of missing corners or stairs, neglecting to put the final polish on chair-legs, or 'slaping floors over' that needed elbow-grease and goodwill. But always she had checked herself with a feeling of shame. It seemed to her not only unlucky but dishonest to count herself free before the chains were loosed. In fact, in the access of zeal following upon her momentary lapse, she was almost sure that she did the same job twice.

Afterwards, indeed, she had allowed herself to come home by the school, though she had passed it without even turning her head, and scarcely so much as straining her ears for a murmur of voices from inside. Martha Jane, however, had no such scruples, as she discovered when she turned the corner. Martha Jane, indeed, was planted brazenly on the doorstep, applying ear and eye in turn to the open keyhole. Not only that—so Mrs. Clapham was told later—but she waylaid the members of the committee as they came in, reminding her allies of their promised support, and attempting to soften the hearts of the rest. She looked slightly abashed for a moment when she saw her opponent, and then gave her a wink and grinned impudently.

'Like to have a peep?' she inquired generously, moving to one side. 'There's nine on 'em sitting in a bunch, and all as solemn as a row of hens! His lord-ship's been pressing 'em to give it to me, and right touching he was an' all. Says I'm one o' them delicate folk for whom life is over-strong!' She winked again. 'I doubt none o' your gentry'll be saying that for *you!*'

Twisted towards her on the step, she looked with a sort of mocking good-humour at the stalwart, motherly woman with the honest face. There was still something of the street-arab about Martha Jane Fell, something that, as it were, turned cart-wheels in even the most sacred presence. But her most dangerous quality was a capacity for passing at will from brazenness to appeal, for seeming to cling even while she defied. Martha Jane could wilt like a weed or spring like a steel trap. She was worn, reckless, and down-at-heel, but she had contrived nevertheless to keep something of the grace of youth, a slimness of form, a fineness of skin, a faint beauty of cheek and chin. Only her eyes betrayed her under her untidy hair, hard even as they laughed at the well-bound figure before them.

After that moment's hesitation, Mrs. Clapham made as if to pass on, but Martha Jane, swinging round again to the keyhole, called her back.

'They're talking about you now,' she informed her kindly, 'saying you're a credit to the village and all that! But they say you've a daughter to see to you in your old age, and I haven't. You'll have to get rid of yon daughter o' yours, Ann Clapham, if you want to best me over the house!'

She spared another second from the keyhole to throw her a fresh impudent glance, but her fellow-candidate did not answer. Turning resolutely away, she marched steadily towards the hill, wishing in every nerve that she could demean herself to stand in Martha Jane's place. She hadn't gone far, however, taking the hill slowly because of her heart, when the school-door had suddenly opened, and, as it were, flung the committee into the road. One or two of them had hurriedly passed her, smiling as they went, and the parson had thrown her a pleasant greeting and lifted his hat. They couldn't have looked at her like that, she told herself triumphantly, if they hadn't given her the house; and the heart about which there was just a little doubt became so thrilled that it threatened to drop her down in a dead faint.

All the evening she had looked for a letter, knowing all the time that it was too early to expect it, and

rebuking herself for impatience and greed. But it had
not come, in spite of her hopes, and nobody she saw
seemed to have the faintest notion of what had
happened. Anyhow, she was sure that there would be
a letter this morning, either by post or hand; or,
instead of a letter, a personal message. She was as
certain about it as she was certain of Heaven. It was
only a question of waiting until the manna should
choose to fall.

Over the muslin half-blind masking the little
window, she saw a telegraph-boy come riding up,
wriggling his bicycle from side to side of the road after
his usual fashion; and, as on the day before, her heart
jumped so that her breath caught and her eyes blurred.
Just for a moment she wondered wildly whether they
could possibly have telegraphed the news, waiting for
the slither of light-descending feet and the batter of
Government on the door. Nothing happened, however, and presently she relaxed her muscles, released
her breath, and rubbed her eyes; reproving herself with
a shrug of her shoulders and a half-ashamed laugh for
being so foolish as to imagine that the wire could
possibly have been meant for her.

But she was still curious about its actual destination,
and presently, when her heart had steadied again, she
opened the door and looked out. The telegraph-boy
was returning by now, whistling and wriggling as he
came, but there was nothing to show at which house
he had left his message. Yet even after he had disappeared she remained on her threshold, partly because the sun and the fine air soothed and stimulated
her in the same moment, and partly because of a sub-
conscious thrill that she could not define. But all that
she received by way of a spectacle was the stiff, dark-
clad form of Emma Catterall, appearing suddenly in
the doorway of a house which always seemed gloomier
than other people's. 'Suddenly', however, was not the
right word to use for Emma. Emma always dawned.

Slowly, when you were not thinking about her, she took her place—an unsolicited place—in your conscious vision; and in the same way, when she had finished with you, she faded before your unwillingly strained eyes.

It was after this fashion that Mrs. Clapham discovered her presence this morning, driven to it by the unpleasant consciousness that she was being watched. Fixing each other with a stare that was almost fascinated in its length, they stood looking across the September sunshine in the sloping street. Then, in the same unaccountable manner in which she had appeared, Emma began to fade, and Mrs. Clapham, with a shake and a fresh laugh, moved likewise and went within.

CHAPTER II

She reacted a little after the episode of the telegraph-boy, who had seemed to be bringing her happiness to her, and after all wasn't. That moment of mounting excitement had left her a little flat, or as flat as it was possible to be on this day of wonderful promise. She still felt rather foolish for imagining that the committee would be in the least likely to telegraph the news. The event was trivial enough to them, after all, however world-shaking it might seem to her. Mr. Baines, the lawyer, who was secretary to the committee, would probably send the news by his clerk; or, failing the clerk, he might slip it into the post. There was also the chance, of course, that he might bring it himself, and Mrs. Clapham quivered with pride when she thought of that. Even then, it would be only another of the wonderful happenings which she felt to be gathering about the central fact. There was the grand weather, to begin with, with herself feeling as grand as the day;

and presently, when she had waited a little longer, there would no doubt be Mr. Baines. . . .

It was no use expecting him yet, however, so she made a determined effort to school herself to patience. Mr. Baines, as all the village was aware, was hardly the sort to rise up early in order to bathe his face in morning dew. Besides, as she reminded herself again, this enchanting dispensation of Providence could not possibly seem as important to him as it did to her. Why, in the pressure of business he might even forget it—let it stand over, perhaps, until to-morrow! Mrs. Clapham could hardly restrain herself from rushing off to sit waiting for him on his office doorstep when she thought of *that*.

She found herself wishing, with a fervour that almost surprised her, that this was Mrs. Wrench's 'day', after all. She remembered how she had chuckled, on waking, to think it was nothing of the sort, but she was not so sure that she felt like chuckling now. Even with Mrs. Wrench it was sometimes possible to slip a word in edgeways, if you tried; and in spite of her absorption in Miss Marigold and Miss Marigold's gowns, she would surely have spared a moment to tell her how matters stood.

But it was not Mrs. Wrench's day, so it was no use thinking about it. It was nobody's 'day', for the matter of that. It was her own day, to do as she liked with from rise to set, and just for the moment it threatened to hang on her hands. She tried to make a bargain with herself that she wouldn't look at the clock for another half-hour, and found her eyes stealing round to it the very next minute. She almost wished —so desperately was she at a loose end—that she had gone up the street to speak to Emma Catterall. She hated Tibbie's mother-in-law as she hated nobody else on earth, but even Emma would have been better than nothing. She went to the window at last, to see whether she had re-emerged, bending her pink face

above the box of pink asters, the Family Bible, and the
clock. But there was no sign of Emma, as far as she
could tell; although, as it happened, Emma, at that
moment, was also peering out. There were no flowers
in Emma's window, but only a few half-dead ferns;
nevertheless, in the blankness and gloom of her dismal
dwelling she was hidden as in a cave.

When Mrs. Clapham could bear the waiting no
longer, she fetched pail and brush from the back
kitchen, and got herself down to scrub the floor. The
place was already so clean that her energy seemed
rather wasted, but, although she was unaware of it,
there was something symbolical in the act. In its own
way it was a sort of dedication, a cleansing of everything round her for the coming event. In any case,
nothing that hadn't been washed since the day before
was ever quite clean to Mrs. Clapham. Yesterday was
yesterday, and to-day was to-day, and nobody knew
better than she just how far dirt could manage to
spread itself in a single night.

At all events, her instinct in the matter had been
perfectly sound, for her nerves calmed as soon as she
touched her tools. As she knelt on her little mat,
scrubbing with strong, rhythmic, stiff-armed strokes,
she felt full of a placid confidence that was infinitely
more pleasant than the foregoing state of thrill. Even
she knew that she was at her best when she was at
her 'job', rough though it was, and low in the social
scale. She felt so soothed that she even sang as she
scoured the flags, giving them just enough water and
yet not too much, as a skilful scrubber should. She
had done the doorstep already, of course—as soon as
she came down—a matutinal rite as mechanical and
natural as washing her own face. She found herself
hankering, however, to wash the doorstep again, and
was only stopped by the consciousness that it seemed
rather silly. Yet the step could not be too clean across
which the wonderful news was certain to come, and

there would be plenty of time for it to dry. The fact that she could say to herself that there was plenty of time showed that she had ceased to expect the news at every minute. She was so pleased with herself when she realised that, that she started to sing again. In her present mood of contented assurance she felt she could wait all day.

She and her little mat had just about finished their perambulation in honour of cleanliness, and she was dipping the brush for almost the last time, when somebody came up the street and gave a birdlike tap at her door. Again Mrs. Clapham's heart warned her that life at this strenuous pitch was not suitable to its constitution, and it was a moment or two before she could force herself to her feet. But she had hardly started to answer the summons before the latch moved in its socket, and the thin little face of Mrs. Tanner came peeping excitedly round the jamb.

'Any news, Ann Clapham?' she inquired breathlessly. 'Have you had t' news? Eh, now, I could hardly sleep for fearing summat might go wrong!'

She slipped into the room as she spoke, pushing the door behind her with a neat movement. There was an almost birdlike activity in every inch of her thin form, and an almost beak-like effect in her pursed-up, toothless mouth. Mrs. Clapham looked simply immense beside her spare little shape, a towering giantess of a woman, broad and wholesome and strong. The rolled-up sleeves of her faded print frock showed her splendid arms, just as her skirt, turned up over her short striped petticoat, showed her sturdy legs. Her clean harding apron struck a note of extreme freshness which was accentuated by the glow of her pink face and the gleam of her white hair. The scrubbing-brush was still gripped in her wet hand, and the zinc pail behind her spoke of her honest trade. Even in her excitement Mrs. Tanner had time for a spasm of admiration. 'Eh, but it seems a shame to put the likes of her in an almshouse!' she said to herself; and then forgot the impression in her eagerness for a reply.

'Nay, I've heard nowt yet!' Mrs. Clapham was one broad smile. 'I doubt it's hardly time. Folks as sit on committees and such-like don't get up as soon as us!'

Mrs. Tanner gave the nod of pained but tolerant comprehension with which one class salutes the idiosyncrasies of another.

'Anyway, it'll be all right. Folks say as it's yours already. . . . I had to look in, though; I was that keen to know.'

'It was right kind of you, Maggie,' Mrs. Clapham beamed; 'it was right kind! Good luck doesn't come every day o' the week, and, when it does, it'd be a queer sort as didn't want everybody to hear!'

Steeped in a mutual kindness that had the warmth of an embrace, they drifted across the fast-drying floor and seated themselves by the small fire. Mrs. Tanner perched herself on the edge of the stiff rocker, while Mrs. Clapham sat in her late husband's chair, bolt upright, her bare arms outstretched, her plump moist hands resting upon her knees. The big woman and the little beamed across at each other, thoroughly satisfied with a pleasant world.

'They'll hear right enough—trust 'em for that! They're agog about it, even now. Mrs. Simmons put her head out as I ran up and said "Hst! Any more about yon almshouse do?"—but of course I couldn't tell her what I didn't know myself!'

'Ay, she's the sort to get up the night before, to make sure of a bit o' gossip!' . . . They had a hearty laugh together at this peculiarity of Mrs. Simmons's, exactly as if it wasn't shared by everybody in the street. But anything was good enough to laugh at on this day that was to be laughter and pleasantness all through. Mrs. Simmons's weakness did as well as anything else. 'But there! I mustn't be counting my chickens afore they're hatched!' Mrs. Clapham said presently, trying to sober down. 'Nice and silly I'll look if I don't get it, after all! Not but what I sort o' feel in my bones as it's going to be all right.'

Mrs. Tanner, at least, had no qualms about tempting Providence.

'Folks all say you're the only person for it,' she repeated stoutly. 'There's a many wanted it, of course, but there's nobody earned it same as you. You'd be fit to hide your face if you knew all the fine things I've heard tell of you these last few days, about you being that honest and straight-living and all that! What, I shouldn't wonder if folks was that pleased they'd go sticking out flags!' she went on, her imagination running away with her—'nay, but they won't. They'll be too put about over lossing your grand work.'

'Ay, well, I can't say I shan't be pleased to be missed. Folks always want to be told there's nobody like 'em when their turn comes to step aside. I'm sure I've done my best for the place while I've been about it!' She chuckled happily, rubbing her hands backwards and forwards over the harding apron. 'There's not a floor can cry out at me as I've ever had occasion to scrub! . . . But I'm going back, all the same, and it's about time I gave up. My knee's been bothering me a deal lately, and my heart's a bit jumpy an' all. I did think of going to doctor about it, but I reckon it's just old age. I'll be right enough, likely, when I'm in my own spot, and no call to bother about the rent!'

'Ay, you've had a fairish hard life,' Mrs. Tanner agreed sympathetically, 'and it's no wonder it's beginning to tell. Not but what you'd have found work for yourself wherever you were, that I'll be bound! You're the sort as always likes things a little hard. You'd never ha' done with 'em soft.'

'I could ha' done with 'em a bit easier like, all the same!' Mrs. Clapham rejoined humorously. 'But you're likely right. I can't abide folks to be mooning around or lying about half their time. I like to see a bit of elbow-grease put into life, same as it might be a kitchen-table! I was brought up to think there was nowt like work, and I can't say I've ever found anything better. My Tibbie's a grand worker an' all, and yon little Libby of hers shapes to frame the same way. ... But folks can't last for ever and that's a fact; and I've always sworn as I'd end my days in them alms-houses on Hermitage Hill.'

The eyes of the two women shone as they met and smiled. They leaned towards each other, a little breathless.

'A pound a week!' chanted the ecstatic Mrs. Tanner. 'It's gone up since t' War.'

'Ay, and as bonny a spot as you could wish!'

'Coal!'

'Such a view as there is, looking right over towards t' sea!'

'No rates nor nothing,' sang Mrs. Tanner; 'and water laid on from a big tank!'

'A flower-garden, wi' a man to see to it——'

'Tatie bed, gooseberry bushes, black currants, red currants, mint——'

'Eh, and such furniture and fittings as you couldn't find bettered at the Hall!' Mrs. Clapham's tone was almost reverent. It seemed to her rather greedy to lay stress upon the material side of her luck, but the excellent plenishings provided by old Mr. T. could scarcely be termed that. It was more as if they were the fittings of the temple which the place stood for in her mind, than the actual chattels of a house in which she was going to live.

They laughed again as they paused for breath, because even for a thing that was sacred nothing but laughter was good enough to greet it. Then Mrs. Clapham checked herself firmly a second time.

'There I go again—making out I've got the place,

when I've never had as much as a word! I'm just asking for bad luck, that's what it is! What, blessed if I didn't find myself singing at my work, for all the world like a daft lass going to meet a lad!' She chuckled again, drawing her hands slowly backwards and forwards over her knees. 'Serves me right if I bring a judgment on my crazy head! ... But I was fair hankering after somebody to talk to when you come in. It's next best thing to my own Tibbie, having you setting there.'

'I'm sure I wish it was Tibbie herself, I do that! Your lass'll be real pleased when she hears the news.'

'She will that!' The charwoman smiled contentedly. 'She's always thought a deal of her mother, has my Tibbie. ... But, bless me, Maggie Tanner, you're every bit as bad as me! Who's to say, after all, as it won't be Martha Jane?'

'Martha Jane?' Mrs. Tanner's wrath and contempt were such that the rocker, hitherto apparently oblivious of her birdlike presence, began to rock as if possessed by some evil spirit. 'Nay, now, don't you talk such rubbish to me! She isn't fit to be mentioned in t' same week!'

'She thinks a deal of her chances, all the same,' Mrs. Clapham returned seriously. 'Ay, she fancies her chances, does Martha Jane. I do think I'm a bit better stuff than her, and that's gospel truth, but seemingly there's some as'd sooner put in a word for her than they would for me.'

'Likely nicked in the head, then, that's what they are!' scoffed Mrs. Tanner. 'I'll believe in 'em when I see 'em. It's true she's seemed mighty full of herself, these last few days, but there's nowt new to that. Nobody in their senses'd vote for her as knew anything about her.'

'There's men on the committee, you'll think on, and she was always one for getting round the men. I remember I could never get my Jonty to say a word agen her, and I reckon it'll be the same with your Joe. Them committee-men won't bother themselves whether she's fit to look after a grand spot like yon; and she's never been one either to cook or to clean, hasn't Martha Jane. She'd let a bit o' piecrust burn any day o' the week if a man chanced to be going past.'

'She's never got herself wed with it all, any way up!' Mrs. Tanner was rocking and fierce. 'Not that them sort o' little details make that much difference to Martha Jane!'

'Not as *I* ever heard of!' Mrs. Clapham supplemented, with pursed lips; and then relinquished the virtuous matron in a burst of happy beams. 'Oh, well, never mind the poor, daft thing!' she finished kindly, rubbing her knees. 'I mustn't get talking nasty on such a grand day as this.'

'Tibbie'll be coming to help you to move, likely?' Mrs. Tanner inquired presently, when by a violently charitable effort they had allowed Martha Jane's frailties to sink out of mind. But Mrs. Clapham shook her head.

'Nay, I don't know as she will. Happen she might, if she could get somebody to see to the children. . . . But there's her sewing, you'll think on, and a deal besides; and anyway she's not that keen on coming back here, isn't Tibbie.'

'What, she was fond enough of the place as a lass!' Mrs. Tanner protested, though less out of contradiction than as if she were somehow taking a cue.

'Ay, she likes the place well enough—I don't mean that. You always think a deal of the spot where you lived as a child. But she'd put the whole world if she could between them children of hers and Emma Catterall. She's never forgiven the way his mother treated Poor Stephen.'

'Nay, now, don't you go calling him "poor", Ann Clapham,' Mrs. Tanner interpolated with spirit, 'and him with his V.C. an' all! Think on how well he did

in t' Army, and what they said about him in t' papers.
What, even Germans, they said, owned up he was
right brave! Tibbie'd give it you, I'll be bound, if she
heard you calling him "poor"!'

' "Poor" was the word for him, though, as a bit of a
lad. . . .' Mrs. Clapham's expression had changed and
become grave and a trifle bitter; and again, as if picking up a cue, Mrs. Tanner found one to match it.

'Ay, he had a terribly thin time of it, had Stephen—
I don't mind giving you that. She wasn't kind to him,
wasn't Emma. Yet I don't know as she ever laid a
hand on him, as far as I've heard tell. Yon half-daft
father of his did, so they said, but I make nowt o' that.
A boy never frets himself much over that sort o' thing.
It's all just in the day's work.'

'Nay, it was something a deal worse.' The charwoman's kind face was troubled and puzzled. 'It was
more the sort o' way she looked and spoke, hinting at
nasty things she could do if she liked. . . . I reckon she
made him feel as if he wasn't *safe*. She didn't feed him
over-well, neither; I doubt he was always going short.
Emma's always been well covered, and will be, I
reckon, when she's in her coffin; but Steve and his
father were as thin as laths. I always kind o' think she
starved poor Jemmy into his grave, though I doubt he
wouldn't ha' been much of a man even on four meals
a day instead of two. Likely she'd ha' done the same
for Stephen, if he hadn't got away in time. There's
nowt breaks a boy's spirit like keeping him short of
food.'

'He'd plenty o' spirit when it come to it, anyway—
the poor lad!' The patriotic Mrs. Tanner fired
again. . . . 'There now, I'm calling him "poor" myself! Germans didn't think him short of it, though,
that I'll be bound! . . . But I don't wonder Tibbie
isn't keen on bringing them children anywhere near
Emma. It's natural she should be sore about it, seeing
how fond she was of Stephen. What, I remember once,

when she was nobbut about ten, seeing her sobbing her heart out in t' street, and when I fetched her in to ax what in creation it was all about, it turned out as she'd seen Poor Stephen looking as thin as a knife-edge!'

'Ay, she never could abear to see anything tret rough-like or unkind. It was that made her look at him first thing. She'd a deal of offers, had Tibbie, as you'll likely know, but she never would hear tell of anybody but Stephen. Once she'd started in feeling sorry for him, the rest was like to follow. He worshipped her an' all, did the poor lad, but I reckon it was Tibbie had to do the asking! She'd to begin all over again from the beginning, so to speak, and make a man of him from the start.'

'And a right fine man she made of him, while she was about it!' Mrs. Tanner crowed. '*Germans*'ll say so, any way up! . . . Them children of his are ter'ble like him an' all,' she went on presently, but more as if she were now offering the cue instead of accepting it.

'Ay.' Mrs. Clapham's hands returned to their slow travel up and down her knees. 'Ay, they're ter'ble like. . . .' She turned her head and stared thoughtfully at the photographs on the shelf. 'It's because they're that like I couldn't get Tibbie to bring 'em here to live. "It's over near yon woman," she used to say, whenever I axed. They come once, though, you'll likely think on, and a fair old time we had of it, to be sure! I went to the lass, of course, after Stephen was killed, but I couldn't frame to stop; so, after a deal o' pushing and pulling, her and the children come for a short visit. But it wasn't very long before she found that *she* couldn't stop, neither! Emma Catterall was always after them children, standing on t' doorstep or hanging about in t' street. She couldn't keep away from them, whatever she did; what, it was almost as if she watched 'em in their beds!'

Mrs. Tanner had turned her head, too, and was

staring out through the slightly open door, through which the sun was pushing its way as if laying a carpet for coming feet. But neither of the women who were sitting there waiting for good news had a thought to spare for that news just now.

'They say Emma makes no end of a stir about Stephen now—showing his likeness and that. Happen she's proud of him now, and happen sorry; leastways, that's what you'd say if it wasn't Emma.'

But again the charwoman shook her head. 'It'd be right enough for most folk—I'll give you that; but it don't seem to fit somehow with Emma. She went on that strange, too, she made you creep. She just hung about waiting all the time—never come in once and sat herself down for a bit of a chat. Of course, we were none of us over-friendly-like; she was bound to feel that; but neither Tibbie nor me is the sort to fly out at folk unless we was pressed.'

'She's not one for ever going into other folks' spots,' observed Mrs. Tanner. 'And I don't know as I ever see her set down in the whole of my life!'

'Ay, well, she never come past doorstep, as I said.... She just hung about, looking on. She's brass of her own, you'll think on, and more time on her hands than most. . . . She'd come sauntering down t' road, as if she was looking for summat, and stop at the door and peer in; and as soon as she'd catched sight o' the poor brats, she'd stand and stare at 'em with her queer smile. They got that upset about it they'd hardly bring 'emselves to go out, and they'd wake in the night, and swear she was in t' room! Tibbie got that desperate about it at last that she took t' bull by t' horns, and took 'em along to Emma's to tea. She thought happen they'd all on 'em be more sensible-like after that, let alone as Emma was Stephen's mother and owed attention an' all. But it didn't work out as she thought, not by a deal. You never see anything like the three on 'em when they come back! The babies had cried 'emselves sick, and Tibbie was white as a sheet. And after we'd sat alongside of 'em for the best part of a couple of hours, and come down agen to the fire—"Mother," Tibbie says sudden-like, breaking out, "it's no use! We've got to go." '

'And she's never been since. . . .' Mrs. Tanner was still staring at the sunlight through the open door.

'Nay, and won't, neither, as long as she's breath in her to say no! Such letters as she wrote me after she got back! . . . I've still got 'em upstairs. They were that fierce they'd have set t' house afire if I'd shaped to put 'em in t' grate!' . . . Tibbie's mother gave her jolly laugh for the first time since the solemn interval, and the rhythmic rubbing began again. 'Ay, well, she's well enough where she is,' she went on placidly. 'She's a good business and a sight o' friends. The folks next door—Rawlinson's what they're called—think the world an' all o' my Tibbie. . . . Nay, she wouldn't come agen whatever I did, though I axed her ever so often. She was right keen on me going to her instead, but I didn't fancy a new spot. I'd summat in my eye at home an' all,' she finished, chuckling; 'and you know what that is as well as me!'

Mrs. Tanner turned herself round now, and chuckled, too. The shadow which had lain for a while over the pair of them—the shadow of something they could not understand—dispersed again in the sun of the coming pleasure. Both their faces and their voices lightened, now that a safe return had been made to the joyful subject.

'I don't know when I didn't know it, come to that! We all on us knew you'd set your heart on that house!'

'Well, it's nothing to be ashamed of, I'm sure!' Mrs. Clapham defended herself happily. 'There's a deal o' things folks want as is a long sight worse.'

'Nay, you'd every right,' Mrs. Tanner concurred, with distinct affection in her tone. . . . 'They say everybody has a dream o' some sort,' she added thoughtfully, 'and that, if they nobbut hold to it fast enough, it's sure to come true.'

'Ay, well, I've held to mine fast enough,' the char-woman chuckled; 'ay, that I have, right fast! What, I've never as much as thought of anything else! I've watched folk marching in, and I've watched 'em carried out, and I've said to myself about both on 'em—"Some day yon'll be me!"' . . . She laughed when Mrs. Tanner jumped as she said that, exclaiming 'Eh, now, Mrs. Clapham, yon isn't nice!'—laughed and laughed until the tears ran down her face, and crumpled the apron over her knees. 'Eh, well, I hope I'll have a run for my money, anyway,' she finished contentedly, as the other rose. . . . 'You're off agen, are you? It was kind of you to look in.'

'Ay, I must be off now, but I'll be back before so long.' Mrs. Tanner's neat little figure hopped briskly towards the door. 'You'll have your work cut out, keeping me off t' step!' she added, turning for a last laugh, and again was struck by the thought that had met her when she came in. 'Eh, but I wonder if you'll like yon dream o' yours when it comes to getting it!' she exclaimed, looking up at the big woman almost seriously. 'I doubt you'll not take kindly to living so soft. Somebody'll be wanting a bit o' help, one o' these days, and you'll be out o' yon almshouse afore you can say knife!'

Mrs. Clapham put out one of her plump hands, and gave her a good-tempered push. 'Get along with you, woman,' she scolded cheerfully, 'and don't be putting your spoke in my grand wheel! . . . Is that postman coming up t' street?' she added swiftly, suddenly nervous. 'Eh, Maggie, my lass, I'm all of a shake!'

' 'Tain't post!' Mrs. Tanner called back, pattering birdlike down the street. 'You're that excited, you can't see. . . . I'll be looking in agen as soon as I'm through, and anyway, here's wishing you luck!'

She disappeared into a house on the opposite side of

the road, and for a while longer Mrs. Clapham stayed
at her door, straining her eyes after the mythical postman whom her imagination had supplied. She had
begun to feel restless again, and as if she could not
possibly wait another moment. Presently, with a sigh,
she went back into the house, but she could not bring
herself to close the door. That would have been a sign
that she still felt equal to waiting, and the mood of
patience had finally passed. Mechanically she put
away pail and brush, and readjusted the rug, but
always with an ear stretched towards the least hint of
a step outside. Afterwards she took off the harding
and straightened her skirt, turned down her sleeves,
and took a clean linen apron from a bottom drawer.
She even went to the mirror beside the fire and
smoothed and tightened the coils of her hair. And
then at last, as if she had done all that could be
required of her, either for the postman or Mr. Baines,
she settled her features into the expression of placid
expectation that was most suitable to the occasion,
and stepped like a kindly victor into the street. . . .

CHAPTER III

Out in the clear September sunshine she planted herself well beyond the doorstep and a yard or two down
the road, feet apart, hands on her hips, and her calm
but interested gaze staring steadily down the hill. She
was not ashamed to be seen standing there waiting for
the great good thing that was certainly coming her
way. There could be nothing forward or lacking in
delicacy in waiting about for what everybody knew to
be your own. The sun, slanting towards her over the
houses, brought out the original lilac of her faded
gown, burnished her hair into actual silver, and caught
at the wedding-ring on her hand. From either side of

the street they looked out and saw her there, and according to their natures were either interested or uninterested, sympathetic or the reverse. None of them, however, could help looking at her for at least a minute. There was something regal about the big, fine, patient figure that was not afraid to go forth in the eye of the sun to meet the possibilities of fate.

Martha Jane Fell, fastening a piece of torn lace about her neck with a bent and tarnished gilt pin, saw her through her cracked panes and gave vent to a cracked laugh. Martha Jane had her own hopes, which were playing havoc with her nerves, and her hands, working at the lace, trembled so much that at last the pin, pressed over-hard, turned like the proverbial worm and ran itself into her thumb. Nevertheless, she laughed again, after the first agony had passed, sucking the wound as she gazed at the figure in the street.

'Looks as if she was waiting for a depitation o' some sort!' she remarked to herself humorously. 'This way to the Monyment of Honest Toil! . . . Thinks she's got yon house in her pocket already, I should say; but I reckon there's still a dip in the bag for Martha Fell!'

And from behind the dusty ferns that were only just alive, and would so very much have preferred not to live at all, Emma Catterall also stared at the figure that was the cynosure of every eye. Its serenity, its dignity, its contented assurance seemed to amuse her almost as much as they amused Martha Jane. Her beady black eyes brightened as they fastened upon it, and slowly there grew on her lips the queer little smile which everybody in the village hated without knowing why. But presently, as nothing happened in the street, she stirred and dropped her lids. 'Ay, well, she knows her own business best,' she murmured to herself, still smiling, as she moved away. . . .

After a while Mrs. Tanner came pattering out to join Mrs. Clapham, followed by young Mrs. James from her grand house that had pillars to its door. This was too much for Mrs. Clapham's own side of the street, which promptly sent forth supporters in the shape of Mrs. Airey and Mrs. Dunn. Martha Jane, heating a pair of rickety curling-tongs at a tallow-dip, was more amused than ever. 'Got her court an' all now!' she observed to the guttering candle as she singed her hair.

The postman might now be looked for at any moment, and excitement mounted in the group in the street. Mrs. Clapham's Court—or, more correctly speaking, her Chorus—was full of good-humoured banter, feeling more and more thrilled with every minute that passed. Mrs. Tanner's thin little voice chirped its jests at dark and haughty Mrs. James, round and motherly Mrs. Airey, and limp and care-worn Mrs. Dunn; while the heroine of the occasion, too nervous to say much, left them most of the talking and merely beamed upon all alike.

Mrs. Tanner, out of the little pursed-up mouth that was so ridiculously like a wren's beak, was of opinion that it was worse than useless to be looking for Mr. Baines.

'Nay, it'll be t' post, you'll see!' she asserted confidently to the crowd. 'Ay, he'll have slipped it into the post. . . . I don't say but what it wouldn't be more an attention like if he brought it himself, but it isn't in nature what you'd look for from Baines. Baines is the sort that first has to be driven to his bed and then shaken out of it. Depend upon it, it won't be Baines!'

Young Mrs. James flushed with annoyance, and drew herself up haughtily. She had a weakness for amiable, short-sighted Mr. Baines, who, at a recent Red Cross bazaar, had made the pleasant mistake of addressing her as Lady Thorpe. . . . 'I don't agree with you, Mrs. Tanner,' she contradicted her coldly. 'Mr. Baines is a gentleman, and he'll do the right thing. Speaking as one as has had personal experience of Mr. Baines, it seems to me a deal more likely that he'll come himself.'

'Nay, it'll be t' post!' Mrs. Tanner persisted, shaking an obstinate head. 'You haven't been here that long, Mrs. James, and you don't know Baines as well as us. He's not like to do for himself what he can shape to get done for him by somebody else. Ay, it'll be t' post!'

'Supposing it's neither?' Mrs. Airey put in with a kindly laugh; and Mrs. Dunn, whose brain was as careworn as her face, observed, 'Supposing it's Martha Jane——?' but was hastily elbowed into silence.

'It don't matter how it comes, as long as it comes right!' Mrs. Clapham answered the lot of them, with her heavenly smile. She soared above them all like a great comfortable hen above bantams and sparrows, growing and gaining in significance as they dwindled and lost. . . .

'Ay, it'll come right, no doubt about that!' At once the Chorus forgot its differences in a breath of united devotion. Mrs. Dunn's remark had been made without her noticing it, so to speak, a kind of side-slip of her deflated mind. . . . 'And there's nobody'll be more pleased than us, Ann Clapham, not even yourself!'

'You're right kind!' the charwoman beamed, turning a grateful glance from one to the other. 'I must say folks is very decent. Mrs. Tanner here come round first thing to ask if I'd heard; and right glad I was to see her, feeling lonesome without my Tibbie.'

'You'll have heard from her lately, I suppose?' Mrs. James asked elegantly; the present belle of the village inquiring politely after her predecessor. Mrs. James was married, of course, but she was the belle, nevertheless; not to speak of the splendid enhancement of having been taken for Lady Thorpe.

'Nay, I haven't,' Mrs. Clapham answered, without turning her head. 'I haven't heard for a while. But she's been making a gown for Miss Marigold's trousseau, so she's sure to have been throng. It's Miss Marigold's wedding-day to-day, you'll think on, and a grand one an' all!'

'Same age as your Tibbie, isn't she?' asked Mrs. Dunn; and added, by way of making up for her late slip, 'but nowhere near her when it comes to looks!'

'Nay, now, Miss Marigold's right enough; she'd pass in a crowd!' . . . Mrs. Clapham was flattered, but she wished to be just. 'Let's hope she hasn't been through the wood that often, though, she's had to pick t' crooked stick at last!' she went on chuckling. 'My Tibbie took t' bull by t' horns, and picked crooked stick right off!'

This evoked a perfect volley of reproach from the shocked Chorus, put finally into intelligible form by Mrs. Tanner.

'Nay, now, Ann Clapham, you should think shame to be talking like that! 'Tisn't right to Poor Stephen, seeing he turned out so grand. Doesn't seem right to your Tibbie, neither, as lost her man in t' War.'

Mrs. Clapham looked slightly conscience-stricken. 'Ay, poor lad—poor lass!' she sighed, by way of amends, and suddenly the shadow of the terrible four years came out of the corners in which it had been dispersed, and breathed a vapour as of shell-smoke over the sunny street. Before the minds of all rose a succession of khaki figures, coming and going; or only going, and getting ever farther away. Young Mrs. James, whose husband had been off to Gallipoli before they were three months wed, looked at that moment not such a very young Mrs. James, after all. The sisters, Mrs. Airey and Mrs. Dunn, drew together and touched hands. Mrs. Airey's lad had come back, and Mrs. Dunn's had not, but even Mrs. Dunn's flattened mind could have told you that the real agony of war is in the suspense and not in the blow. The mental horizon of all stretched itself again, demanding that strained, painful vision which had looked so long towards India, Salonika, Palestine, and France. They felt again that atmosphere which is like no other on earth—that mixture of bewilderment and intense interest, terror and exaltation, utter helplessness and secret pride. And, sighing, they sighed as one, chiefly with relief, but also with an unconscious regret for the heady wine of drama that had once been poured into the white glass vials of their colourless lives.

'Stephen wasn't much to crack on when he was here,' Mrs. Tanner continued, 'I'll give you that; but he was a good lad, all the same. Ay, and need to be, too, or he'd have murdered yon mother of his long before!'

The fresh outbreak of shocked expostulation was this time addressed to her, accompanied by quick, half-scared glances at Emma Catterall's door. 'Nay, now, Maggie, you're going a deal further than me!' Mrs. Clapham protested, but Mrs. Tanner remained unmoved.

'What's the use of shutting me up about a thing as everybody knows?' she demanded boldly, 'barring perhaps Mrs. James here, as is over-young? It's a wonder the boy stayed right in his head, the way he was tret!'

'Mrs. Catterall's set up enough about him now, anyhow,' Mrs. James said, throwing another glance up the street. 'What with cramming his likeness down everybody's throat, and taking flowers to the War Memorial and the Shrine, you'd think he'd been her own pet lamb and a mother's darling from the start!'

'I never rightly knew what it was she *did!*' Mrs. Dunn said in her flat tones, giving vent to the inevitable remark which had its place in every discussion of Emma's doings. 'I don't know as I ever heard her lift her voice to him once, and she isn't the sort to lift a hand. 'Tisn't shouting and leathering a lad as does him that much harm, neither; nay, nor even keeping him a bit short o' grub. I've seen a many as fair throve on it, and that's a fact—laughing and whistling and making right fine men an' all! It wants summat else to take the heart out on 'em as it was took out o' Poor Stephen.'

'It's not feeling *safe* as does for a child,' Mrs. Clapham said slowly, repeating rather reluctantly her statement of less than an hour before. 'I was saying so to Maggie Tanner just now. . . . A child's got to be growing and learning things every day, and without knowing he's doing either; and if he don't feel certain he's doing the right thing, what, he stops doing it altogether. That's how it was with Stephen, I reckon. He just stopped. . . . It was like as if he was always holding his breath.'

'Doctor says there's some folk should never have charge of children at all,' Mrs. Airey put in with sudden and ghoulish emphasis. 'He says they sort of destroy them just by living with 'em—fair suck the life out on 'em, so to speak!'

Mrs. Clapham stirred unhappily.

'Eh, for t' land's sake, don't talk like that, Bessie!' she besought her anxiously. Fear came over her after that last speech, the sense of a sinister presence brooding over the street that was very much worse than the shadow of the War. A look of almost clairvoyant apprehension came into her eyes, slaying their happy prevision of beautiful things. . . . 'It don't seem quite fair to be talking like that of folks as live so close.'

'She gives *me* the shivers right enough, anyway!' Mrs. James broke out, laughing nervously, and casting yet another glance at the dreaded door. 'It's that smile of hers . . . and the way she watches to see what you're at! There's something at the back of her mind as sneers and laughs at you all the time. . . . As for yon tag of hers about knowing your own business best, all I can say is it fair makes me want to scream!'

'I've known a many as was feared of Emma,' Mrs. Tanner followed on; 'parson's wife, for one—ay, and parson an' all! I've seen district visitors and suchlike coming out of yon house looking for all the world like a bit o' chewed string. Ay, and one day—yon time when parson had a curate as was more than a shade soft—I see him come shambling down t' steps fair crying and wringing his hands. I was in t' street at the time, clipping yon bit of box we have at the door, and he stopped alongside of me, and said, 'Mrs. Tanner, that woman's a devil!' I was fair took aback by such language, as you might think; but when I looked up there was Emma smiling behind her ferns, and watching yon snivelling lad like a cat wi' a half-dead mouse. It was so like the way she carried on wi' Poor Stephen, it fair give me a turn; so for Stephen's sake I took curate into t' house and give him a cup o' tea and all the gossip I could lay my tongue to, and sent him off home with Emma clean out of his mind, and chuckling as throng as a laying hen!'

'There's only one as has never taken much count of her,' Mrs. Airey said, when they had stopped laughing about the curate, 'and that's Martha Jane Fell. I've heard her reeling off stuff at Emma as just made you catch your breath, and Emma's smile getting lesser and lesser with every minute. Ay, and I've seen her bolt into yon house like a rabbit into its hole, just to get away from her long tongue!'

' 'Tisn't to be expected Martha Jane should have fine feelings same as us!' ... Young Mrs. James tossed her head with a fiercely-virtuous air. Being acquainted only by hearsay with the informalities of Martha Jane's past, she naturally supposed them to be more momentous than was actually the case. Nor were the rest of the Chorus averse to encouraging her in this supposition. The post still lagged, and the time had to be passed; so presently they were drawn nearer and nearer in the road, lowering their voices and nodding their shocked heads. Mrs. Clapham kept saying, 'For shame, now!' and 'Can't you let sleeping dogs lie?'

breaking every now and then into her hearty laugh.
'I must say, though, I do think I've more claim to that
house than her!' she added, after a while, getting
hungry for fresh encouragement as there was still no
sign of the post.

'I can't think how they ever considered her for a
moment! . . .' Mrs. James thrust her head above
water, so to speak, and then eagerly plunged it back.
The feet shuffled in the road, and the heads whispered
and bobbed, with every second that passed getting
farther from the truth. Martha Jane, pulling up at the
back the skirt that instantly slipped down, and down
at the front the blouse that instantly slipped up, came
out of her door and stood watching them with a
sardonic grin.

'Talking about me, I'll lay!' she observed to herself,
half bitter, half amused. She had seen too many heads
close together in her vicinity not to know when it
meant scandal about herself. Often enough some of it
happened to get round to her again, and there were
times when she had a malicious joy in speeding it on
its way. 'I've heard that much about myself and my
goings-on,' she remarked once, 'that I don't know by
now which is gospel and which ain't! Anyway, it
wouldn't be safe for me to swear it on t' Book, I know
that! I reckon I'll be as surprised as anybody when t'
Judgment Day comes round!'

Suddenly turning her glance up street instead of
down, she beheld Emma Catterall's furtive gaze
sliding away from her like a half-felt hand, afterwards
focusing itself on the gossiping group. 'Wonder what
she's gaping at *me* for?' she said to herself, rather
uncomfortably, and then winked and grinned. 'The
Queen *and* her ladies-in-waiting!' she remarked with
a jerk of her head towards the little throng. 'Ann
Clapham's mighty sure things is going to be O.K.
Seems to think she'll simply romp home over yon
house!'

Emma Catterall made no attempt to reply to this effort of wit; did not, indeed, look as if she had even heard it. She merely began to dissolve into thin air, and disappeared even as Martha stared. The latter, however, was used to this vanishing trick on the part of her neighbour, and only laughed. But she, too, was hungering for an exchange of words with somebody; feeling, as Mrs. Clapham had felt earlier in the morning, that even Emma was better than nothing. She waited a while, therefore, hoping that she might reappear; and then, as she gave no further impression of life, took her courage in her hands, and sidled cringingly down the street.

'There's no telling, after all, as it mightn't be me!' she was saying to herself, by way of keeping up her pluck, though, in point of fact, she had very little hope of anything as splendid as almshouses ever coming her way. But Martha Jane was never the sort to cry beaten before she was down. She, too, had awakened that morning with an unwonted sense of something about to happen, some forthcoming miracle already launched upon its path. She, too, had felt upon her cheek the far-off brushings of the wings of romance. She had done wonders—and more than wonders—with the committee, as she knew, and it might be that even one vote more than she had counted upon would suffice to put her in. The weight of the village was against her, of course, heavy with laden tongues, but village opinion would matter nothing if she had got the vote. Little indeed would she care for the whole lip-pursing lot, once she was safely possessed of the house on Hermitage Hill!

She thought of all that it represented—mental and physical comfort, as well as prestige—and longed for it with a passion that was almost angry in its desire. Life for Martha Jane had consisted chiefly not of things which had been given her, but of the things which she had taken, and for once in that life she wanted a free gift. She had always preferred to achieve her ends by crooked ways and doubtful means, but she wanted a straight road to lead the way to this. The house on the hill had not been her dream, as it had been Mrs. Clapham's, but it had its glamour, nevertheless. Her chances could hardly be called favourable, however, as she was bound to acknowledge. She wasn't the 'almshouse sort', she said to herself, with a cynical sigh; followed—just *because* she wasn't 'the almshouse sort'—by a cynical grin.

But at least the grin raised her spirits, since her courage consisted largely of her sense of humour, and she came sidling down upon the group with the cringing yet flaunting air which she kept for her own sex. As soon as a member of the opposite sex appeared, the flaunting vanished as if by magic. Then Martha Jane became at once a faded but sweet blossom, a bruised petal patiently waiting the fall of a manly foot. She wilted, so to speak, withered under your eye, producing the same impression of appeal as in the more forward and less subtle attitude of seeming to cling. It had been this air of shrinking from life, of being beaten back by every zephyr that blew, that had been Martha Jane's chief weapon in dealing with the committee. But there are limits to the marvels that may be accomplished even by the ghost of a vanished grace, and Martha Jane was pretty sure that hers had stopped at the extra vote.

The Clapham contingent stiffened when they saw her coming, sliding down upon them with that amazing mixture of provocative humour and fawning appeal. But she was a neighbour, in spite of her morals, and still had her rights, no final pronouncement from some august mouth having set her definitely beyond the pale. Moreover, she had every reason to suppose that she was in the running for the coveted house, and on that ground alone she had authority to be present. Once in possession (always supposing such a thing possible), she would have to be treated differently; would *be* different, in fact. The more imaginative and calculating among them visioned a Martha Jane in genteel black, visited by parsons' and governors' wives, a prominent figure at village sewing-parties, church pill-gills, and the altar-rail. They drew a little apart, therefore, though quite unable to look pleased, allowing the chief actors in the forthcoming drama to line up side by side.

Martha Jane threw a mocking glance sideways at the fine bulk of Mrs. Clapham, towering above her like a great merchantman beside some beaten yacht. 'You're waiting for t' post, likely?' she inquired innocently. 'It's getting about time. I thought I'd like to be along with my few well-chosen words when t' news comes as you're in.'

Mrs. Clapham laughed kindly, as at an intended joke, but her cheek flushed, nevertheless. Again she was conscious of outrage that this worthless specimen of humanity should be bracketed with her in the great event. She was a tolerant woman, and not one at any time to drive a sinner to the wall, but there was no getting past the fact that Martha Jane was a blot on the fine beauty of the day. Her slovenliness, with the tawdry touch which was somehow so peculiarly Martha Jane's, was in itself an offence against the pure delicacy of the morning, but it was the mocking quality of her mien that especially sullied the fine air. Mrs. Clapham began to wonder whether she wasn't being merely absurd in trying to take her beautiful day so beautifully. Martha Jane gave her much the same uncomfortable feeling as that curate of Mrs. Tanner's used to give her in church; the same feeling that she might have had if a clown had been introduced into a Bethlehem Play.

'It's right kind of you, I'm sure,' she replied, as she had already replied right and left, but with none of the usual heartiness in her voice. 'Happen it'll be t' other way about, though,' she added politely, but with an effort, 'and me as'll be the one to congratulate *you!*'

'Likely—I *don't* think!' spurted forth from Mrs. James, who had fully intended to preserve a dignified silence while in the polluted propinquity of Martha Jane, but found it quite impossible when it came to it. She stiffened herself, however, as if violently conscious of a background with pillars, and although there were no men to be seen, Martha Jane wilted, staring pathetically into the distance where possibly they might lurk. . . . 'It'd be queer if they passed *you* over, Mrs. Clapham, for anybody round here!'

'It's real nice of you to say so,' the charwoman thanked her, a trifle uncomfortably, 'but there's a many as good as me. I'm a deal older than Miss Fell here, though, and I reckon that gives me the better right.'

'Not to speak of a sight of other things as well!' . . . Mrs. Tanner pursed up her tiny, sharp physiognomy until it was more like a bird's than ever. 'They'll never go past you, and that's all there is about it. Martha Jane'll have to wait a bit longer, I doubt; ay, and happen another bit after that!'

The latter suddenly stopped wilting, (nobody of the male species having put in an appearance), and straightened into a brazen fierceness.

'There's them as says I just can't *miss* getting it,' she announced, flushing; 'his lordship, for one! What, he very near promised it me, there and then, but I couldn't go taking it behind Mrs. Clapham! " 'Twouldn't be fair," I says to him, firm but kind, "not to go letting her have her chance." . . . Alms-houses is *meant* for folks like me, his lordship says,' she went on, the toss of her head infinitely more impressive than anything in that line achieved by Mrs. James— 'folks as can't frame to fight their way. 'Tisn't everybody as has titles voting for 'em, and coronets shaking hands!'

'It's about all you *will* get, I reckon! . . .' Mrs.

James's tone was more venomous than she intended, for not only was she a kind enough woman at heart, but there were those chances of Martha's to be considered. But her private piece of vainglory as typified by Mr. Baines was threatening to lose in glamour beside this lordly support. . . . 'I don't mind betting yon feather boa of mine as you can't keep your eyes off, every time I go past, as you never set foot inside t' almshouse door!'

The unconscious but none the less telling malignancy of this thrust almost brought the tears to Martha Jane's eyes. She was not quite herself, this morning, not quite her own armoured and viper-tongued self. Slight as was her hope of success, it was still sufficient to soften her fibre, to fray her nerves and make her generally more susceptible to attack. It was only for a moment, however. Her body's trick of wilting was seldom anything but camouflage for an unwilting spirit. When she had conquered her tears she turned upon Mrs. James such a stream of vituperation that that refined lady was fairly driven backwards by it, as by a hose; and heads came out of windows and round corners and through doors that had hitherto been hiding themselves discreetly behind arch or curtain or jamb.

The furious storm, sprung out of nowhere in the calm September street, was brought to an end by Mrs. Clapham laying a kindly hand upon Martha Jane's shoulder. On any other day, perhaps, she might not have interfered; might even have found it rather amusing. Racy vulgarity getting the better of ultra-refinement is always a rather inspiriting sight. But to-day it seemed dreadful to her that her splendid moment should be prefaced by this sordid scrap. It hurt her that there should be this unpleasantness at the climax of her honest life; and moreover there was always the fear at the back of her mind that somehow it might break her luck. . . .

Martha Jane's speech snapped like a bent twig when the charwoman's hand came down upon her. With her mouth still open, as if it were indeed the mouth of a hose from which the water had been switched off, she stared weakly into the pleasant face. It was a long time now since any woman had touched her, especially a woman like Mrs. Clapham. The last time she had been touched, if you might call it a touch, had been in a quarrel with the drunken Mrs. Johnson, of Lame Lane. Mrs. Johnson had blacked one of Martha Jane's mocking and cynical eyes, and Martha Jane had pulled out a lock of Mrs. Johnson's none too plentiful hair. Not that Martha Jane was in the habit of doing these things—they only happened sometimes; but that last occasion contrasted with this was enough in itself to make her wince.

Mrs. Clapham, for her part, was thinking that Martha Jane's shoulder was nearly as thin as a young girl's. Not such a shoulder as Tibbie's had been, of course, because Tibbie's shoulders had never been thin. They were plump, laughing, expressive shoulders, which talked almost as much as Tibbie herself. Nevertheless, it was of her absent daughter that Mrs. Clapham thought, and the tenderness that was in her heart went into her hand and so down into Martha Jane.

'Now, Martha, don't carry on like that!' she rebuked her authoritatively, though on a motherly note. 'You'll be finely ashamed, making such a to-do, if you find you've got the house, after all. Anyway, it'll be a good day for one of us when t' news *does* come along, and we don't want it spoilt by nasty words. If it's me as gets it, I hope you won't take it too hard; and if it's you'—her voice faltered a moment as she tried to envisage the fearful conditions in which such an event could ever occur—'I'll be right glad to help you with moving in; ay, and to scrub floors for you an' all!'

The generosity of this offer produced an outburst of admiration from her satellites. 'Eh, now, if that isn't kind! . . . Real Christian, *I* call it! . . .' and 'If that isn't the kindest thing I ever heard!'—this last from young Mrs. James, retired within escaping distance of her pillars. Martha Jane looked spitefully round the group, and then back for a moment at Mrs. Clapham's hand. The sun played on the wedding-ring as she looked, flashing it in her eyes, and suddenly she gave her shoulder a little twitch, so that the hand slid off it and dropped.

'Thank you kindly, Ann Clapham!' she jeered; 'I'll be sure to think on. I'm not very set on cleaning, myself, so I'll be glad of a hand. Folks is different, of course, and I wasn't brought up to it, same as you. Some on us is finer clay than others, as his lordship says, and I reckon my sort o' clay wasn't intended for scrubbing floors!'

There was another outburst, though one of resentment, at this grateful and gracious speech, and the charwoman turned away with the colour hot in her cheek. The heart that had felt so tender only a moment ago now seemed full of nothing but angry disgust. Martha Jane was certainly doing her best to spoil the beautiful day, first of all by turning it into a ribald joke, and then by setting the company by the ears. Just for the moment Mrs. Clapham felt thoroughly vexed with the whole world—with Martha Jane, with the post, with his lordship and Mr. Baines; and even, though quite unjustly, with the admiring Chorus itself. Even the lovely morning seemed to fade because of her wrath; taking with it, as it dimmed, the perfect certainty of her hope. . . .

And then suddenly there rose before her eyes a picture of Tibbie laughing at Martha Jane—Tibbie, who had always refused to look upon Martha Jane as anything but the village clown. She had even been known to say that they ought to be grateful for Martha Jane, but she could hardly expect her mother to be grateful to-day! The thought of Tibbie, however,

brought the smile back to Mrs. Clapham's lips, and
her sense of miracle slowly returned. She told herself
with a gallant boast that was at the same time rather
grim, that she would certainly scrub the floors for the
poor, daft thing if she got the house! But even while
she played with the thought, she knew that she
troubled herself for nothing. She could no more
picture Martha Jane in her temple of hope than she
could picture her beautiful Tibbie in her coffin.

Putting the matter from her, she settled once more
to her patient watching of the street, only to be conscious instantly of a fresh commotion. Mrs. James,
who had started again upon Martha Jane, came to a
dead stop, and darted back to the charwoman's side,
while the rest of the women gathered around her like
chickens about a Buff Orpington hen. Mrs. Clapham
turned a surprised head, and looked over her shoulder.
Emma Catterall was coming slowly towards them
down the hill.

CHAPTER IV

IT was hardly surprising that Emma's approach
should have caused panic in the little group, for it
was only on the rarest occasions that Emma ever
approached anybody. As for making one of a party,
she never did that—as Mrs. Clapham had already
observed. The utmost that could be seen of her, as a
rule, was a hint of her presence behind the ferns, or
ebbing and flowing in the pool of shadow behind her
door. Sometimes, on very urgent occasions, she might
be found in the street, but even then she only hovered
on the edge of things. She never plunged right in and
became one of the crowd, as the alarmed intuition of
her neighbours warned them that she intended doing
to-day. She just hovered on the fringe of whatever
was going on, paralysing its energies with her queer

little half-smile. Beneath that smile the bride instantly became convinced that there was something wrong with her hair or her gown; while the widow, hitherto upheld by the dignity of her woe, burst into fresh tears. Into the consciousness of each came a vision of the things that stand about human life, aloof and yet close as Emma was aloof and close, and standing and smiling, perhaps, as Emma Catterall stood and smiled. . . .

There was something portentous, therefore, about this alteration in Emma's methods, and the Clapham contingent felt it in every nerve. It was as if she brought with her some news which they had not anticipated, some revelation for which they were not prepared. For, great occasion though this undoubtedly was to the people concerned, it was not, after all, such a *very* great occasion. Events of far wider and higher importance had failed to fetch Emma from her lair—such as Armistice Day, the bolting of the bus-horses, or the King's visit to Cautley School; most important of all, the packing of the six-foot music-hall man into a twenty-four inch box on a brougham in the Market Square.

At first glance there seemed nothing sinister about the short, roundabout figure in its white apron and dark gown, the smooth face and bands of dark hair which showed little sign of turning grey. A respectable, self-controlled, self-respecting woman, you would have said, looking at the still face and folded arms, and hearing the quiet, expressionless voice. It was only after a while that you began to feel troubled by the personality behind, to shiver under the passionless scrutiny of the beady, black eyes, and to long to break up the little suggestive smile which hovered continually on her lips.

Heads were turned as she came up, and curt sentences exchanged; etiquette demanding, as in the case of Martha Jane, some slight recognition of her presence. It was not because of any social ostracism that Emma had never acquired the genial habit of 'joining on'. In spite of the widespread feeling regarding her treatment of Poor Stephen, nobody had ever found courage to say much about it. They had hinted, of course, subtle hints or broad, low hints or loud, but they had never accused her to her face. Perhaps they felt that there was nothing to be gained by direct attack, or else in the fits of anger and pity that swept them from time to time, surely somebody would have spoken. Martha Jane *had* spoken, of course—they all of them knew that; but unluckily Martha's morals were such that her speaking could hardly count. The other women had simply contented themselves with private arraignment and the casual hint, together with such kindnesses to Poor Stephen as happened to come their way.

Yet even now Emma did not actually penetrate the group—an impossible feat, indeed, seeing that the Chorus was crowded about Mrs. Clapham like saplings about an oak. The latter threw her a 'Well, Emma, how do you find yourself this morning?' with the heartiness of a bluff English sea-dog to some cynical Spanish don, and then turned again to the street. It was Martha Jane who finally broke the uncomfortable silence with her usual patter of mocking speech.

'Save us, Emma Catterall! You don't mean to say you've ventured out to see what's coming to me and Mrs. Clapham? I wonder the skies don't fall—I do that! Me and Mrs. Clapham feel real honoured, I'm sure. You're in plenty of time, if you want to know; you'll be in at the death; though, if post didn't happen to be late this morning, you'd likely have missed it, after all!'

'In at the death, am I?' Emma repeated in that uncannily-still voice which did not so much seem to speak as only to happen. 'In at the death? . . .' The little smile came to her lips, as if at some peculiarly agreeable thought. . . . 'Ay, well, that's where we all come in, one time or another. . . .' Her eyes slid up and down and away from each of the group, and came to a halt on Mrs. Clapham. 'Seeing you all that throng made me quite curious-like,' she continued, after a pause. ' 'Tisn't everybody has the time to be standing about that early in the day; but there, as I always say, I reckon you know your own business best. . . .'

A kind of spasm ran through the group at the phrase which they had all long since learned to hate. They were all strung-up and sensitive by now, and the phrase tightened the tension beyond bearing. Mrs. Airey's face lost its comfortable, motherly look, and Mrs. Dunn's grew longer and flatter. As for Mrs. James, in spite of the house with the pillars, she gave the impression of actually creeping under the wing-feathers of Mrs. Clapham.

'No harm in waiting for t' post, I suppose?' yapped Martha Jane; 'especially when folks has important business!'

'Depends on who's waiting—and what for!' Emma's tone was silky, but dreadfully full of meaning, and Martha Jane suddenly wilted. 'A man isn't less of a man because he's a bag on his back and a bit of red to the front of his coat. . . . He's ter'ble late, anyway, isn't he?' she went on smoothly, leaving her cryptic statement to drive pleasantly home. 'I've noticed a deal o' times that, when news is long on the road, it's like enough because there doesn't happen to be any at all.'

For the second time that morning Mrs. Airey and Mrs. Dunn drew together and touched hands. They who had hungered for news through the Great War knew the terrible truth of that. Mrs. Tanner, however, perked up her head.

'What, there must be news sometime, you'll think on!' she chirruped bravely. 'It's only a matter of who brings it. There's some think it'll be Mr. Baines.'

'Baines?' The smooth, sliding tones seemed to convey, even in that single word, that it would be better on the whole if the devil himself brought the news, rather than the amiable lawyer. 'I've never known anything but bad luck come o' news brought by Mr. Baines. There was that time, you'll think on, when he come to tell Alice Alderson as she'd a bit o' money left her by her aunt; and, after she'd got engaged on the strength of it, and run up a ter'ble big bill, Mrs. Clapham, with your Tibbie, an' all, round he come again to say it was all a mistake. Then there was that mighty queer tale about Polly Green, which I shouldn't as much as mention if we wasn't friends. Baines had looked in to say as her husband was coming back from abroad, after twenty year, and she went and hanged herself, right off the reel. Ay, and yon other time, you'll think on (now you'll surely remember *this!*), when he come to tell Ann Machell as she'd got the same house you're after now; and blest if she didn't have a stroke with excitement that very night!'

The spirits of the whole company were at zero by now. Even Martha Jane seemed crushed for the time being. Some of them, indeed—Mrs. James, for one—cast longing glances at their dwellings, and thought to themselves that they might just as well be waiting inside. It seemed mean, of course, to desert Mrs. Clapham, and at the critical moment, but nobody could be expected to put up with Emma. They could not understand why she made things seem so hopelessly wrong, as if nothing splendid could possibly happen. It was as if that little smile of hers brushed all the colour out of life, hinting that it was something different from what you had thought. It couldn't be just that she slanged everybody as their names came up, because they were more than equal to that themselves, and would, if they were honest, admit that it left them all the brighter and better. It was that queer something at the back of Emma's mind that made you feel so low, something that hinted at knowledge you didn't possess. It was like being shut in a dark room with somebody you couldn't see. It was like being a mouse and thinking you knew the whereabouts of the cat; conscious all the time from your head to your tail that it was watching you from somewhere else.

As for Mrs. Clapham, her knee was beginning to ache with the long standing, and there was also a grumble about her heart. She, too, had almost begun to wish that she had never come into the street at all, but had stayed quietly inside her cottage. It seemed to her suddenly that she was making an exhibition of herself, standing there with that crowd of women. Not that she actually lost faith in the wonderful outcome that was to be; it was only that the perfect approach was being spoilt. First of all, there had been Martha Jane, turning her handsprings like a clown; and now unexpectedly there was Emma, with her prophecies of ill-luck. . . .

So crushed, indeed, was the whole group, that it seemed for the moment as if nobody would ever have courage to answer. But even the most oppressed will fight to the last ounce for a thing that has touched their imagination, and Mrs. James had again been injured in her ideal. 'Mr. Baines'll bring no more bad luck than most folks—that I'll be bound!' she burst out sharply, even twisting herself from under the feathers to glare. 'Bad luck comes of itself and with nobody's help; we all on us know that. But, speaking for myself, I'm not sure as even bad luck brought by Mr. Baines wouldn't sound like good!'

Emma said nothing for quite a long time, but just stood staring with her little smile, while the embarrassed red grew in the other's face. . . . Her crossed hands, cupping her elbows, did not so much as twitch.

'I'm not saying it's what Mr. Baines *brings*,' she answered at last, as Mrs. James dived back; 'it's what he *leaves*. He comes up all nice and smiling and sweet-spoken like, and you feel rarely pleased. It's only after he's gone you find as things isn't what they seem.'

'They can seem any old how they choose, so long as I get t' house. . . .' This was Martha Jane, recovered a second time from her wilting. 'News can come through a dozen Baineses, so long as it says I'm in!'

Mrs. James being to all intents and purposes invisible, Emma had plenty of time to attend to Martha Jane.

'I'm surprised, I'm sure, to think of you being after one o' *them* houses!' she remarked sweetly. 'When I heard tell about it, I could hardly believe my ears. The folks in them houses is expected to keep 'em spick as a pin, and I can't rightly see you putting your hand to that. You'll have governors and their wives calling and ferreting round to see what you're at; and a nice to-do there'll be if things isn't just so. Seems to me you'll have to alter your ways in other things, too, if you mean taking yon house. . . . But there, after all, I reckon you know your own business best. . . .'

'Ann Clapham's offered to scrub floors for me as a start-off!' Martha Jane laughed. 'That'll give me a leg-up! . . .' She changed her tone suddenly to the professional whine, as if for the benefit of somebody not present. 'Folks isn't all as hard as you folks seem to think. There's Mr. Audland promised somebody should see to me if I was ill; and his lordship'll send me one of his own gardeners if him as belongs alms-houses is overpressed.' She caught Mrs. James's sniff from under the feathers, and grew in defiance. 'Right kind about it his lordship was, I'm sure! Says I'm a deal too delicate to lift a finger myself.'

'No use counting on it, and so I tell you!' Mrs. Tanner put in briskly. 'Ann Clapham's going to get yon house—not you!'—and Mrs. James snorted 'Ay, I should think so, indeed!' terribly rankled about the lordship; and other comments followed at which Martha bridled and brazened and wilted by turn.

When they had all finished, Emma began again in her expressionless tones.

'Ay, Ann Clapham'll get it; there's no doubt about that. . . . I don't say but what I couldn't have had it myself, but there, thanks be, I don't need other folks' brass. Ann Clapham's had a hard life, though, and deserves a bit o' quiet. I don't know as she'll take to it just at first—being a lady and all that; but there, I reckon she knows her own business best. . . . She isn't as young as she was, neither, and folks as works over hard wear out ter'ble fast. Ay, she'll get t' house, will Ann Clapham; there's no doubt about that.'

There was another uncomfortable pause when she had finished, and Mrs. Clapham cast an uneasy glance at her over her shoulder. What Emma was saying *sounded* all right—at least, for Emma—so she was at a loss to understand why it should fill her with apprehension. Yet, instead of strengthening her own conviction of coming fortune, in some mysterious fashion it undermined it. She began to feel that, if Emma continued to say that sort of thing, she would not only lose all confidence in her luck, but would find it lacking in flavour if established. She really wished now that she had been patient enough to await the news indoors, and was even beginning to turn on her heel when she was called to attention by Mrs. James. 'There he is!' the latter was saying from under the feathers, disappointed yet thrilled. 'Look ye! Look ye, Mrs. Clapham! There he is! There's t' post!'

The uniformed figure of the postman had suddenly appeared round the curve of the street, and at once Mrs. Clapham and Martha drew together, as if conscious that neither for the lucky nor the unlucky would it be possible to meet this moment alone. Mrs. James slipped her hand through Mrs. Clapham's arm and gave it an excited squeeze, and the charwoman flushed a deep crimson and paled slowly again. Martha Jane, however, to whom excitement was the breath of life itself, looked for the moment strangely brisk and young. A hint of the old rose-colour came into her cheek, and a youthfully-brilliant sparkle into her eye. Mrs. Tanner and her colleagues broke into little twitters and chirps. . . . 'Eh, but he's taken his time! . . . Which on 'em will it be? . . . Eh, but I'm right thrilled! . . .' While at the back of them all, where she stood silent and still a little apart, Emma uncrossed her hands and let them drop to her sides.

And still the postman was taking his time, rapping at this door, and poking papers through that; handing in letters, when he did hand them, as if he were meting out orders of execution. He was a dour, silent person, who seemed to regard letters as an unnecessary luxury, for which the recipients should be made to pay; and though during the War he had gone so far as to admit the need of the post to mothers and wives, he seemed to expect them to do without it now that the War was over. It was impossible that he should not have noticed the thrilled group of waiting women, even if he had not felt the current of excitement sweeping towards him down the street; but, for all the attention he paid them, they might not have existed. He stayed quite a long time at Mr. Baines's office at the foot of the street, grumpily handing in document after document, and (apparently) concealing the last of them in his bag. Even the gaze of seven passionately-interested females did not seem able to hurry him by a second.

'Ay, he's taking his time!' Mrs. Tanner repeated sardonically, after a short pause, and in the tenseness of the atmosphere every one of the others jumped. The electric tremors passing between them ran and raced like sunlight on flashing wires as the postman finally turned and came heading towards them. Even now, however, he seemed quite oblivious of their existence, and on a sudden impulse Mrs. James stepped out from under the feathers as if to block the way with her arms. But before anything could be said he was

up to them, by them, and then unmistakably past.
'Nowt for none o' ye!' he snapped, without even
turning his head, and vanished up the alley that led
to the 'Black Bull'.

Martha Jane's laugh led the chaos of sound into
which the disgruntled Chorus broke; but, brazen
though it was, it was also slightly relieved. The passing of the post left her with still another chance, still
another moment in which to preen herself on her
possible success.

Mrs. James was asseverating—'Didn't I say it
wouldn't be t' post? You mark my words now! . . .
It'll be Mr. Baines . . .' and Mrs. Tanner was chirping
—'Did you ever see such manners? He might ha'
given us a word!' with the twittering anger of a furious
wren. Mrs. Clapham said nothing, but her mouth
dropped at the corners like that of a disappointed
child, and behind her Emma lifted her arms and
folded them slowly again across her waist. . . .

'I always said he'd bring it himself!' Mrs. James's
voice was happy and high. 'Not because of the stamp
and suchlike rubbish—Mr. Baines ain't the sort to
stick at a stamp—but because he's a gentleman and
likes everything just so. Folks can't be more than
gentlemen, nohow,' she finished, glaring at Martha
Jane, 'even if they do happen to be lordships an' all!'

The flaw in the last sentence passed Martha Jane
by, but she was ready for battle, nevertheless.

'You wouldn't expect lordships to be doing *clurk's*
work, I reckon?' she demanded scornfully, 'or handing
in notes as if they hadn't a footman to their name? . . .
He says he'll call when I'm in and see as I'm properly
tret,' she delivered her final blow; 'and I shouldn't
wonder if he stopped for a cup o' tea!'

A fresh spasm, evidenced by pursed lips, went
round the shocked throng, exactly as if they had been
drilled by some rapped-out word of command. Mrs.
James looked at Mrs. Tanner, and Mrs. Airey at

Mrs. Dunn. Martha Jane went furiously red, and tossed her head so violently that a hairpin flew out. Only in the background Emma went on smiling her Mona Lisa smile. . . . 'Lordships and suchlike have their own way o' doing things,' said her expressionless voice. 'Seems to me calling on such as you is more a parson's job than a lord's. . . . But there, no doubt he knows his own business best. . . .'

'Anyway, I'll lay my best new rubber hot-water bottle as it'll be Mr. Baines!' Mrs. James was still faithful and valiant, but her voice sounded a little flat. It was a bitter pill not to be able to fling back the statement that Mr. Baines would be calling on *her*. Martha Jane might be lying, of course—and probably was—but still there was no knowing what lordships might choose to do. For the first time Mrs. Clapham's friends began to entertain doubts as to her divine right, and to wonder whether by any possible chance Martha Jane *could* come out top. Mrs. Clapham must have felt the doubt in the air, for she turned again as if meaning to steal home. Once more, however, she was arrested by Mrs. James's voice, and this time there was no mistaking its unmixed pleasure. In the tone of a herald proclaiming some royalty to a waiting court, Mrs. James made her announcement of '*Mr. Baines!*'

Once again the group drew together, breathless and tense, though always with the exception of Emma, a little in the rear. Mrs. Tanner broke into a fresh series of excited chirps, and for the second time the years fell away from Martha Jane. Mrs. Clapham, however, uttered a sharp sigh, as if aware that repeated drama on this scale was hardly the thing for a doubtful heart; and Emma behind her neither chirruped nor sighed, but again unfolded her arms and let them hang by her sides.

Mr. Baines had suddenly appeared at the bottom of the street on the way to his office, holding a skipping little girl by a fatherly hand. He was a well-dressed, pleasant-looking man, with a buttonhole and a smile; and the little girl was pretty and pink and fair, with a sky-coloured silk jersey over her little white frock. When they reached the office he let go her hand and pointed in the direction from which they had come, and she stood on one leg and pouted, and then suddenly skipped again. They argued a moment or two, with more pointing and pouting and skipping, and then both their heads turned as if pulled by a string. Forgetting their differences, they stood looking up towards the women in the street.

Mr. Baines laughed when he saw them and put up his pince-nez, while the child stared at them gravely, a finger seeking her mouth. Mr. Baines hesitated a moment, blushed, looked at his office-door as if thinking of his clerk, and then back again at the breathless group. To the two at the bottom of the street there was something almost intimidating in the concentrated expectancy of the obviously-set piece. Mr. Baines pushed his hat slightly to the back of his head, feeling embarrassed and perplexed. Really, he hardly felt equal at that early hour to facing a posse of seven women, and with both the almshouse candidates there to boot!

At last, drawing a letter from his pocket—('*The* letter!' gasped the impassioned Chorus)—he stooped and gave it to the child, obviously issuing instructions, and pointing delicately to the set piece. The little girl looked reluctant at first and then suddenly eager; nodded her comprehension and poised herself for flight; while Mr. Baines, smiling and blushing all over his clean face, took off his hat with a wave to the set piece, and vanished thankfully into his office.

The child came speeding up the street, serious, and clutching the letter tight; and suddenly the tension of the women broke in a general smile. From doors and windows faces came peeping again, and they, too, smiled at the flying messenger. Even Mrs. James smiled, hurt though she was by the unexpected and—almost—cowardly defection of Mr. Baines, and trying to console herself with the assurance that the wave had undoubtedly been meant for her. Martha Jane smiled wistfully, ingratiatingly, wilting in every limb, in case either Mr. Baines or his clerk should be looking out of the office window. As for Mrs. Clapham, she smiled through a blur of tears, because the little child skimming towards her reminded her so of Tibbie; while in the background Emma continued to smile, too, though with an amazing difference of expression. Unheard by the others, her breath came in short gasps, and her hands twitched as they hung at her stiff sides. . . .

She alone stood firm as the group broke to receive the child, so that, carried along by her rush, the latter ran almost into her arms. Emma laid a hand on her shoulder and bent to look at the note, but the child backed away so sharply that the hand tore the frill at her neck. 'Not you!' she exclaimed, frowning and clutching the letter, and actually looking at Emma as if she hated her. Nevertheless, Mrs. Catterall did not seem disturbed. The smile on her lips seemed suddenly to hold some added element of satisfaction, and slowly her hands came up from her sides and fell placidly into place. . . .

The contact, however, seemed to have upset the little girl, for she stood looking around the group with dubious eyes. The women waited patiently, smiling kindly at her confusion. Once, indeed, Mrs. Dunn began 'Now then, dearie'—in her colourless tones, but was instantly elbowed into silence by her sister. Again the child looked round, caught Martha Jane's appealing glance, and broke into a brilliant smile. Darting forward with the same butterfly lightness, she thrust the note into her uncertain hand.

The world swung round Mrs. Clapham; the ground

tilted under her feet. As for the Chorus, its feelings
had vent in an actual scream, which was followed at
once by a paralysed silence. Only Emma retained her
satisfied air, and her hands stayed quiet at her waist.
. . . And then, out of the mists surrounding and over-
whelming her, Mrs. Clapham heard Martha Jane's
laugh. . . .

' 'Tain't for me, dearie . . . you've made a mistake;
thanking you kindly, all the same! . . .' The laugh was
nearer this time, and a thin, long-fingered hand came
under the charwoman's nose. 'No use being dishonest
under the circs!' said Martha Jane. 'Here, Ann
Clapham! You may as well have what's your own.'

The thin hand thrust the letter into the groping
plump one, and then Martha's face backed away with
a twisted smile. 'Sorry I can't come scrubbing your
floors,' she finished, discordantly cheerful, 'but I don't
mind going so far as to wish you luck!'

Her voice broke on a note like that of a cracked
dish, and she edged quickly away with trembling lips.
The child ran after her, however, saying 'She tore my
frill! Look, my frill's all torn!' and casting angry
glances at the imperturbable Emma; and Martha
Jane, stopped by the clutching hands, made a valiant
effort to struggle with her tears, and bent herself to the
woes of little Miss Baines.

Right over Mrs. Clapham and to the ends of the
earth the sun came out for ever and ever. Her hands
shook as they tried to open the envelope and failed,
and the Chorus grabbed it and did it for her. In the
same piecemeal way they read the letter aloud, peering over her elbow and under her arm, while she
laughed and wept and gasped, and thanked God and
the governors and the world in general. Of what was
actually in the letter she heard very little, except the
fact that the house was undoubtedly hers. Mrs. James,
of course, was inclined to dwell upon the flowers of
speech which she guessed to have emanated from

Mr. Baines, expressing the committee's appreciation of the successful candidate's worth, and wishing her happiness under her new roof. The other women, not being burdened by an ideal, dwelt practically if ecstatically upon such details as the allowance and the coal; but Mrs. Clapham heard little of either. All she did was to exclaim 'Ain't that grand, now? That's real nice! Ay, that's right kind!' whenever the rising voices seemed to expect it. All that mattered for the moment was the fact that the dream had not failed her, that never for an instant had her confidence been misplaced. She had been sure that the right things happened in the right way at exactly the right time, and now she could go on being sure as long as she lived. People got what they wanted all right if only they had enough faith—that was another beautiful thing that the letter had proved true. She forgot the long wait and Martha's clowning and Emma's sinister looks, and only remembered that all was right with the world and God emphatically in His smiling heaven.

And in the background Martha Jane bent to the complaining child, murmuring soothingly and making quaint little jokes with quivering lips. Taking the crooked gilt pin from her own dirty lace, she fastened the snowy frill of little Miss Baines. It had been a bad moment for Martha Jane when she was offered the letter by mistake, but there was no sense in blaming the child. She wasn't 'the almshouse sort', she reminded herself again; and again, *because* she wasn't the almshouse sort, was able to raise a smile. . . .

She pressed the pin-point into a safe place (pricking herself again), and the little girl, with a word of thanks, skipped away down the street. The women around Mrs. Clapham were falling silent at last, too much exhausted to find anything fresh to read or invent. Behind them Emma was receding rapidly up the hill, making her way back to the dark house and the dying ferns. . . . Martha Jane braced herself for a final effort.

'Off again, are you?' she called after the retreating figure. 'The vanishing trick, eh? as per usual? . . . Ay, well, you got all you wanted, I reckon!' she laughed harshly. 'You were in at the death-rattle, after all!'

Emma, now on her steps, turned at the last words, and it seemed to her tormentor that her smile deepened. That was all the answer she made, however—if it could be called an answer. Even as Martha Jane watched, she began to fade, dwindling and gleaming and glooming, until at last she was out of sight.

PART II

THANK-OFFERING

CHAPTER I

By the time the Chorus had talked itself to rags and a dribbling finish, and Mrs. James had remembered her pudding and Mrs. Airey her hot irons, and Mrs. Clapham had had time to think of her knee, and how she was tired with standing, and how it would be just as easy to enjoy the news sitting down—both Emma and Martha Jane had vanished utterly from the scene. It was the charwoman who noticed their disappearance first, wiping away the last glad tears from her shining, glorified face.

'Eh, now, if Martha Jane hasn't made off, and I never thought on to say I was sorry she'd lost! I was that taken up wi' t' letter I couldn't think of nowt else. She'll be feeling bad about it, I reckon, will poor Martha Jane. I wish I'd had a word wi' her before she slipped away!'

'I shouldn't worry myself. . . . Likely she'll go whingeing to yon lordship of hers, and get summat instead!' Mrs. James looked back from between her pillars, anxious, in spite of her pudding, for a last slap at Martha Jane. 'Anyway, I was right about Mr. Baines bringing the news,' she went on proudly; 'or next best thing to Mr. Baines! A bonny little thing, that little girl, isn't she now?—and that like him an' all! . . . Ay, well, Mrs. Clapham, I'm main glad it come out right, and there's a deal more I'd like to know if it wasn't for yon pan. . . .'

'Eh, and yon irons o' mine'll be fit to scorch!' . . . Mrs. Airey bestirred herself also at the departure of Mrs. James. 'I'm as throng as I can be to-day, an' all. Folks is that put about if they don't get their washing on the tick, you'd think they'd only a shirt and a pillow-slip to their names! . . . Step along in with her, Maggie, and get her a cup o' tea,' she added to Mrs. Tanner, as she and her sister moved away. 'She's a bit upset wi' it all, and a cup o' tea'll pull her together. Folks is easy put out about good news— I cried a deal more when my Teddy come back from t' War than I ever did when he went—even if they don't all get strokes and such-like just by clapping an eye on poor Baines!'

There was a last burst of laughter in the street at that, the last that it was to hear that morning, the last, perhaps, that it was to hear that day. . . . 'Ay, Emma was right creepy with her nasty tales!' Mrs. Clapham concluded meditatively, when the sisters had gone. '(I can manage right enough, Maggie. Don't you put yourself out!) She's cleared off again, I notice, and with never a word. She must just ha' waited to hear the news, and then made back.'

'There was summat queer about her ever coming at all!' . . . Mrs. Tanner lingered, cogitating, in the empty street. 'What, she never stirred foot even for t' Coronation, you'll think on—(Edward was it, or George?). You and she have never been that thick, I'm sure, that she should turn out to wish you luck!'

'She talked that strange, too,' the charwoman puzzled, thinking back, 'praising me up and so on, and yet wi' a scrat in it all the time! She fair made me begin to think things was going to go all wrong.'

'It's that way she has of making you feel she knows summat important as you don't. It's like as if she give you plenty o' rope to hang yourself, and then stood about smiling, waiting for the pull. Ay, and what you'd feel right sore about when it come to it wouldn't be as you was hung, but feeling you'd made a fool o' yourself with yon woman a-looking on!'

'Ay, that's summat like it,' Mrs. Clapham murmured. 'That's it, I reckon. . . .' She threw a glance up the street at the silent, ill-omened house. 'It's no wonder she made such a wreck o' Poor Stephen.'

The Saga of Poor Stephen who had fallen in the War began all over again, with precisely the same zest as if sung for the first time. It was a sort of duet into which they fell quite naturally whenever they happened to meet, and however often it was repeated it never palled. Conversation is almost the only form of artistic expression open to most of the poor, and on this subject at least these two had reached a high level. The Saga of Poor Stephen was, indeed, their star performance. Knowing it like their prayers, they played up to each other with mechanical ease, yet found always some shade of inflection which might possibly be bettered, some sentence introduced or eliminated which shed new light upon the whole. And always, as soon as they had parted, their minds set to work again upon the scene they had just played, half consciously rehearsing it for its next public appearance, and seeking some fresh touch which should cause it to live anew.

However, they rang the curtain down at length, and drifted apart—Mrs. Tanner backing towards her door with that almost unconscious movement of street-gossips—as if she was pulled by a string—and the charwoman turning joyously home to her own dwelling. She reached it in less than a dozen strides, but even in that short distance she produced the effect of a full-rigged ship coming buoyantly into port. Crossing the step, she had a passing twinge of remorse because she had neglected to give it its second scrub; and then she was once again in the little kitchen, with the door closing behind her back.

It was a wonderful moment for Mrs. Clapham when she came back again to her home, bearing her sheaves with her. The early morning had been wonderful, too, but in a totally different way. It had been splendid, of course, full of rapture and hope, but she knew now that at the back of everything there had been a fear. That sudden bout of laughter and tears had testified to the strain. The early-morning phase had been bought at its own price. But this moment was all splendour without terror, glory without pain. Steeped in wonder, it was yet perfect in satisfaction; shot with ecstasy, it was yet peace. . . .

Presently, perhaps, when the supreme moment had passed, she would wish for that earlier phase all over again. *That* would seem the supreme moment to her, looking back, the most poignant, the most dramatic, the most worth having because of its thrills. She would forget the scorch of the chariot of fire in which she had left the earth, and only remember the sweep of it as she ascended to heaven. Nevertheless, this was the really great hour of her beautiful day, and she recognised it while she had it. There is no moment like that in which one runs home through a shining world to hide behind a shut door with the glad fulfilment of an innocent dream.

With it, however, came the realisation of what she would have felt if things had happened the other way about, and even the thought of it was so terrible that it turned her faint. Reaching the rocking-chair, she dropped into it with a thankful sigh, and the anything but thankful chair uttered a protesting creak. But the horror soon passed and the glory returned, so that she hardly knew whether the gold motes dancing in the kitchen were made by the sun, or whether the whole world had turned golden in essence because of the splendour in her brain.

With smiling lips, and half-closed, tear-wet eyes, she sat rocking herself to and fro, while the over-burdened chair uttered its almost human shrieks of protesting rage. But she was too happy to notice it, too happy to move; too happy even to get herself the cup of tea which she dearly craved. She knew vaguely that her head ached as well as her back and her bad knee, but these also were beyond notice. The most they could do was to force her to own, chuckling, that it was a good thing miracles didn't happen every day of the week. But then she did not want them to happen every day; she did not want them ever to happen again. Once was all she had asked for in the whole of her life, and that once was proving itself most gloriously enough.

Undoubtedly her chief joy, half-conscious though it was, lay in her supreme and perfected confidence in the workings of fate. Human beings are never so happy, so soothed, and so unafraid, as when they seem to identify themselves with the Ruling Mind. The soul, swerving blindly from fear to fear, clings thankfully to the least vestige of a plan, whether for good or ill. It was not often that Mrs. Clapham had felt afraid of life, but it seemed to her at this moment that she would never feel afraid again. It was muddle that frightened people, she thought to herself, torn edges and jagged ends, suddenly-twisted threads that on every count should have run straight, and meaningless blows from a vague dark. Mrs. Clapham was of those who prefer to be hit firmly on the head by an Absolute Will, rather than to be sent flying into space by the blind bursting of a mindless shell.

But for her, at all events, life had proved itself faithful up to the very hilt. Week after week, year after year, she had held to her great belief, and in the due moment of promise it had been fulfilled. The right thing came at the right time and in the right way—always she came back again to that. A little earlier, perhaps, or a little later, and the whole thing would have been less perfect; would not have found her so ready or left her so secure. Even a splendidly-sudden surprise would not have been really so splendid, because unable to fix in her this precious certainty of success. Sudden surprises are wonderful in their way, opening the doors of fairylands and heavens, but they do not create security or make for peace. On the contrary, they, too, suggest chaos after their own magnificent fashion. The highest pinnacle is that which is reached after earnest endeavour, patient provision, humble yet certain hope. The charwoman felt satisfied in every inch, seeing life and the justice of things fitting each other like lock and key. She felt as one feels at the end of a sunset or the close of a song. She felt as one feels when one shuts the door of a room in which a child has fallen asleep. . . .

She wished that the man who had thought of her long ago could know that both his wish and hers were going to be fulfilled at last. He, too, had been one of those who find their greatest pleasure in watching the Universe work out even; so that the news that his forty-year-old plan was coming into effect would have afforded him a personal satisfaction. She felt sure that he would have nodded his head with his grim smile, saying, 'Right you are, Jones! Meant you to have it. Pleased. D—d glad!' feeling that, in this one thing at least, he had been able to give the sometimes-recalcitrant cosmos a shove on the right road.

She thought gratefully, too, of those who had voted her the house, trying to call up, though with a touch of shyness, the kindly things which they must have said, not only in committee but in the privacy of their homes. Some of them must have gone into the letter which they had written through Mr. Baines, but so far she had heard so little of that wonderful letter! It was still in her hand, of course, too precious to put down, and presently she would find her glasses and read it with quivering joy. But for the moment she needed no further stimulant for her happy mind. The ecstasy in her soul required no extra assistance from the elegant phrasing of Mr. Baines.

She thought also of the body of public opinion which was said to be at her back, and felt for the time being as if every soul in the place was a personal friend. It was wonderful, even for a short time, to feel the thoughts of all those well-wishers turned simultaneously towards herself. That was another thing she felt certain she would never mistrust again—the genuine joy of the many in the genuine joy of the one. There were the four women, for instance, who had stayed with her so long, swelling her triumph, when it came, by the mere fact of their kindly presence. They had, as it were, lifted her in their eager arms, ready to thrust her into the chariot before it had touched the ground. They had been like children, with a fifth who had won or was winning a coveted prize; like bridesmaids, speeding and cheering a happy but trepidant bride. . . .

That last word made her think of Miss Marigold up in town, who would even now be getting ready for church. Her mother would be helping and watching her, no doubt, as Tibbie's mother had once watched and helped. Miss Marigold, however, was no longer young, while Tibbie had been young as a first summer bird. Miss Marigold was to wear the uninteresting garments which so many brides wore now, but Tibbie herself had been dressed in white. Not satin, of course, or a wreath, or the over-grand ornament of a veil— both Tibbie and her mother were too sensible for that. But nobody who had seen Tibbie that day, whether in London or Timbuctoo, would have been stupid enough to take her for anything but a bride. She was the real, loving, loved, bridal thing that trod actually on air, so that one seemed, as it were, to see her spurning the earth, and to hear all about her the uprush of fine wings. . . .

The picture of Tibbie in her wedding-white was so present to her mind that she was surprised, when she opened her eyes, not to see her there in the flesh. She was so puzzled, indeed, that she stopped rocking and sat up, until presently, as her glance strayed about the room, the knowledge came to her that it was Tibbie's photograph that she sought. She did not seem able to visualise it in its usual place, and she got to her feet, wondering whether the emotion through which she had just passed had somehow shortened her sight. The photograph was there, however, she found, when she moved across, but had slipped on the shelf and lay on its back. She set it up again and stood looking at it, and Tibbie looked, too, but it hardly seemed to her that that was Tibbie's face. Tibbie's real face was the one she had just seen when she was half asleep, which had hung above her and kissed her . . . and laughed . . . and kissed her again. . . .

The photographs of the children were as usual stiffly erect, but she scarcely glanced at them as she turned away. It was impossible, with that vision of laughing girlhood still in her eyes, to think of them as belonging to Tibbie. Indeed, their utter unlikeness to her—always a source of grief—turned them, at this particular moment, into actual strangers. They were so tragically the counterparts of that unfortunate Poor Stephen, to whose comfort and help Tibbie had rushed like an indignant angel. There seemed little but pity and the attraction of opposites to account for the strange marriage, for the young couple had been like creatures out of two totally different spheres. Tibbie had come out of a House of Laughter and Stephen out of a House of Pain; and in spite of their love it was the image of pain that still looked out of their children's eyes. . . .

Her mind went back at that to her late talk with Mrs. Tanner, conning its weak points, and preparing it once more for the next occasion when they should be called upon to 'say their piece'. She was busy with it all the time she was brewing and drawing the tea, and even while, glasses at length unearthed, she pored joyously over the letter. Between her gasps of pleasure at each newly-discovered tribute, such as 'hard-working citizen', 'good neighbour', 'praiseworthy mother', and 'kind friend', some door in her mind kept swinging and standing ajar, showing her the pale-faced little boy who had lived through Heaven knew what misery in the house at the top of the street.

In the confidence born of the perfect happening at the perfect moment in the perfect way, Mrs. Clapham wondered how it had been possible for anybody to be as much afraid as Poor Stephen. She was almost inclined to feel impatient with him, looking back, though she had been sorry enough, and even fiercely indignant, at the time. In common with others in the street, she had done her best to see that Stephen was fed, that his clothes were mended and brushed before he went off to school, that there was a fire for him to sit by in cold weather when he chose, and sometimes a penny slipped in his pocket for buying sweets. But Stephen had been hard to help, as are all early-abused, early-cowed young things, and it was not often that he could be decoyed into other people's houses even for his good. It was almost as if the contrast between what he found there and what was waiting—or wasn't waiting—for him at home, was more than his wounded spirit was able to bear. In any case, he had avoided their kindly designs whenever he could, choosing his moment to slip past when they weren't looking, or creeping back again at night with ears deaf to their shrill calls. Often and often she had seen him stealing by in the winter dusk, resolutely turning his eyes from their open, fire-streaming doors. Even in the September sunshine Mrs. Clapham shivered at the thought of that going home, back to the dreary house in which he had been born afraid.

It was many a year now since she had set foot in Emma's house, but, gradually feeling back, she got its atmosphere again. She could remember little, indeed, of how it had looked; she could only remember how it had felt. Going into Emma's was not so much going into a house as letting yourself into the four walls of Emma Catterall's mind. Everything that was in it

looked as it did because of Emma, so that the tables
hardly seemed tables, or the chairs chairs, or the beds
beds. Even Emma's husband had somehow had that
effect, had suffered a sea-change simply because he was
Emma's. Jemmy Catterall had been weak and foolish
as a young man, but he had not been the inhuman
monster he appeared later. Marriage with Emma had
turned him shortly into a sullen brute, subject to fits of
fury which stamped him wrong in the head. That
undependableness of mood had been a sorry atmosphere for Stephen, combined with that terrible
sensing of something that wasn't sane.

Yet Jemmy—or so at least Mrs. Clapham had been
known to insist—would have been right enough but for
Emma. He was never a star, of course, either in looks
or brains, but he was right enough as men went, seeing
that in most cases they didn't go far. It was hardly
credible that he should have turned into the mad
skeleton of his later years, peering at people from
behind the ferns, or, later still, from a room upstairs.
When he wasn't peering he was emptying water-jugs
upon callers' heads, or throwing things at the passers-
by. It seemed an eternity that he had leered and
peered, until finally his amusements had come to an
end behind the shut door of a coffin-lid. . . .

Well, that had been Stephen's father—not much of a
father for anybody, if it came to that, but least of all
for one so inexpressibly in need of help. Yet, even at
his worst (and it was a most unpleasant worst), it was
unanimously agreed that he was nothing to Emma.
Mrs. Clapham could remember how they had all been
afraid of her, even as a girl, because of that thing in
her mind which watched and hid. Tibbie, too, had
complained that Emma spied on her while she slept,
just as her own babies had cried themselves sick about
it, later on. But the child out of the House of Laughter
had not troubled herself about Emma for very long;
quite early the obsession had turned into interest in

Poor Stephen. Even in those days she used to talk to her mother about the little boy who was always afraid; later still, when they were going to the same school; and later again, when they were grown up and gone to work. And then suddenly the happy, chattering voice had stopped of its own accord, dumb in that last, sweet, waiting stillness before the rushing confession of love. . . .

Upon that desolate Poor Stephen, sunk in his misery and mental murk, Tibbie's choice had had the effect of a silver clarion in the dark. The conferring of her love was like the conferring of a kingly robe and crown. The change in him was so startling that it was almost as if one saw the gold and the jewels shimmer about him as he moved. Tibbie was a strength-giver, just as Emma was a strength-stealer, but she did a great deal more for Stephen than that. She drew out of him by degrees the courage that was in himself, as well as the graces and charm which make a man loved wherever he goes. The long-latent force, crushed and shrivelled in youth, had gathered itself at last into that splendid battle-deed; but when the time came for her to lose him, as she had known it would have to come, it was the fact that he had been loved by his fellows that Tibbie had valued most.

Taken altogether, it was a strange tale of the breeding of pluck, especially such pluck as had set Stephen's name in newspapers without end, on Rolls of Honour and brasses, memorial crosses and shrines; even on the rough little wooden cross which the Germans had raised to him themselves. Only on rare occasions had Tibbie tried to tell her mother what Stephen had suffered in the past, and then it was always by request. It had been hard enough, even, for Stephen to tell his wife, and it was harder still for Tibbie to pass it on. Then, too, it seemed like sending him back to the house of bondage again, to keep even a hint of it in their thoughts. And it was all such a story of patches when it was told, a dreary and mean muddle like streaks on a sordid pane. They were such queer, quiet, sinister things that Emma had chosen to do—things that were yet as demoralising in their effect as any of Jemmy's wild water-jug-throwing moods. What the other children had suffered only in imagination had really happened to Poor Stephen, for his mother had actually spied upon him while he slept. Night after night he had started awake to find her in the room, a motionless dark figure set at the foot of his bed. She had said nothing; she had done nothing; she had just stood in the shadow and smiled; and he, gasping with fear in the bed, had yet managed to keep silence, too. Quite early he had known her for his enemy, both by night and day, but in the shadow at the foot of the bed she was something worse. The whole sinister powers of darkness seemed to be concentrated in her form, coming to brood above him while he was sound in his first sleep. . . .

This horrible travesty of motherly tenderness had frightened Tibbie Clapham as nothing else had frightened her in life; turning her, even in its recital, into a bitter, white-faced woman whom her mother hardly knew. Evil is never so sinister as when it touches the beautiful natural things and makes them strange. The story of those nights had impressed Tibbie with such cruel force that there was a time when she was almost afraid to approach her own children as they lay and slept. . . .

The nights had been hardest to bear, so Stephen had said, but Emma had watched him everywhere else as well. Indeed, after a while, he had grown to feel that even distance could make no difference; that, no matter where he went, he would never be free of her eyes. The whole circumstances of his life, with their lack of comfort and food, contributed to the obsession, doing their share in keeping his nerves unnourished and his bodily strength low. Then, too, there was the miserable meanness which hid whatever he needed and watched his face while he sought it; that murmured alike whether he was at home or abroad; that crept upon him or made sudden noises; that hinted at evil in connection with every name that he knew, sliding back, in the final event, to hint at it also with his own. . . .

But it was always the watching that he minded most, and that would have finished him in the end, sending him, but for Tibbie and marriage, either to suicide or drink. Even when he had left the place and was happily settled somewhere else, Emma's eyes had seemed to go with him. Not until long after he was married, Tibbie had said, had he ceased to feel that he was being watched.

'But he never felt it in France,' she said to her mother, after Stephen was dead. 'He told me—he even wrote about it—that he never felt it there. It was as if there was some big angel between them, making her keep away. Oh, mother, it was harder than words can say to let him go, but I used to feel so glad for him when he was in France! . . .'

CHAPTER II

THE rocking had begun again, the slow, rhythmic rocking that seemed to draw the past out like a charm, in spite of the continuous protest of the angry chair. It altered in character, however, after a while, the swing of the rocker dwindling at times until it almost stopped, and then beginning again with a gentle push. It was as soothing as the sleepy surge of a summer sea, urged by some impulse into a gentle swell, only to smooth itself out into stillness and slumber again. Even the angry chair seemed to be getting drowsy as well, and was silent at times for as much as a minute. At the end of the minute it would break out again into a raucous yelp, like the spasmodic effort of a tired dog. Gradually, however, both rocker and rocked came to a trance-like quiet. In the gold of the morning sun and of her own special private glory, Mrs. Clapham sat and slept.

She slept for about an hour, and was unaware that more than one person had been near her while she dreamed, peeping in at her through the window, or laying a gentle hand on the loose latch. Members of the Chorus appeared from time to time, only to back away again with an impressive finger on their lips. Mrs. James, indeed, at a second attempt, had actually penetrated into the sacred place, with infinite care setting at Mrs. Clapham's elbow a covered plate of soup. The young school teachers had looked in for a word on their way home, and had gone on again with hushed steps, taking with them that vision of tired thankfulness and infinite peace. Mrs. Clapham, of course, knew nothing of all this, but it soothed her even in sleep. The atmosphere of kindly interest, combined with the sun, lay softly about her like a silken shawl.

It was the rush of the children that awoke her at last, the feet of the home-coming children on the hill. Twice a day they streamed past Mrs. Clapham's cottage, and always the sound of their coming was like the sound of a river in spate. One said to oneself, 'What is it? What is it?' and then knew it to be the feet of the new generation on the road. The patter and clatter of those feet wove themselves into the last of Mrs. Clapham's dream. She heard the clink of clogged soles, the lighter slither of leather, the whistles and cries of the boys, the running chatter of little girls. And, long after the stream had passed on, it seemed to her that she heard other feet on the hill—the thin little dragging feet of little Libby and Baby Steve. . . .

She was almost sorry when she found that she had slept, for there is no divider, either in joy or sorrow, so great as sleep. The first ecstasy of her pleasure was over and gone. She felt almost as if the tremendous event had happened yesterday instead of to-day, and was vexed to have missed even a moment of the precious thrill. At the same time, she felt better for the rest, both in body and mind. Both her back and her knee had ceased to ache, and her head felt business-like and cool. The pleasure was still there, of course, and would rise to transport again, but just for the moment her brain was at work upon it rather than her soul.

It is true that the sense of miracle came hurrying back when she discovered the plate of smoking soup. The poor, however, are accustomed to presents of this kindly sort, and it was important only because it had happened to-day, when kindness kept adding itself to kindness, and beauty to beauty, and joy to joy. She knew it was Mrs. James who had brought the soup because it had come in Mrs. James's best wedding-present china. *That* was the miracle, if you like; the thing that would not have happened on any other day, but that simply couldn't help happening on a day like this. Mrs. Clapham felt touched almost to tears by this exhibition of delicate taste, running her fingers appreciatively over the flowered border. It was like Mrs. James's refined ways to have brought her the best china, knowing that even the best food tastes better out of a beautiful dish.

She drank the soup gratefully, glad that she had no need to set about any cooking for herself, and ate a piece of her own excellent currant bread. Her currant loaves, indeed, were quite famous in the district, so much so that there were people who ordered them from her every week. Miss Marigold was fond of them, too, and so was Tibbie—Tibbie, who wrote that even the children said she could not make them like Granny! Miss Marigold was to have a loaf as a wedding-gift when next she came home; in the excitement of moving she must not forget that. But once up at the new house she would have plenty of time for her loaves—loaves fit to set before the King, if by any chance the King, or the local gentry, who unconsciously ranked so much higher in her country mind, should honour her with a call.

She felt so energetic after the sleep and the soup that she longed to begin pulling the cottage to pieces at once. The almshouse was furnished, of course, and after a fashion that took your breath, but she had no doubt that there would be room for her few bits of sticks as well. They would be Tibbie's and the children's after she was gone, and in any case she did not want to part with them just yet. The apparently lifeless furnishings of a house register always the joys and sorrows of those to whom they belong, and everything in the cottage was beautiful to Mrs. Clapham because here Tibbie had lived and laughed.

But of course there could be no moving for a day or two yet, even although already she was hungering to be off. It would seem almost indecent to grab at the house like that; greedy, anyhow, and not quite nice. In any case, she felt sure it would have to be cleaned first, just as the spot she was leaving would have to be scrubbed throughout. Still, there was no reason why she shouldn't take a look at the place, and amuse herself by making her joyful plans. Her heart rose and danced again at the pleasing prospect, as the motes danced in the silently-passing sun. With hands that trembled a little she washed Mrs. James's china and set it aside to return, and then climbed the stairs to the little bedroom to tidy herself and change.

She took off the print dress and put on the gown that Tibbie had made for her long ago, a soft black gown with a little white at the throat and wrists. Even on Mrs. Clapham's large figure it fell into the graceful lines which seemed to come as a matter of course into everything that Tibbie touched, even the cheapest satin or the harshest serge. Yet, although it was Tibbie's work and a labour of love, Mrs. Clapham couldn't help feeling that it was rather funereal to-day. She had worn it at Tibbie's wedding, and it had seemed gay enough then, but at this moment of coloured splendour it seemed almost sad. She felt that she wanted to flaunt forth in something light—something more like Miss Marigold's pale blue *crêpe de chine*! The thought of herself, however, clad after that fashion, reduced her to helpless mirth, and after shaking with laughter until she actually shook the room, she relinquished the *crêpe de chine* and recaptured her common sense.

She felt even more restless upstairs than she had felt down, and it was all she could do to keep from dragging the battered tin trunk from under the bed and beginning to pack. All the time she was dressing she kept looking about, telling herself to remember this and not to forget that. It was absurd, she said to herself, to feel as if she were leaving, that very day! It wasn't as if she hated the cottage and was thankful to go; it was more than likely that she would weep her heart out when the time came to say good-bye. Already she was inclined to be jealous of the future tenant, wondering if she would keep it as it ought to be kept. Not that she could possibly keep it as Mrs. Clapham had done; that was beyond hope. The most that could be looked for was that she wouldn't make it an actual by-word in the row.

She planted a bonnet—the generic Bonnet, black, with a bit of velvet, a bit of ribbon, a bit of feather, a bit of jet—on the silvery smoothness of her parted hair, and was ready at last to set forth on her triumphant journey. With a humorous laugh she told herself that it was just as well she had changed her gown, or she would have been scrubbing that almshouse before she knew! Her promise to Martha Jane came back to her with the thought, making her realise how confident she had been. As if she would ever be likely to scrub floors for a woman like Martha Jane! . . . But again she was conscious of the narrow line that divides fortune from misfortune, triumph from disappointment, victory from defeat; and in the light of that rash promise was more thankful than ever for her escape.

With all her glory about her, however, she could afford to feel sorry for Martha Jane, and now that she had begun to think about her again, she did feel dreadfully sorry. It would have been unbecoming in a generous victor not to throw her a pitying thought, and Mrs. Clapham did more than that. She began to cast about in her mind for an olive branch of sorts, but could think of nothing available but a currant loaf. It was a small enough offering, of course, but currants were currants, nowadays, and flour was flour; and in any case a loaf of her baking would have its own prestige. In its homely way it would convey the same delicate touch that Mrs. James's wedding-present china had conveyed so pleasingly to herself.

Making up her mind at last, she wrapped the loaf in a cloth and went briskly out. The morning sun was beginning to leave the street as she emerged, tending to become an afternoon sun and moving slowly towards the west. Nevertheless, she did not feel that it was deserting her because it was passing on. It had stayed with her all the morning, like a royal guest at a humble feast; now it was going before her to shine for her in her new home.

Exalted though she was by her recent great success, she could not help feeling a little nervous about her visit. Martha Jane might possibly refuse to let her in; insult her, perhaps, or, at the very least, try to take the gloss off her conquest with ribald jeers. On the other hand, she might possibly find her crying—a lonely, unwanted woman, hurt by another of life's jars. Mrs. Clapham felt like crying herself when she thought of that. Of course she might have gone out to pour the tale of her wrongs into some sympathetic ear, and in that case there would be nothing for the bearer of branches to do but to turn again in her tracks. But the latter had scarcely swung round on her step before she became aware that at least she must be at home, for, outside the kitchen window that was almost level with the road, Emma was standing, bending and peering in.

Fear, devastating and intense, came upon Mrs. Clapham when she beheld Emma. There was something almost gloating in the way she stooped to the low window, something of the intent Roman waiting for 'thumbs down'. So interested was she that she did not hear the closing thud of Mrs. Clapham's door, or even the sound of her footsteps coming up the street. There was no smile on her lips as she stooped and stared, and for once its absence was actually more alarming than its presence. Mrs. Clapham's picture of Martha Jane crying or cursing gave place to others infinitely worse. Now she beheld her dangling from a hook in the ceiling or prostrate with prussic acid on the floor. Her heart beat so violently that she could scarcely breathe, and her stout arms dithered so that she nearly dropped the loaf. . . .

She was close upon Emma when the latter suddenly saw her and straightened herself with the click of a clasped knife. 'Eh, but you give me a fright!' she began, gaspingly, and then stopped. An extraordinary change came over her as her eyes fastened themselves on Mrs. Clapham's bonnet and gown. Her arms dropped to her sides as if torn away by some unseen hand. Her mouth opened, her jaw dropped . . . her eyes went dead, her face white. . . .

Mrs. Clapham was more frightened than ever when she saw Emma looking like that. 'There's nowt wrong, is there?' she cried at her sharply, shaking with fear. 'What's making you look so strange, Emma? Is owt wrong with Martha Jane?'

But the amazing transformation which had come upon Mrs. Catterall had passed even before she had

finished. The dull colour came back into Emma's
face and the watchful yet blank look into her eyes.
Her arms came up slowly and folded themselves to
their usual place. And then, as Mrs. Clapham still
stood panting and shaking, she started her slow
smile. . . .

'I don't know as *you'd* call it wrong,' she answered
her gently, in her expressionless tones, 'though I
wasn't brought up myself to consider it right. But
there, I reckon every one knows their own business
best,' she went on, moving to one side. 'Anyway, as
you're here, you'll happen look for yourself. . . .'

CHAPTER III

FEELING slightly ashamed of herself, but too frightened
and curious to refrain, the charwoman stepped forward and took Emma's place.

The hill, rising beside the window, seemed to surge
along its sill as a rising wave surges along the bows of
a vessel, and she had to bend almost double to see
through the dirty panes. Even then she could discern
nothing at first because of the brightness without, but
gradually, as she stared, the figure of Martha Jane
came into being. She was seated beside the table,
with her head laid on her arms, and her flushed face,
twisted towards them, showed her sunk in a sodden
sleep. Her hair was coming down, her blouse had
slipped up, and she had lost a shoe; while the lace collar,
which she had robbed of its pin for little Miss Baines,
was hanging airily down her back. Within reach of
her outstretched hands stood a bottle without a cork,
from which they seemed only this moment to have
slipped away. . . . Mrs. Clapham clicked her tongue
between her teeth when she saw that bottle. There
could be no mistake about Martha Jane. . . .

'The right sort for almshouses, I *don't* think!' Emma

was saying in smug tones behind the charwoman's back. 'Seems to me mighty queer they should ever have thought her in the running at all; but there, I suppose they reckon they know their own business best. . . .'

Mrs. Clapham straightened herself rather painfully, and looked at her with dismay.

'Eh, dear!' she exclaimed dismally. 'I'm right sorry she took it like that!' She stepped back into the road, an expression of real trouble on her honest face. 'It's a real pity, that is; ay, it's a sad pity! She must have been a deal keener on yon house than ever I thought.'

'She wasn't never the sort for almshouses,' Emma repeated stolidly, unperturbed. 'One o' them Homes or such-like is the right spot for Martha Jane; not to speak of yon Home in partic'lar as is under lock and key.'

Mrs. Clapham gave an involuntary but unhappy giggle. 'Nay, now, Emma Catterall,' she protested, 'it's not kind to speak like that!' For the time being the ecstatic joy had gone out of her face, leaving it looking worried and almost guilty. It was true that she was spared the shadow of a dangling Martha Jane, but even Martha Jane drunk was enough of a blot on her beautiful day. 'The poor thing's done nowt to deserve being shoved into prison,' she went on lamely. 'I doubt we all on us make out she done a deal more than she ever did in the flesh.'

She saw Emma's smile beginning to broaden pleasantly, and pushed on again hurriedly.

'She keeps her cottage a fair sight, I'll give you that, but then it was nobbut a poor sort o' spot when she first come. Once up at t' almshouse she'd likely have shaped a good deal better. I've often noticed how folks perk up when they get a good spot, and a few nice sticks as they think is worth their while. And I don't know as I ever see her drunk in my life, though they *do* say as she likes a drop with her tea. . . . Nay,

I doubt it's just disappointment and nowt else. It's driven her to it, that's what it's done—me beating her over yon house!'

'She wasn't suited nohow,' Emma repeated firmly and almost mechanically, her eyes still running over the other's bonnet and gown. They were calm enough now, however, as was also her voice. Whatever had been the cause of that strange upheaval, it had passed and left no trace, yet the charwoman still moved uneasily under her gaze, feeling as if the beady black eyes were pricing her toilet from head to foot. She was thankful at least that there could be no question about the soberness of her gown, and more than thankful that in no circumstances whatever could there have been any question of a pale blue *crêpe de chine*.

Emma's eyes completed their tour by coming to rest on the currant loaf, which was hastily produced by its owner from its snowy cloth.

'I brought her a bit o' my currant bread,' she explained awkwardly, and with a somewhat embarrassed laugh. 'I thought it'd show there was no ill-feeling! . . . Door'll be locked, though, likely,' she added, with her hand on the latch. 'I doubt I might just as well take it back.'

'A lot *she*'ll want with currant bread!' Emma returned sardonically, but Mrs. Clapham took no notice. 'Nay, it's open right enough,' she said, as the door yielded. 'I'll just slip in and pop it on t' table. . . . I'd nowt else I could bring,' she added, looking back for a moment with a second laugh. 'I've been that sure I was going off I couldn't bother about food!'

Pushing the door gently, she advanced into the kitchen as quietly as her weight would allow, though, from the look of Martha Jane, it seemed hardly likely that even an air-raid would have power to stir her. Just so, she thought to herself, had Mrs. James slipped into her own cottage with her gift of soup, to find her sleeping the little cat-sleep that had come on her unawares. The comparison brought a return of her morning indignation, as she stood looking down at the snoring woman and round the dirty, neglected room. It was certainly a troublesome flaw in her beautiful day that Martha Jane should continue to parody her all through.

But before long her indignation passed into a troubled wonder as to her own duty. Perhaps she and Emma between them ought to try to get Martha Jane to bed, or at least to dispose her gracefully on the sofa. She did not like to think of her sitting there to be gaped at by the passers-by; and, even as an object-lesson, she was scarcely a suitable sight for the children returning to school. She felt pretty sure, however, that Emma would refuse to touch her, nor did she feel over-inclined to touch her herself. In the end, therefore, she compromised by drawing the blind on its crazy roller, and, whipping the cloth from under the loaf, cast a last look at the sublimely-indifferent figure and went out again into the street.

Emma was still there, she found, still puzzling her with that air of interested focus upon herself.

'What was that you said just now about going off?' she inquired, almost before Mrs. Clapham was well outside. She spoke tranquilly enough, though her hands twitched under her elbows as if demanding to be released.

'Going off?' The charwoman looked puzzled, and then swung round again to the door. . . . 'Eh, now, if yon smell o' drink hasn't fair followed me into t' road!'

'You said you'd been that full of going off you'd done no cooking or owt,' Emma reminded her stolidly, ignoring her comment. Her eyes, fixed on the other's face, seemed to be willing her not to look at her hands. . . . 'I didn't rightly know what it was you meant.'

Mrs. Clapham gave the same half-ashamed laugh. 'I only meant I was that throng with plans and such-like about the new house! Not that I *did* owt, you'll understand, such as packing an' all that. I was only thinking about it and turning it over in my mind.'

A large sigh seemed to make a stupendous struggle and emerge diminished through Emma's lips.

'Ay, well, it's a good thing you didn't turn it over *that* often it tumbled out!' Already she was beginning her usual backing towards her steps, and Mrs. Clapham backed, too. She could hardly believe her ears when she heard Emma concluding smoothly—'No use asking you in, I suppose, for a bit of a chat?'

The charwoman stared blankly for a moment, and then flushed, changing her weight with an embarrassed awkwardness from foot to foot.

'I thought of just going up to have a look at the house,' she hesitated at last. 'It's a bit grasping, likely, going up so soon, but I'm fair aching to have a peep. That's why I'm all donned out in my Sunday black!' she finished with an apologetic smile.

A second sigh that had begun as an outsize in Emma's mouth issued in miniature on the soft September air. She nodded gently.

'I don't know as it isn't wise. Things don't always come off, and it don't do to chance a slip. . . . Seems to me, though, you might spare a minute to step in. You've all afternoon before you, and you can do a deal o' looking in that.'

Mrs. Clapham hesitated a moment longer, and then capitulated. Even the Emmas of life were hardly to be refused on this her beautiful day. She was in the mood, too, to believe that even Emmas might have their moments; that, in spite of intuition and other more definite evidence to the contrary, they might yet end by proving themselves honest and true friends. . . .

'Ay, well, I'll see what I can do,' she agreed, though still rather doubtfully, looking down at the cloth on her arm. 'I've a deal to see to, though; I shan't be able to stop. Anyway, I'd best slip home first wi' t'

clout, and I've a pot o' Mrs. James's to return an'
all.'

She hurried off as she spoke, throwing the last words
backwards, almost as if afraid that she might be
dragged into Emma's on the spot, swam down the hill
with great noddings of the black feather and billow-
ings of the black gown, and disappeared; while Emma
herself stayed watching her until she was out of sight,
and then faded towards the steps, and up the steps, and
through the doorway into the dark beyond. . . .

Mrs. Clapham was so busy turning over in her mind
the why and wherefore of Emma's request that she
failed to notice various forms scuttling into their
dwellings at her approach—forms which bore a
decided resemblance to members of the Chorus. But, by
the time she had deposited the cloth, locked the door,
and gone on to leave the china with Mrs. James, she
discovered that the street had not been by any means
empty during the foregoing scene. The younger
woman received her thanks with that kindly self-
satisfaction which forms the usual interpretation of the
dictum that it is more blessed to give than to receive,
and hurried on to a subject of greater interest.

'What in the name o' goodness were you and Mrs.
Catterall doing outside o' Martha Jane's?' she
inquired eagerly. 'You seemed terribly interested in
something or other, I'm sure! Not that I've been
spying or owt, so don't think it. I leave that to our
friend Emma! But I was just looking out, thinking we
might be going to have a—a spot o' rain, and I see you
and her together, as thick as thieves. Mrs. Tanner
was looking out, too, and much about the same time,
seeking yon cat of hers as she sets such store by, you'll
think on; and we were both on us fair puzzled what
the two on you could be at!'

'Nay, it was nowt,' the charwoman answered
hastily, feeling decidedly mean in refusing the tit-bit
for which her supporter obviously yearned, yet

resolved in her own mind not to give Martha Jane away. 'I just slipped up with a bit o' my currant bread as a peace-offering like, and a sop to my conscience at the same time!' She tried to laugh with her usual open heartiness. . . . 'As for Emma, she's as queer as Dick's hatband to-day. I reckon she was just up to her usual tricks, spying on other folks' doings for want of some of her own!'

'Well, she seemed real interested, she did that—as throng as throng! Mrs. Tanner and me couldn't help noticing how interested she was. . . . Likely you found Martha Jane at home when you slipped up with the currant bread?'

'Ay, she was at home right enough!' Mrs. Clapham replied, hoping that her tones did not actually convey the ironic emphasis with which they rang in her own ears.

'Ay, she was, was she?' Mrs. James looked politely eager. 'And—excuse me asking you now—was she grateful an' all that? She wouldn't be best pleased at the way things has shaped, I'm sure.'

'She didn't say much one way or t' other,' Martha Jane's defender lied (if it could be called lying) with desperate ease. 'She was a—a bit quiet-like,' she went on firmly, 'not feeling like visitors, I reckon. . . . I expect she'll be glad enough, though, of the bread, when it comes to eating it. 'Tisn't often, I *will* say, as folks sniff at my currant bread!'

'No, indeed! It'd be queer if they did,' the other assented, though with a somewhat abstracted air. 'It was right nice of you, I'm sure, though I don't know as I think she deserves it. Mrs. Tanner and me never thought it was anything like that, but then we wasn't taking that much notice. . . . Not but what we might ha' made a sort of a guess, knowing your kind heart.'

'Nay, if it comes to hearts, who fetched me yon soup?' Mrs. Clapham inquired playfully, glad of the chance to strike the key-note again; and got out into the street on a wave of fresh mutual blandishments, such as 'Ay, and your best china an' all! Too good, by half . . .' and 'Nay, now, as if anything I had could be too good for the likes of *you!*'

'I'm off to have a look at t' house,' she added, by way of making a second apology for the black gown. 'Likely it seems a bit soon to go rushing up, but folks should make the most o' their time when they're not as young as they was!'

'That's so. Not but what you'll have many a happy year there, I don't doubt!' Mrs. James finally capped the conversation, and remained at the door watching her as she swam away. Everybody seemed to stand and watch her to-day, Mrs. Clapham thought, self-conscious in every limb as she climbed guiltily towards Emma's. She felt guilty because, side by side with her reluctance about the visit, was a half-formed curiosity as to what Emma could have to say. It was because of this latent curiosity in herself that she had not mentioned the invitation to Mrs. James. It made her uneasy in some inexplicable way, just as the strange little scene which had just passed had made her uneasy. It was as if something within her warned her of some approaching event, in which she and Emma, neighbours for years and yet almost complete strangers, should be brought sharply together and carry the principal parts. . . .

She went up the steps slowly, and with a distinctly ashamed air, feeling the eyes of the Chorus glued to her turned back, not knowing that Providence had already seen to it that they should be otherwise engaged. Mrs. Airey and Mrs. Dunn were at that moment holding anxious converse over a scorched frill; Mrs. James was recalled indoors at the critical point by a bump as of something violently-fallen up-stairs; while Mrs. Tanner, although drawn to the window by some psychological pull, was hurled back again, as it were, by the awful spectacle of the cat on the shelf with the beef. . . .

CHAPTER IV

THE whole world had seemed bright with the fine September day which had been sent to bless Mrs. Clapham, but there was no September day in Emma Catterall's. Most houses take on a different character with the seasons, and are either cosy or dreary in winter, sunny or stuffy in summer; in spring, perhaps, full of unexpected light and shade, and in autumn of the after-glow of sunsets or the splendour of windows framing some golden tree. But in Emma Catterall's house the year went by without ever setting foot inside her door, never once renewing the atmosphere or cleansing it by a breath. Going into it was like going into some primitive cave, where all that the centuries seemed to do for it was to make it ever more dark and damp, and to add to the whispering bats that clung about its walls.

Mrs. Clapham, with all her varied experience of dwellings behind her, knew that there were people who made houses dark simply by living in them, and others again who seemed to fill them with a sort of hard-edged light. She knew this by the half-conscious effect which they had upon her; so that, leaving the one, she was always glad to get out again into the sun, and hurried away from the other to find a shadowed corner of her own. But the atmosphere of Emma Catterall's had a quality that was altogether different. Going into it was less like going into a house than into the terrible lodging of some human—or, rather, dreadfully inhuman—mind.

Yet the dwelling itself was extraordinary enough, in all conscience. There are some houses so curiously, almost insanely, built, that the brain simply refuses to grasp them; and others again full of some strong influence which seizes upon you as you go in. Mrs. Clapham knew of at least one abode in which, after years of scrubbing and cleaning, she still found herself

unable to distinguish between the doors; and another
in which, directly she got inside, she turned instinctively to mount the stairs. Emma's house seemed
to share both these idiosyncrasies after its own fashion.
Not only was it thoroughly mad in construction, but it
was full of some queer power. There were people who
said that it was an ancient slaughterhouse turned into
a dwelling, and even now it was neither house nor
cottage. It had bulging walls and unequally-placed
windows, and lead spouts ornamented with strange
heads; and, instead of standing in line with its neighbours, it had edged its way out until it narrowed the
street. There it had turned itself round to command
a view of the hill, as if, like Emma herself, it must
always be on the watch.

From the stone steps you came to a landing with a
couple of doors, while directly in front a mean little
stair went creeping away from you into the dark.
Both doors were closed when Mrs. Clapham arrived,
and that in itself seemed rather strange. They were
oak doors, apparently never polished, so that, instead
of shining like mirrors, they looked dirty and dead;
and Mrs. Clapham had long ago forgotten which was
which. Emma might at least have left one of them
ajar, she thought to herself rather indignantly, staring
irresolutely from one black latch to another, as well as,
almost as if fascinated, at the depressed-looking stair.

It was one of those stairs which, after inviting you
to ascend, suddenly dart round a corner and vanish
nobody knows where. The only difference was that
this stair did not dart; it barely even crept; scarcely,
indeed, seemed willing to behave like a stair at all.
And as Mrs. Clapham stood gazing at it, waiting for
Emma to appear, she remembered the little boy who
also had only crept, cold to his very bones at the
thought of his spied-on bed. . . .

She herself had never seen the comfortless room in
which Stephen had slept and wept, but it was easy

enough to imagine from what Tibbie had told her. According to Tibbie, it had had the same dirty and dead door, and the sort of upsetting floor that catches nastily at your feet. The paper had hung in mouldy festoons from the leaning walls, and in the darkest corner of all had stood the rickety, half-clothed bed. Even in summer the long, narrow place had been almost dark, and full of a trap-like effect produced by a window too small for the room. And all up and down had been scattered possessions of his mother's; so that, whether she was in or out, the atmosphere was still Emma's. There was an army of old clothes, for instance, which Stephen had simply loathed, because of that likeness which old clothes keep to their former wearer. Even when Emma had stopped staring and gone away, the old clothes had stared instead. Stephen had seen them swollen and swung into life by some passing breeze, or as limp and dreadful old Emmas, hanging slackly by skinny necks. . . .

And still there was no sound or vestige of life from behind either of the dead-looking doors. . . . She put out her hand to knock, and dropped it again, intimidated by the silence, and fell instead to staring afresh at Stephen's stair. Her imagination, unusually stimulated by the day's events, presently went so far as actually to show her Stephen himself. Through the dusk his thin little hands gleamed as he tugged himself up by the dirty rail, and his thin little legs gleamed as he dragged them from step to step. His eyes travelled towards her as he reached the curve, and she nearly dropped; for it seemed to her as she looked that it was not Stephen whom she saw, but the terrified, haunted face of his little five-year-old son. . . .

The thought of Stevie in that place frightened her so much that she was hurried into instant action, and, choosing at random, she knocked at the door on her left. Later, as nobody answered, she knocked again, and was lifting her hand a third time when a faint noise drew her round. Facing about, she discovered that the door behind her had opened without her knowledge, and that Emma was standing watching her with her Gioconda smile.

'Eh, now, you did give me a start!' she remonstrated almost crossly, crimsoning with annoyance and an inexplicable sense of shame. Emma, however, did not deign to reply, but merely backed, smiling, through the kitchen door, opening it just sufficiently to allow the other to squeeze through.

'You've been such a while, I made sure you didn't mean coming at all,' she at last condescended to answer, when they were in the kitchen—a queer-shaped room with a sloping and knotted floor, a window that looked out at nothing more inspiring than the side of a barn, and another, which held the ferns, overlooking the street. It was gloomy, like everything at Emma's, and Mrs. Clapham, who was usually so neat on her feet, found herself first kicking the dresser, then bumping the table, and finally catching her toe in the torn rug. She was thoroughly flustered by the time she had sat herself down in the chair indicated by Emma, while the fact that Emma herself did not sit down, but remained standing beside the table, disquieted her more than ever. But then, as she and Mrs. Tanner had already agreed, Emma never *did* sit down. Even at night you could not think of her as sitting in front of the fire, knitting, perhaps, or simply dreaming of old times. Even at that hour you felt sure she would be on the watch, stealing about the house and peering into the rooms. Standing by empty beds, too, Mrs. Clapham thought, with a shiver, and possibly pretending to herself that they had suddenly been refilled. . . .

Seated uneasily in her chair, she hardly knew where to turn, for, repugnant as she always found it to look at Emma, it was even more distressing to look at the room. It was always something of a trial to her to go into other folks' 'spots', because they so seldom came up to her personal standard. More than once, when calling upon a sick neighbour, she had scrubbed the house from ceiling to floor; not so much out of sheer kindness—sometimes, indeed, in spite of protest—but because of the thirst for perfection by which she was driven. So now, seeing in spite of herself the dirty windows and floor, the unpolished brasses and steels, she positively ached for bare arms and an old frock, a new brush and a full pail. Time and again she found her hands stealing unconsciously to her tidy cuffs. . . . It was strange how totally different slovenly houses could be, though houses that were thoroughly clean were much the same. It was astonishing, for instance, how Emma's dirty home differed from Martha Jane's. The latter was dirty, of course, even dirtier than this, and certainly it was a great deal poorer. Yet even at its worst there was always a dashing touch about Martha Jane's—the glint of a cheap brooch flung carelessly on a table, or the gaudiness of an Easter egg swinging crookedly from a bracket. Once, indeed, at the turn of the year, Mrs. Clapham had seen through the open door a bunch of snowdrops in a broken glass. . . .

Then, too, the seasons came and went in Martha Jane's; Nature, at least, did not pass it by. But Emma Catterall's house, with which Nature would have nothing to do, ought not to have been dirty, and was certainly not poor. Financially, she was said to be better off than anybody in the street, and her furniture, though neglected, was most of it good and sound. Out of the tail of her eye Mrs. Clapham could see a bow-fronted chest of drawers which she would almost have given her almshouse to possess; and she felt pretty sure that Emma's own bedroom would be comfortable enough, whatever sort of a hole she had thought fit for Stephen. Yet nobody who had lived in Emma's neighbourhood would dream of buying her furniture when it came to the hammer. They would be too much afraid of seeing her roundabout figure standing behind some chair, or her black eyes watching and peering from some suddenly-opened drawer. . . .

'Ay, I thought you didn't mean coming,' she was saying again, loosing one hand from her waist and leaning her weight on it on the table. 'I made sure you'd given me the go-by, and gone to look at yon house.'

Mrs. Clapham reddened and began to rub nervously at her knees. 'Ay, well, I don't mind owning I'm a bit set up about it,' she acknowledged frankly. 'It's a grand day for me and no mistake—best day I've had for years!'

Emma nodded with amiable condescension.

'We've all on us known you wanted it a long while back now. It's been a reg'lar joke up and down t' village, has Ann Clapham's house. Committee could hardly ha' gone past you, knowing you so keen.'

'I've earned it, anyway!' Mrs. Clapham broke out, reddening again. Emma was being simply loathsome already. . . . 'Everybody says I've best right, along with them last words of Mr. T.'

'I've heard a deal o' them last words, one way and another,' Emma responded, gloating over the half-angry face before her. 'Them kind o' last words is often enough somebody else's second thoughts. . . . Not but what you've the best right, as you say,' she continued smoothly, seeing the charwoman's eyes flash. 'Likely you've wrote committee a letter by now, telling 'em you accept?'

'Nay, what, I never thought about it, I'm sure!' Mrs. Clapham answered, suddenly crestfallen. 'I've been that busy shaking hands wi' myself, I've had no time for nowt else. . . . But they'll know I'll accept right enough,' she added, plucking up spirit. 'Why ever should I have axed for t' house if I didn't mean to take it?'

'Folks change their minds.'

'Happen they do!' The charwoman's voice was slightly defiant. . . . 'But I shan't change mine.'

'There's never no telling, though, what may go and put you about. What, I remember when Mary Taylor got t' house next door to yours, she went up to have a look at it, same as you, and when she come back she wouldn't have it whatever. She went up like when it was getting dark, and she swore as she'd seen a coffin in t' middle of t' best bed!'

'I shan't change my mind for all t' coffins in the kingdom!' Mrs. Clapham's voice rang out on a note that was almost fierce, and, perhaps because of its violence, Emma coloured slowly. Even in her own ears the charwoman's voice sounded boastful and harsh, so that she shrank a little and felt ashamed. All that morning she had thought of herself as a somewhat splendid and interesting figure, but the sound of that voice seemed to reduce her to the rough, red-armed worker who stands as the prototype of her class. 'I shan't change—not me!' she repeated, but less boldly, staring uneasily at her tormentor.

'I'm not saying you would,' Emma assured her quite peaceably. Her plump hand pressed a trifle harder on the table, but her little roundabout figure stood taut and straight. . . . 'I'm not saying you would. You're the sort as goes right ahead when you've once started. All the same, it might be just as well to drop t' governors a line. Even if folks don't change their minds for themselves, there's things happen as changes 'em for 'em.'

'My! but you're a regular croaker, Emma Catterall!' the other burst out impatiently. 'Whatever *should* happen, I'd like to know. . . . Governors'll never look for letters and such-like from *me*,' she went on more temperately, and trying to laugh. 'They'll know well enough I'll be jumping out o' my skin!'

Emma nodded again, as if in agreement, but her

hand left the table and wandered up to her waist. 'There's such things as politeness and that, I suppose,' she reminded her gently; 'but there, when all's said and done, you'll know your own business best. . . .'

Mrs. Clapham winced openly at the usual formula, though not, as it happened, for the usual reason. She had always prided herself on her excellent manners, and it was dreadful to be called to account about them by Emma. Discourtesy, in any case, was simply not to be thought of on her beautiful day. With a downcast face she turned to throw a glance at the empty street, and behind her Emma's arms slowly unloosed and dropped, only to lift slowly and couple themselves again. . . .

'Ay, well, you're likely right!' The big woman swung round again with recovered spirits. 'It does seem as if summat thankful ought to be said. The worst of it is that I'm that bad with my pen! It'd ha' been as easy as wink if I'd had my Tibbie.'

'You'll ha' heard from Stephen's wife lately, I reckon?' Emma inquired casually, and again Mrs. Clapham winced. It was so like Emma, that reaching out and laying a finger on your most precious treasure. . . . 'Nay, I haven't heard for a goodish bit,' she answered stiffly, looking away. 'She's always a good deal to do, what with her job and her children an' all.'

'Children take a deal o' seeing to,' Emma agreed smoothly. 'They're a deal o' work. Nobody knows what having their hands full means till they've one about.'

'I can't say as I ever found my Tibbie much trouble!' Mrs. Clapham's tone was again defiant. 'What, she could see to her buttons and tapes nigh as soon as she could walk, and, as for her needle, she took to it like a duck to a pond!'

'Ay, well, you see, mine was a lad. . . .' Emma's glance left her neighbour's face and rose to the mantelpiece, where Poor Stephen, in khaki, looked from a silver frame. Mrs. Clapham's glance followed suit, and it seemed to her that the sad eyes shifted as the mother's gaze came up. . . . She had winced again at Emma's last words, and begun her usual rubbing of knees. In common with many women during the Great War, she had felt ashamed of not owning a son to add to the general loss. Stephen and Tibbie had done their best to make her feel that Stephen was really hers, but there was no getting past the fact that he was really Emma's. Certainly, here in the gloomy room, where the silver frame was the only thing that was polished and shone, there was no disguising the knowledge that he was really Emma's. . . .

The latter, as if subconsciously aware of this recrudescence of war-time shame, suddenly left the table and moved across to the hearth. Reaching up for the photograph, she looked at it for a moment, and then handed it to the visitor. Stephen's mother-in-law took it reverently, if reluctantly, feeling the silver setting smooth and cool against her hand.

'You'll happen not have seen Stephen's last likeness,' Emma remarked smugly, deliberately ignoring the fact that in all probability Mrs. Clapham had one of her own. 'It was took after he got his commission, as you'll see, and there's none could look more of a gentleman, I'm sure. His lordship come to see me after Stephen was killed, and he was rarely taken with yon picture. "He's the very spit and image of you, Mrs. Catterall," says he, sitting there, wi' t' likeness in his hand, same as it might be you. "The spit and image," he says, "and right proud you must be to think as your face is one as the whole British nation takes its hat off to, to-day!" (T' likeness was in t' *Daily Sketch*, you'll think on, and a deal more papers besides.) "The only son of his mother, and her a widow!" his lordship says soft-like, and looking that grieved and kind. . . . Then I showed him photo as Stephen's wife sent of Stephen's children, and I give you my word he very near started to cry! "Stephen'll never die as long as them children are alive," says he. "What, the little lad's that like him it might be Stephen himself come back again from the dead!"'

Mrs. Clapham said nothing while the smooth voice held blandly on, full of that strange something that always hinted but never spoke. With the shining frame in her worn hands she sat staring at the shadowed young face that she remembered so well. Her duplicate copy at home had never risen to a frame, but when she took it out of its drawer in the sunny kitchen it always seemed to her to smile. Here, however, imprisoned a second time in the House of Pain, there was no vestige of laughter on Poor Stephen's lips. They were haunted eyes that looked at her out of the costly frame, and that day by day watched Emma stealing about the room. There was courage in the set of the figure and the line of the shut mouth, but there was neither exhilaration nor even hope. Over the whole printed presentment which was all that the War had left, was the unmistakable stamp of his unforgettable past.

'I thought happen you mightn't have seen it. . . . You've not been near me for so long. . . .' Emma's voice was still flowing smoothly from hint to hint, gently conveying reproach for a wrong to a bereaved mother ('and her a widow') which even a real live lordship had been too human to commit. 'There's a deal of others besides . . . some on 'em when he was a Tommy . . . ay, and after he got his stripe . . . ay, and here's one wi' his platoon.' The Army terms came easily from her lips, as they had come from so many mothers' lips during the War, and the woman who had had no son from whom to learn them felt a second twinge of shame. 'Here's t' card they sent for putting in winder to say as your son had joined up; and this here's what t' Mothers' Union presented to them as had lost their lads. . . . Ay, and here's Libby's and Stevie's photos, as took his lordship so aback. I reckon there's no mistaking they're Stephen Catterall's barns.'

The little roundabout figure passed from spot to spot, handing the precious objects to Mrs. Clapham, who received them silently, setting them on her knee, and thinking, as many were thinking, now that the War was done, how small were these relics of those terrible years. Also she thought of what Emma did not know, that it was only after a fight with herself that Tibbie had sent the pictures at all. As for the offering from the Mothers' Union, she knew very well what the Vicar's wife, who was its head, had had to say about *that!* She could have laughed, even now, recalling Mrs. Wrench's disgust when faced with Emma's name on that royal list.

Not that she really felt like laughing in the least, for every minute that passed left her more troubled and ill at ease. There was something so calculated about the whole conversation, the setting forth of the relics, the deliberate exclusion of herself. Emma's methods made her feel self-conscious and yet stultified at the same time, leaving her as they did no loophole for self-defence. From Emma's egotistical speech you would never have guessed that Mrs. Clapham had anything to do with either Stephen or Stephen's children; not even, indeed, with Stephen's widow. In the case of the children the exclusion was made even more pointed by the continual dwelling upon that unhappy likeness. It was perfectly true that in those sad little photographs which Emma handled so gloatingly there wasn't a trace of Tibbie or Tibbie's mother. All the love or the hatred in the world couldn't deny the stock from which they sprang. Undoubtedly they were Emma's grandchildren more than they were Mrs. Clapham's, and as the latter looked at them she was seized by doubt and almost dislike. The spasm passed in a moment, however, leaving her penitent and ashamed. She remembered their plaintive but sweet voices, their shy but endearing ways; tricks of speech which, young as they were, already showed their minds as far removed from Emma's as the Poles. It came to her, too, that it was a terrible thing to carry a likeness to somebody you hated and feared, so that, no matter what you did, or how far you happened to go, that somebody was always waiting for you whenever you looked in a glass. . . .

'Ay, children make a deal o' difference in a house.' Emma reverted to the original discussion. 'Stephen's wife won't have that much time for anything else. Not that she'll mind the trouble, likely, any more than me. I was always one for liking a child about the place.'

Mrs. Clapham's flesh positively crept at the audacious, smooth-spoken words. The colour sprang to her lowered face. Once again she seemed to see the pale-faced boy on the stair, and repelled the vision with actual fright. More and more she was beginning to wonder what was the purpose behind all this. . . .

But at last Emma's wholesale commandeering of everything that she loved had aroused her to open resentment. 'Ay, and me an' all!' she broke out sharply, yet remembering even in her vexation to handle tenderly the relics of the War. 'There's nowt like coming home to a child's funny little ways. What, there's times even yet I can't hardly believe I shan't find Tibbie on t'other side when I push the door! Folks never forget as has once had a child about the spot, and the older they grow the more like they are to think there was nowt to match it.'

'That's only just thinking back, though,' Emma replied, returning each of the photographs to its place of woe. 'Old folks can't really do with children in the flesh. They make a deal o' work, as I said just now, and old folks can't do with that. They want their bit o' rest and quiet. You'd find a child real tiresome nowadays, Ann Clapham.'

'Not me!' The charwoman flung out her answer with stout scorn. 'I was never one to mind a bit o' noise at any time—nor work neither—and shouldn't now. I like to hear young things singing and shouting up and down the world. Folks's barns where I scrub near always look to me for a bit of a lark. And I'm a long way from being an old body yet, even though I'm not as young as I was!'

'You've aged a deal lately, though—ay, more than a deal!' Emma had finished her setting of her sorrowful prisoners to rights, and was now returned to her post at the table. (Would she *never* sit? Mrs. Clapham wondered exasperatedly.) 'You're not as lish on your feet for one thing—I've noticed that. Think on how you kicked table-leg or summat when you come in. And there's a look about you I don't like, same as I've seen in a deal of folks as was quick took off. What, there was one day I see you coming back from your job, I was feared you'd drop down dead in the street! Walking dead lame you was, and with your hand on your heart, and as for your face, what, it was the colour o' putty! I made sure I'd see doctor at your house afore so long, and I was right surprised when he never come. You kept house for a while, though, didn't you?—ay, so I thought. There's no denying you were mortal bad.'

Again the smooth voice and the black eyes held Mrs. Clapham captive, allowing her no point at which to speak; and again, as she listened, she felt the old trouble at her tiresome heart, and was conscious of the old grumble in her tiresome knee. She was ashamed, in any case, on her beautiful day, to remember that other day of depression and giving-up; but that Emma should know of it made her doubly ashamed. She had forgotten, as she toiled miserably up the empty street, that quite probably Emma would be watching her from some hidden place. She said to herself that, if only she had known it at the time, she would have got home somehow without giving herself away! The thing in itself had been hard enough to bear, setting a dread in her life that she would never afterwards escape; but it made her fear greater and the wound deeper that Emma, of all people, should have seen her shame.

'Eh, well, folks all has their bad times,' she answered at last, in a defiant tone that yet, in spite of her efforts, held a distinct element of apology. 'I don't know what was the matter, I'm sure. A touch o' 'flu, likely—there was a deal about. Anyway, I got over it mighty sharp,' she went on valiantly. 'If you know so much, I reckon you'll know that! There's not many can get through the work I can, even now, and that's the truth. As for kicking table and such-like, your spot is a bit dark, Emma, coming out of the sun.'

'Seems like as if there might be summat amiss with your eyes,' was all Emma's response to this, fixing her with her own beady, black orbs which looked as if they would last to the Judgment and beyond. 'It's queer how folks don't always notice when they're breaking up. I've known some on 'em go on exactly the same for years and years, and then all of a sudden stop like a clock. There was Mr. Perry, you'll think on, reading lessons on Sunday evening as throng as a crowing cock; and almost before you could speak he was going about with a stick and a dog. Then there was that fine, big Mrs. Chell, much the same build as you, dancing as light as a bubbly-jock at the Farmers' Ball, and next day stiff as a board. Nay, when folks is most certain, yon 's the time to look out; so don't get boasting, Ann Clapham, for fear of a judgment.'

'Nay, but I'm not boasting—nowt o' the sort!' The charwoman's hands, at work again on her knees, actually threatened to rub a hole in the good black gown. 'I've never been one to get above myself, and I'm not now. I'm just thankful, that's all—cheerful and thankful I'm so fit and well.'

'Ay, well, don't think so much about it, that's all I'm meaning to say. Don't count on it overmuch. What, you'd never have put in for yon almshouse if you hadn't felt you was done!'

'I put in for it because I'd earned it—not because I was wore out!' Mrs. Clapham's face was almost purple, and her hands worked like a rubbing-machine. The suggestion was intolerable to her that she was something come to an end, a finished, miserable object creeping into a hole. Again she forgot that she had ever felt that she couldn't go on . . . forgot that Emma had seen her when she felt she couldn't go on. . . . 'I might be a broken-kneed bus-horse, the way you talk!' she concluded with an attempt at humour, though with all her fighting spirit aroused by the assumption that she was no longer worth her salt.

Rather to her surprise, however, Emma retired from battle on this particular point.

'Ay, you've earned it, that's true,' she answered amiably, and almost eagerly, 'and I'm sure I hope you'll be right happy! I only meant it was lucky you hadn't to go on with your job. Likely you'll live to be ninety when you get up to yon house.'

'There'll be a deal of folk put about if I hang on to it till then!' Mrs. Clapham chuckled, her natural good temper responding at once to the other's change of tone. 'I don't know as it'd be quite nice to go on filling up charity-houses as long as that. . . . But it grubs me a bit, you piling it on as I'm over old for my job. Come to that, you're only four or five year younger yourself!'

'I've had a deal easier life, though,' Emma returned, in the same unprovocative tone, 'a deal easier, you'll think on. I've never had to do a hand's turn for any-body but my own. You was in service ten year or more afore you was wed, and then, after Jonty died, you took to this job. Things has been a deal softer for me than that; and then I've my bit of brass. I've good health, too—wonderful good health. Doctor says I'm as sound as a bell.'

'You look it, I'm sure!' Mrs. Clapham agreed as politely as she could, conscious as she was of a painfully-jealous grudge. Emma had done her best to make her feel that she was done, and now she was boasting of her own good health! At all events, she would go out of Emma's feeling a great deal older than when she came in; might, indeed, have to be carried out, if she stayed much longer! Her nerves were all to pieces, as it was; there were moments when she even wanted to scream. It was absurd, of course, seeing she could so easily get away; but then the trouble about Emma's was that it sapped your courage for getting away. . . .

But again she was visited by the vision on the stair, and again it flustered her into action. She got to her feet hastily, feeling as if in that dark house the night was already near, and that while she chattered and dallied her day had already passed. 'I'd best be getting on; time's going by,' she explained, edging her way to the door. 'It's a step to the almshouses, you'll think on, and a bit of a pull an' all.'

Emma, however, made no attempt to move, and in some mysterious manner her complete immobility had the effect of arresting the other's progress. 'What way did you think o' taking?' she inquired coolly. 'By t' Post Office, or through the fields?'

'Nay, what, I hadn't thought about it, I'm sure!' Mrs. Clapham's voice was suddenly wholly joyous, as if even the question was a sort of release. 'Likely I'll choose t' fields,' she added quickly; 'they'll be nice and fresh. Were you wanting anything at Post Office, by any chance?'

'Me?' Emma's eyebrows rose to a great height above her beady eyes. Her arms were clamped like iron across her waist. . . . 'Nay, not I. I was just curious-like, that's all.'

'We haven't much use for Post Offices, you and me!' Mrs. Clapham chuckled amiably, able even to bracket herself with Emma, in the sheer delight of getting away. 'Not but what I must get a letter off to Tibbie, one o' these days, to tell her of my luck.'

Thinking about the letter to Tibbie, she did not notice the deep flush which came into Emma's face, creeping all over it from the roots of her dark hair to the collar-band on her short neck. Her voice, however, reached her calmly and unemotionally.

'Ay, she'll think it a rare piece o' news, I don't doubt. Likely she'll feel, same as me, as it's time you gave up your job. But think on about letter to the committee, while you're about it. T'other to Stephen's wife can wait.'

'Ay, I'll think on!' Mrs. Clapham pulled a wry face, sighed, and then laughed. She moved on again, sailing with her air of a great ship towards the kitchen door, but spoiling the effect by kicking the dresser as she passed. 'Eh, now, if I'm not clumsy!' she laughed ruefully, over her shoulder. 'Likely you're right, and I'm getting blind or a bit daft!'

At last she was on the landing again, with her hand reached to the outside latch, and Emma—who seemed not so much to have moved as simply to have faded from one spot to another—a yard or two behind. And as they paused before speaking their final words, friends to all outward seeming and yet enemies to the bone, the single note of a bell was struck from the church-tower. Instantly Emma crumpled sideways against the wall, her face twisted, her eyes wide. 'Passing-bell!' she contrived to get out in a choked voice.

Mrs. Clapham's own heart gave a violent jump, and she threw up the latch quickly and opened the door. The next moment she broke into a relieved laugh as the bells crashed into a peal of joy.

'Passing-bell!' she jeered kindly at the disgruntled Emma. 'What, them there's Miss Marigold's wedding-bells, that's all! She's getting herself wed in London to-day, if you'll think on.... Ay, and look ye! They're gettin' t' flag up on t' tower an' all!'

The bells thundered and pealed as she went slowly down the steps, looking up at the bright flag above the clean grey stone of the tower. An extraordinary sense of happiness seized upon her as she came out again into the sunny day. It seemed to her at that moment that it was for her and not for Miss Marigold that the flag had been run up; that it was of her happiness and enrichment the bells were telling their tale. . . .

'I never could abide t' death-bell!' Emma was explaining smoothly, upright and composed again, from the shadow behind. 'Likely I had a fright along of it when I was a child. I've felt a deal worse about it an' all since my poor lad was killed in France.'

'Come to that, it give me a bit of a turn myself!' Mrs. Clapham laughed, descending the last step. 'I don't know as I'd ha' liked to hear t' death-bell to-day. It'd ha' seemed for all the world as if it was bringing me bad luck!'

She threw a nod of farewell towards the shadow which she believed to contain Emma, and set herself to the hill and so to the short cut across the fields. All the way behind her as she went the bells clanged and clamoured Miss Marigold's joy; and Mrs. Clapham smiled as she listened to them, and then wept as well, because of that note of finality in the wedding-peal which is almost all that the married woman hears. The passion of its rejoicing speaks so vehemently of something brought to an end, a road closed, a door shut, a sharp cutting as with a knife. The joy of the wedding-peal must needs be emphatic and loud, because it is a joy that demands utter fearlessness if it is to remain joy at all. So across the fields Mrs. Clapham went smiling and weeping, but especially weeping; shedding the tears of all mothers for the end of the road of youth. . . .

PART III

THE TEMPLE

CHAPTER I

SHE drew great breaths of relief as she made her way through the fields, treading the little worn paths between the sloping stretches of green. Between the warm fastnesses of the hedges she felt sheltered, but not cramped—those close coverts of life which wore so rich and crowded a look. The bright line of the sky barring the tops to the west told her that very soon she would see the sea. Indeed, the broad, lifted, lightened sense which belongs to a coast was not only in the look of things but in the feel. There was a thrill in the air as of something running towards freedom of breath and limb. The very land itself seemed to rush on-wards rejoicing to its escape.

Unpleasant as the experience had been, she could almost have found it in her heart to be glad of the 'little chat', because the walk through the fields seemed so gracious by sheer contrast. Like most country women, she very seldom walked for walking's sake, merely going mechanically wherever necessity happened to take her. But she appreciated the country well enough when she had time to look at it, and if she did not think of it very often it was because it was always there. To-day, however, there was some·thing almost poignant about coming out of Emma's cave into this sweet openness and spacious peace. It was almost like leaving a prison to walk direct out of the house that was Emma Catterall's mind into this wide and wonderful house that was the Mind of God Himself.

As she went along, with the bells clashing and clanging behind her back, she tried to shed all those thoughts of Emma which tugged at her brain like spiked brambles at a skirt. Indeed, it seemed to her, after a while, as she got further away and higher, that she shed not only Emma, but the whole of the village as well. Up here in the clean fields she seemed alone in a new world, with nothing of any importance but the free road to her desire.

But before she reached that desirable point her mind had still a good deal to say about Emma and Emma's detestable behaviour. There had been times, indeed, when she had felt as if it were Emma's 'day' instead of her own, so completely had Emma contrived to pervade it! Yet there seemed no possible reason why she should have chosen to take a hand in passing events. All her proceedings had been puzzling in the extreme, and none of them more inexplicable than the 'little chat'. Neither her natural intuition nor the shrewdness induced by a long and strenuous life had been able to provide Mrs. Clapham with a clue to her neighbour's purpose. Emma had depressed her, of course, made her feel ill-tempered and ill-behaved, reminded her that she hadn't a son, and—almost, indeed!—that she hadn't a daughter! But all that, after all, was only just what she knew to be Emma, that mixture of stabbing and subtle suggestion which represented her queer character. It did not account for the 'little chat'. Possibly she had meant nothing more than to make herself thoroughly nasty; to roll a log, as it were, in the way of a march past. But there was more than one point in the recent talk which this explanation did not cover, such as the troublesome letter to the committee. Mrs. Clapham still felt more than a little heated upon this particular subject. It would be strange indeed if, at her time of life, she had to begin learning manners from Emma!

At one of the stiles she encountered a young soldier, wearing the khaki which was still to be seen about the country, and he stood on one side to let her through.

Like most stiles, however, it was meant for the young and slim, and presently, as she struggled and chuckled, he put out his hand and gave her a pull. 'You look mighty pleased with yourself, mother,' he commented, as she squeezed past. 'That's a wedding-peal they're ringing there, isn't it? Have you been getting wed?'

The remark struck her in her happy mood as a very jewel of humour. 'Better than that!' she chuckled, still panting but full of smiles. 'I've finished wi' that a long while back. It's a deal better than that!'

'Well, good luck to it, whatever it is!' he wished her, springing over the stile, and as he went on his way again she heard him begin to whistle. He had a thin, dark face that reminded her of Poor Stephen, stamped with that strained, sleepless look which was the legacy of the War. He had not been whistling when they met, but he was whistling now, as if the very sight of a creature so happy had somehow made him feel happy, too. It was not a loud whistle, indeed, not the noisy, almost unconscious whistle of thoughtless youth. It was rather hesitating and wistful, a little doubtful, a little afraid. It was not the full note that almost deafens the ear when the earth is at last the birds'; it was the first ripple of robin's song when the year is on the turn.

The sight of the haunted face that bore such a likeness to Poor Stephen set her thinking again of the sad photograph in his mother's room. Absurd as it seemed now, she had felt, at the time, as if it had wished her to take it away. Yet most people going in—people like his lordship, for instance—and seeing it in its silver frame, would never doubt for a moment that Emma had loved her son. They would take off their hats, as it were, to her glory and grief. Even if you had told them the truth, and with an army of witnesses at your back, they would still have averred that at least Emma was sorry now. Yet nobody who had known her as Mrs. Clapham had known her would believe that it was possible for her to be really sorry. It was true that Mrs. Tanner had hinted at some such possibility only that morning, but she herself would be the first to say that she had meant nothing by it. As for the charwoman, whose love for her only child was as crystal-clear as running water, she could see nothing that looked even remotely like love in the sorrowing Emma. She was not the only one, of course, who had been puzzled of late by the queer psychology of war-time love. So much of it seemed to be merely clutching and coarse, as if it was the body that mattered and not the soul. Emma, indeed, seemed to be still clutching at Stephen even after his body was gone, and not only clutching at Stephen but his widow and children as well. . . .

She met nobody else while she was crossing the fields, and presently even the young soldier who was so like Stephen became fused with him in her mind, so that she thought of him at the end as no more than a photograph or a ghost. The sense of poverty and humiliation which had so oppressed her in Emma's left her completely now she was in the open. Indeed, she seemed to herself to grow bigger and more important with every step, and as if the very cattle grazing on either side were there merely to pay her tribute. The birds sang for her, the flowers grew for her, the long slopes of grass were green. She was the fortunate being whom the gods had decided to bless, and as such she loomed large as the broad universe and high as the tall sky.

Both consciously and unconsciously she was drinking it all in, knowing that never again would she feel like this. Never again would the earth seem so wholly hers, set as a background for her personal joy. Never again would she loom so large, or tread so buoyantly with royal feet. This was the perfect day of her whole life, and she could not expect to have it repeated. Perhaps on some fine September evening a touch of the ecstasy might return, but, though it would always be thrilling, it could never be quite the same. It would be looking back on the beautiful moment instead of living it, breathing it in. No power on earth could bring her the actual moment back. By that time it would have receded among those memories of life which lie bathed in a golden light, but which, lovely and comforting though they be, lack the magic grip of the great hour.

Yet, just ever so small a twist of Fate's easily-twirled wheel, and all the wonder and beauty might have fallen to Martha Jane! Things *did* happen like that, as she knew very well, impossible as it seemed to her at the present moment. The crown *did* fall on the wrong head, the sceptre thrust itself obstinately into the wrong hand. Now that she realised the supreme greatness of the occasion, Mrs. Clapham could not help feeling innocently-thankful that it had not been wasted on Martha Jane. Not that it *could* have been, of course—not by her newly-proved rightness of things— she recognised that. What seemed more than a little strange, looking back, was that Martha Jane should not have recognised it too.

Not that Martha Jane, if for some reason the gods had chanced to see crooked for once, would not have recognised the occasion *as* an occasion. The trouble would have lain in her method of dealing with it. She would have been pleased, of course, and even grateful after her fashion; but it would not have been a very delicate fashion. Martha Jane, to put it vulgarly, would have made a beano of it. She would have had a crowd about her at once, not only outside the house but also within; a slatternly, noisy crowd, as loose and degenerate as herself. Men would have looked in to drop her a ribald word of congratulation; grinning boys and inquisitive girls hung with cocked ears about the sill. And when finally she had set out to look at the house she would not have been alone, as

Mrs. Clapham was alone; so much alone that even a passing soldier had turned to a photograph or a ghost. Some of her own sort would have been with her, without doubt, slovenly, down-at-heel, loose-moraled, loose-tongued. Their loud laughter over the fields would have startled the grazing cattle and fluttered the tranquil birds. Meeting the young soldier, they would have stopped to tell him the news, so that the current of beano-mirth would have caught and gathered him in. Would he still have been made happy, the charwoman wondered, by the blatant happiness of Martha Jane? Would he still have whistled his little tune when he had left them and gone on?

As for the house itself, awakened from sleep by the noisy crew, she hardly dared bring herself even to think of it. Suddenly it would have heard them passing from room to room, those still-sacred rooms from which death had so recently gone out. Gradually the neighbours would have run to listen and look; passers-by pause in the road or come to lean on the little gate; until presently, by the end of the day which should have been all beauty and peace, Martha Jane would have made a cheap-jack booth of Ann Clapham's House of Dreams. . . .

The wedding-bells came to a lingering close as she got to the last stile; sliding, after a last, almost subdued peal, into a cadence of three notes, as if neither ringers nor ringing were able to stop; and followed, just when the ear had become perfectly sure of the end, by the single note that had frightened Emma. The tiny pause gave it both a purposeful and an accidental sound, and in both cases seemed to set it apart in meaning. It seemed somehow to leave the whole peal hanging in mid-air, and yet it had nothing to do with the peal at all. It was like a word spoken at a song's end, that had nothing to do with the finished song, but was quickly and firmly beginning a new. . . .

Presently, however, the long stream of vibrations had shredded itself away, and into the air came that sense of completion and rest which the single bell had seemed to deny. Mrs. Clapham paused at the stile under the same rush of feeling at the cessation of the bells as had seized upon her when they first started. 'Over . . . it's all over . . . it's all over. . . .' The silence seemed to say that even more poignantly than the sound. . . . The ringers would be paid for their work to-day, but when they had rung for Tibbie, they had rung for love. Tibbie's mother had wept for Tibbie as well when she heard the bells, because for her as for Miss Marigold, it was 'all over'. It came to her, suddenly that, in all probability, there would never be any bells either for Tibbie or Miss Marigold again, until that last slow-speaking bell of all which loved and unloved share alike. . . .

CHAPTER II

THERE was no young soldier to tug her through the last stile, but she would have got the better of it even if she had had to climb it, for on the far side lay the long, white hill which was topped by the House of Dreams. Nearly topped, that is; for the almshouses, in point of fact, although close to the summit, were also under the slope. No really lovable house is ever set precisely on the top of a hill, for the winds to jostle on every side. The true house nestles a little against the arm of the land, high enough to look out, and yet low enough to be warm and safe.

The four houses, indeed, were sheltered on three sides, for north and west ran a spur of hill rimmed by ranks of larch; while on the far side of the road raised fields protected them on the east. But south and south-west the land dropped away before them until it reached the village, so that, looking across the roofs, you could see the park with its wooded hill, the long lines of the marsh, the sands, and the distant sea.

Houses, like folk, age quickly in the rigorous north, and these had already acquired the stamp of time. Already they had become part of the landscape in which they stood, had struck their roots downward until they seemed to grow. Their good grey stone was thickly-creepered in parts, and the gardens had already arrived at the real garden repose. The sun, which had gone before to make ready for Mrs. Clapham, was standing steadily over the scene, showing the autumn flowers brilliant about the walls, vivid almost as jewels against the softer colours of the land around. There was an amazing freshness about it all, something delightfully clear and clean. It seemed as if a wind that was salt and yet soft must always be blowing on Hermitage Hill.

Now that she actually saw the house standing above her, it seemed impossible that it could be hers, easy as it had been to believe when it was only a picture in her mind. Seized by a fear that it might suddenly vanish, she set off towards it with such ardour that she nearly finished the climb in a dead faint, reaching her goal just in time to cling thankfully to the iron railings. She stood there for a little while, with the house heaving and blurring before her eyes, and then stumbled uncertainly through the gate and knocked feebly at Mrs. Bell's.

The latter, who had noted her approach through the holes of a lace curtain upstairs, allowed a decent interval to elapse, and then appeared with an air of surprise.

'Eh, now, Mrs. Clapham, that's never you?' she began elaborately, lifting her hands; but stopped her acting at once when she saw the other's exhaustion. 'Come in . . . come in . . . you look real done up! . . .' She bustled her anxiously into the kitchen. 'What in the name o' fortune fetched you up so fast?'

'I was that keen to get here!' the charwoman acknowledged, half-laughing and half-crying, and thoroughly thankful to get her cotton-wool legs to a place of rest. 'You'll have heard they've given me t' house?' she gasped presently, taking out a large white pocket-handkerchief and wiping her face. 'I'm right anxious to have a look at it, and they said as you'd have t' key.'

'Them as comes up the hill fastest like enough goes down it soonest!' Mrs. Bell observed grimly, ignoring the key, and speaking with the wisdom of one who had seen many cheerful acquirers of the house descend the hill again much less cheerfully—in coffins. She was the oldest tenant—by tenure—at the moment, and prided herself accordingly. 'Not but what it'll be a long time before your turn comes,' she added graciously, having made her point; 'that is, as long as any of us can hope to look for. Folks on pensions and such-like live for ever, they say—leastways, that's what *they* say as has the gift o' the pensions—but I can't say it's been my experience. I've seen a ter'ble lot o' coming and going in my time up here; in at one door and out at t' other it's been, so to speak. What, there's been whiles when I haven't even rightly known what folks was called, until I'd read their names on their tombstones after they was gone!' . . . She paused for appreciation, which the visitor supplied weakly. . . . 'Ay, we heard as you'd got t' house,' she continued, condescending to answer at last. 'Mr. Allen the butcher got it from Mrs. Walls—her as is office-cleaner for that Baines.'

'Mr. Baines sent a note by his little girl. . . .' Mrs. Clapham contrived to sit up, and began a shaky but lengthy account of the great event. Mrs. Bell, at least, looked as though she would live for ever, she thought to herself, surveying the wiry old woman in her multitudinous clothes. 'Meeting was yesterday, as you'll likely know, and Mr. Baines se..t word to-day.'

'Ay, well, I don't doubt you've as much right to it as most,' Mrs. Bell assured her patronisingly, for all the world as if the disposal of the almshouses were actually in her gift. 'I don't know as we could have gone past you, taking it all in all. Me and Mrs. Bendrigg and Mrs. Cann have been talking it over, and we come to the conclusion as we couldn't have done better.'

The recipient of this extreme favour responded with a grateful beam.

'You'll find me decent enough as a neighbour, I reckon, even though I says it as shouldn't. I like a bit of a chat now and then, but I'm not hasty with my tongue. I'm not above doing a hand's turn for others, neither. I don't think you'll find me bad to do with, taking me all round.'

'Nay, I don't doubt but what we'll get along grand.' Mrs. Bell permitted herself the ghost of an approving smile, pleased to find that the new-comer was obviously taking things in the right spirit. 'Me and Mrs. Bendrigg and Mrs. Cann—we've all settled as you'll do. But we're mighty particular up here, all the same,' she added hastily, as if fearful of being too lenient. 'We've a right to be, come to that, being folks *chosen*, as you might say. For instance, we don't hold wi' being out after ten o'clock——'

'Nay, what, I'll be in my bed by nine!' Mrs. Clapham interjected quickly.

'—Or having over-many callers——'

'I don't look for a great deal.'

'—Or taking on followers or such-like rubbish——'

Mrs. Clapham began to chuckle at that, partly involuntarily, and partly from a desire to please, but stopped hurriedly when she discovered that the remark had not been meant for a joke.

'Not that there's many rules of any kind,' Mrs. Bell continued, ignoring her mistake; 'not, that is, as was framed by old Mr. T. There's no children allowed, of

course, and we have to be right strict about not using
t' washhouse out of our turn. But there's one or two
customs and such-like as has kind of grown up among
ourselves. For instance, we've a sort o' rule not to go
popping over often into each other's spots. (Nay, I
can't tell you *how* often *too* often is; you must bide
and see for yourself.) Not to borrow over-much from
other folks, neither—I've seen a deal o' bad blood
come o' that. Not to be peering at other folks'
gardens to see if they're shaping better than ourn, or
to take up more o' the man's time than our rightful
share. Not to go setting t' kitchen chimbly afire, or
chattin' to people out in the road——'

'I don't fancy I'll give any trouble over any o' them
things,' Mrs. Clapham put in, feeling she simply
couldn't stand another sentence just then that began
with the word 'not'. It was just Mrs. Bell's way, she
was saying diligently to herself, and she must do her
best not to mind it. Nearly everybody had their 'way',
which you had to poke through before you discovered
the person underneath. When she had succeeded in
poking through Mrs. Bell's, they would no doubt get
on like smoke. Martha Jane, though, would never
have understood Mrs. Bell's peculiar 'way', and it was
more than certain that Mrs. Bell would never have
understood Martha Jane's. In the safety of possession
Mrs. Clapham could afford to chuckle at the thought
of Martha Jane faced with these various ordinances—
Martha Jane, who never bought anything she could
manage to borrow, who was throng as a magpie about
other people's affairs, and was always idling and
chattering out in the street!

'Nay, you'll find me easy enough to do with,' she
hastened to affirm again, fearful that Mrs. Bell might
fish up another rule. 'I've had a pretty hard life, one way
and another, and all I'm asking for is a bit o' quiet. It'll
be summat new for me to find myself with only my own
spot to see to, and such a handsome-like spot at that!'

She looked admiringly, as she spoke, round the cosy little kitchen with its excellent furniture and sensible grate, and its owner had to repress a quiver of pride before producing the requisite sniff.

'They're well enough as they go,' she replied loftily, 'though I'm not saying they haven't their drawbacks. Seems to me they might have made the rooms bigger while they was about it, and put in a deal more cupboards and shelves. Furniture's right enough, I suppose, though I don't hold with oak myself. Mahogany's a deal more tasty,' Mrs. Bell finished, with her nose in the air; 'but there, you couldn't expect an old gentleman to go thinking o' things like that!'

'Ay, but that's just what he *did* think about!' Mrs. Clapham defended him stoutly, hurt by this callous assessing of the old man's gift. 'I was at his Lancashire place more than once, and, my goodness, but wasn't it grand! And he took every bit as much pains wi' these spots as he ever did with his own. I reckon he chose oak for t' houses because he thought it would last.'

'Ay, but fashions change, even in almshouses,' Mrs. Bell observed, truthfully enough, and with a sententious air. 'I don't say they won't last our time. I don't say they're not good enough for you and me. But it's queer to me, all the same, if the folks as come after don't want summat a sight different!'

'Ah, well, they'll do *me* all right, and a bit over!' Mrs. Clapham laughed, getting ready for stirring. Her heart had settled back into its usual stride, and her legs felt really like legs, instead of bundles of cotton-wool. 'I'll best be moving on again, though I've been glad of the rest. Happen you'll be kind enough to give me the key.'

Mrs. Bell moved reluctantly to the mantelpiece, and from a large canister extracted a small door-key with a dangling label. As the oldest tenant she had charge of the keys whenever the houses fell vacant, and it was only with the greatest difficulty that she could bring herself to hand them over.

'I hardly reckoned on you being up so soon,' she remarked rather crossly, and still retaining the key. 'Folks don't always come the first day; I don't know why, I'm sure. Happen they don't care that much, or they feel a bit delicate-like about claiming their rights. . . . Not but what you can do as you choose,' she added quickly, as the charwoman flushed, 'so don't go thinking I mean to be nasty.'

'I just *had* to come!' the other answered, almost apologetically. She was now on her newly-restored legs, and drawing nearer the precious key. 'Come to that, the house has been mine a sight o' years, after a manner o' speaking!' she finished, with spirit. 'And anyway, I can't rest till I've seen about getting it cleaned.'

'Nay, what, you'll find it clean enough, if that's all!' Mrs. Bell exclaimed eagerly, moving the key farther out of her reach. 'When anybody dies, the governors always has it done special.'

'Not what *I* call clean!' . . . Mrs. Clapham's voice was regal and her head went up in the air. Her tone was that of the recognised artist, whose dictum on his own subject is beyond dispute. 'Governors mean well enough by it, I don't doubt,' she admitted kindly, 'but it'll be mighty queer, all the same, if it's clean enough to suit *me*!'

She held out her hand firmly, but her hostess still clung to the dear possession. 'Ay, well, then, I'd best come and show you round,' was her last desperate expedient; but Mrs. Clapham would have none of that, either.

'I'd rather go by myself,' she told her amiably, but in the same indisputable tone. 'You're right good, I'm sure, and I'm hoping as we'll be friends; but I think when I first see t' house, I'd like best to see it alone.'

She extended her hand farther, and after a pause she laid the key in her palm, much as if she were handing over the keys of some beleaguered city. She was a trifle offended, as the charwoman had expected, and she was also decidedly disappointed. Showing the new tenant over her own house would have fanned for a while the flicker of dying importance. But she was aware that Mrs. Clapham came with testimonials that couldn't be bettered, and she was also impressed by the fact that she had known old Mr. T. And in spite of herself she was impressed by her royal attitude towards the cleaning. The layman gets the better of the artist in four cases out of five, but this happened to be the fifth.

'Ay, well, it's your own affair, after all,' she replied, at length, with a touch of dignity, but nothing worse. The speech, however, was too reminiscent of Emma to be perfectly pleasant, and the visitor winced. Later, thinking things over, it seemed to her strange that she should more than once have noticed this echo of Emma in the totally-different Mrs. Bell. It was as if the grip of Emma's mind upon hers had been working silently even here, making the same subtle demand upon her that it had made insidiously all day. . . .

'You'll drop in again, though, for a cup o' tea?' Mrs. Bell, still loth to lose sight of the treasure, followed both it and its owner to the door. 'Eh, but the folks I've seen walking away with that very same key! First was Mrs. Wells, as went and died of cancer the very next year; and then Mrs. Saddleback, as broke her leg in the first week. Then there was Mrs. Green . . . nay, likely, 'twas Mrs. Brown. Ter'ble bad neighbour she was an' all . . . nay, likely, 'twas Mrs. Green. . . .'

Mrs. Clapham had withdrawn herself now, with the skill of her class, but Mrs. Bell was still at her heels. 'Then there was Mrs. Phipps,' she was saying lustily, 'her as is just gone. A right good soul she was an' all, barring that she was a bit cracked. Still, there's folks *do* say as when them dies as has lost their minds, it's happen only the body as gets took away, and the mind, happen, stays behind. . . .'

'I don't reckon it'll do me much harm if it has!' Mrs. Clapham threw at her cheerfully, as she hurried away. 'I'll just have a look round and see what's what; and if you can spare me a cup o' tea, I'll be right glad of it when I'm through.'

She left Mrs. Bell still looking longingly after the key, and, turning the corner, arrived at her own door. Michaelmas daisies and asters lined the flagged path at either side; purple, clean-coloured faces not yet touched by the frost; but beside the door itself was what she knew to be a flowering currant, that first flambeau of glory which Nature flings to us in the spring. She had wanted one all her life, and here was one set for her at her very door. When it flowered again in the spring it would be just as if old Mr. T. had made her a personal present. More than ever it seemed to her as if the whole thing were emphatically 'meant'.

With a shaking hand she inserted the key. It turned smoothly and kindly with a welcoming click. . . .

CHAPTER III

She drew in a long breath as she slowly opened the door, feeling for that which was waiting for her on the other side. Then slowly she let it out again with a sense of blissful relief. The house was a little close through having been shut up, but it smelt friendly and it smelt clean. The soul of a house is in its own peculiar smell, and certain people can no more live with certain house-smells than with a disagreeable flower. Mrs. Clapham, however, smelt the soul of this house, and knew that it was all right. Before long, indeed, the house would have a different smell—the smell of soap and furniture-polish and recently scrubbed boards which followed Ann Clapham about as the scent follows the rose; but it would be only a surface smell, after all. Under it the smell that was the soul of the house would continue to rise and fall, the soul which reached out to her a welcoming hand, and murmured and crooned to her as she went in.

She let the door slip to its place, and it shut behind her with a second click. Now she was all alone in her own house. . . . Whether she turned to right or left of the little hall the rooms were hers, and when she went up the little stair the rooms upstairs would be hers, too. Now she knew for a fact that all life had just been a leading-up to this. At last she was in the temple to which she had climbed so long, and which had waited there steadfast until she was able to come. . . .

She went first into the kitchen, as befitted her practical mind, but also because in the kitchen she would know definitely whether the smell of the house-soul was all right. But the neat, pleasant kitchen yielded nothing that could possibly disturb either nose or eye. It had been lived in, obviously, but it had not been neglected. Some of the furniture was a little worn, but it was furniture that was all the better for being worn. She could hardly contain her delight at sight of the closed range, the handy pot-rails and cup-boards, the stout dresser and strong chairs. She laid an awed touch upon spoons and forks, on dishes and plates, and stood back to gaze through excited tears at the pans shelf-high on the coloured wall. It seemed to her, as she passed enraptured from find to find, that she would never want anything more as long as she lived.

As she moved about, crying and smiling, giving little sobs of excitement and gasping—'Eh, did you ever now!' and 'Eh, now! look at *them*!' she became ever more thankful that she had succeeded in staving off Mrs. Bell. She could never have let herself go in that carping and sniffing presence, and half the pleasure consisted in letting herself go. Alone with the house, she could be as undignified as she chose; the house did not mind—the homely, welcoming house. In the thrill of the moment it seemed to her like a September-time Santa Claus; with herself, no more than a little child again, laughing and crying like a child. . . .

It was like old Mr. T. to have seen to it that the kitchen had a wooden floor, and an elegant block floor of the best pitch-pine at that. He knew how warm and easy it would be to ageing feet, how smart to the eye, and how simple to keep clean. It was like him, too, to have ordered thick curtains for the window facing the sea, knowing what draughts would come sweeping in when the gales were at their height. But no matter where she turned she found continual witness to his careful thought. There were a hundred practical details in which she recognised his mind— the mind of the Lancashire business-man who did well whatever he touched.

It was like the other side of him, too, Mrs. Clapham thought, peeping at last into the parlour, to have provided a room like this for the tenant's pride. There were people who said that poor folks didn't need a parlour, but of course they couldn't have understood what it really meant. Old Mr. T., how-ever, had understood, although you couldn't have driven him into his own beautiful drawing-room even with whips. He knew that a parlour was a kind of private church, where you locked up the things that were precious to you, and went away happy because they were safe. So he had always insisted upon a parlour in each of his houses, though he took care to make it the right size; not too big so that it would mean worry and work, and yet more than sufficiently big to hold treasures and dreams.

With an almost hushed step she went open-eyed

round the room, laying a light finger upon tables and chairs, and stooping reverently to feel the pile of the carpet. There were ornaments and lace curtains, pictures, a 'best' tea-set in the cupboard; but she did not dwell on them for very long. The parlour would need hours of worship all to itself, and she could not possibly spare them now. Coming out, she found a last touch of the 'parlour' side of old Mr. T. in the white china handle and finger-plate of the parlour door. She had a really helpful cry-out when she noticed these, sobbing contentedly against the wall.

Curiosity, however, soon got the uppermost of emotion, and presently, feeling very much better, she set off upstairs. The stair-carpet was not down, she was glad to see, for the third time that day feeling her hands itching for brush and pail. The stairs themselves were just the right width and depth for shaky old feet, and there were knobs on the rail to which, on occasion, feeble old hands might cling. A window at the turn prevented the staircase from being dark, and at the same time satisfied a deep-seated human need by allowing a peep at a neighbour's affairs. There was an oak press on the landing, and a grandfather's clock ; and the little brass handles of the doors shone to greet her like lumps of gold.

She chose for herself the bedroom that looked out towards the sea, and then wept again when she was in that, although for a totally different reason. Ann Clapham had not found herself missing her husband for years upon years, but quite unexpectedly she missed him now. He had died so soon that it was hard to remember that he had ever happened; and although she had been fond of him while he was there—a quiet, pleasant man who contrived to be humorous whilst saying little or nothing—he had not left much of a blank when he went away. Even the wedding-bells of to-day had recalled Tibbie's wedding rather than her own; but now, coming into a strange house, as she had done on her marriage, she looked instinctively for the departed Jonty.

But it was not easy to see him at first when she found herself looking back, because he had receded so far into the eternal distance. She had to forget that she was old before she could see him at all, forget her wrinkles and her white hair, her large bulk and her tiresome heart. Even then it was difficult to realise that she had once been loved by a lad; for it was finally with a lad's face that he kept appearing out of the mists. For quite a long time it seemed to her that she must be staring at the son which she and Jonty had never had, so little bond seemed there to be between this youthful vision and herself.

But presently, as she sat on the bed and dreamed, the soul of her slid away from the flesh and joined Jonty in the eternal bounds. There she walked with him, light step for light step, hearing her own youthful voice and laugh, knowing her own youthful form and face. Once more they were lad and lass—first, children together; then courting; then married. . . . And finally—the last test of the true dream, and also the last thing the dream-powers grant—she put out her hands to touch him and found him present and living and warm. . . .

From her husband her mind passed naturally enough to Tibbie, but she could not persuade it to grasp her for long. Always it seemed to slip away, to move on; to ignore, as it were, her very existence. Neither would it condescend to dwell upon Stephen, or even the children. Hitherto they had all been vividly in her thoughts, but here in her new quarters she couldn't see them at all. It was just as if something refused to let them come in; as if they couldn't or wouldn't—perhaps *wouldn't*—come in. . . . She couldn't offer to see them against the background of her future home; and presently, though without knowing it, she gave up trying. All the rest of the time she was there she never thought of them once, making her pleasant plans as if they had never been.

She amused herself for a while seeing how easily the cupboards opened and locked, how the drawers ran on a grain of silk and the beds slid on smooth wheels. Sound workmanship throughout—that was the hall-mark of the house; dry walls, firm floors, well-fitting windows, furniture of the best. Again and again she said to herself that it was all exactly what might have been looked for from old Mr. T. And always first and foremost he had thought of the houses as places where old folks would have to live. The windows, therefore, were broad but low, so that no clean-curtain-loving housewife should be tempted to dally with a pair of 'steps'. The foundations were good, but there were no cellars into which shaky old legs, descending daily, could do their best to break shaky old necks. Coal-house and larder were both within easy reach of the kitchen, and there, as everywhere, all the floors ran level. Nowhere was there a sudden step going down or up; not even a passing unevenness that might possibly stub old toes.

Old Mr. T. had known that half the quarrels among women are conducted from the safe standing-ground of their own thresholds; so, as far as possible, he had set the doors of his almshouses back to back. His whole object, indeed, had been to make the old folk feel private, without ever letting them feel alone; and although he had been bound to make the wash-house in common (always a fearful source of anguish of soul) he had hedged it about with terrific instructions which only the thoroughly-graceless would dare to break. But, in spite of Mrs. Bell's intimidating list, the wash-house was almost the only thing about which there was any definite rule. Old Mr. T. had known that you can generally trust a decent woman to look after a decent house; but that, where wash-houses are concerned, no woman living is always perfectly sane.

He had known, too, that old folk usually like to see a 'bit of life', and that nothing bores them so much as to be shut away to look at nothing. So wherever he could he had put the kitchen to face the road, defying the social tenet which says that this is the sole privilege of the parlour. He knew that the old, who had stopped running about on their own account in life, could weave chapters on end about somebody running about with a Gladstone bag. With all their experience, all their knowledge of human nature behind them, it seemed hard to him that they should not use it. Age is the natural harvest-time for the observer and looker-on, and it would have seemed as cruel to him to have denied it its fruit, as to deny dancing and singing to buoyant youth.

But he had known also that the old have their hours of weary withdrawal from life, as if all in a moment somebody hailed them to look beyond. It was then that they wanted wide, tranquil skies, rolling lands and the distant sea—all those spacious country things which speak of a wider country still. So in Mrs. Clapham's kitchen at least he had set that second window towards the west; the eye that looked to the marsh and the park and the dim blueness of the bay. He knew that sometimes, when the evening came, the old would let down the blind of the window that looked to the road, and sit in the other that looked to the sky in the west. Through the window behind them they would hear hoofs and wheels, voices and young laughter, footsteps and talk; but their eyes would be fixed immovably on the thing 'beyond'. At that hour they would not raise a corner of the blind to look at 'life', because they would be looking at something so much bigger than life. Leaning back in one of his easy chairs, with half-dropped lids and quietly folded hands, they would sit staring at the colour and light, the shining mystery of evening peace. He liked to think that some of them might even pass like that, without any nuisance of doctor and sick-bed; that, soothed and content, alone and yet not lonely, ready yet not afraid, they might step straight out of the house which he had built into those other houses not made with hands. . . . He built many almshouses during the course of his long life, but it was only when he built the last of them in his old age that he came finally to think of that.

Mrs. Clapham remembered now, as she came back to it again, that it was in that very kitchen he had called her a 'd—d good sort'. The almshouses were just finished but had not been allotted, and one morning, as she waited on him at breakfast, he had asked her if she would like to see them. A little later, therefore, they had found themselves walking out, and although she had felt coy and abashed, the old gentleman had not cared a button. 'Come along, Jones! Step out!' he had ordered her, when he found her attempting to hang back. 'Short life. . . . Short days. Put your best foot foremost, Jones! Step along; step out!'

He had taken her over each house in turn, jerking out explanations of his ideas, and watching her keenly all the time. He had waited patiently while she lingered and stared, and over and over again he had asked her opinion. Presently she made an effort and ventured a shy hint, and with mixed horror and pride watched him enter it in a book. Finally, she had blurted out that nobody would ever believe the houses to have been planned by a man, and suddenly his eyes had twinkled, his lips parted, and he had chuckled grimly and looked pleased. . . .

It was in the corner-house kitchen that their tour had come to an end, and there he had really started to talk—that is, as much as anything that ever came out of that taciturn mouth could truly be termed talk. It seemed to her that she could see him now, standing in the west window, a still sturdy and square figure, although getting a little bent. At least she was almost sure she could see his clothes, with their bulging pockets and bagged knees—clothes which were yet so full of character that, in brushing them, she had always felt as if she was brushing old Mr. T. And although they were shabby and out of shape, they were made of such stuff that they couldn't wear out— never *did* wear out, indeed, as far as the charwoman knew. For years she had traced those clothes, first on the back of one person and then on another, and always, no matter who was inside them, looking exactly like old Mr. T. . . . His square hands had been thrust behind him under the tails of his square-cut coat, and his square grey hat had been pushed to the back of his square head. From under his thick eyebrows his keen grey eyes had stared at the view, and from between the white whiskers rimming his shaven chin he had jerked the stiff speeches from his obstinate mouth.

'Best of the bunch, eh, Jones?' he had demanded proudly. 'Long chalks the best of the bunch! It's that window makes it . . . thought it would . . . felt sure. Felt d—d sure, in fact, but the architect wouldn't have it. Had the devil of a lot of trouble with that architect, taking it all round. You know what a devil of a lot of trouble I've had with him, don't you, Jones?'

'Jones' murmured respectful assent, remembering with awe terrible battles overheard through the study door, together with the lurid comments of old Mr. T. after the architect had gone away.

'Couldn't be made to see old folks should have the best. Couldn't grasp anyhow that they had groggy knees . . . blind eyes . . . shaky old hearts. Would have sent them climbing here and diving there—acrobatics all over the place—if he'd had his way. He's too young—that's what's the matter with *him*; forty years too young. It takes the old to build for the old; young folk can't understand.' He took a hand from his coat-tails and pushed his hat farther to the back of his head. 'My first almshouses ... not a patch on these ... too d—d young myself. But he'll begin to see what I was driving at in another forty years.'

'Jones' had been young, too, in those days, and in spite of her commendation she had not really understood, either. She had had to wait until to-day to grasp what his patience and insight had really meant. She, too, had had to wait forty years. But at all events she understood now, with admiration and grateful tears. In the heart of this one of his numerous 'Joneses' at least, Mr. T. had his due reward.

It was somewhere about this point that he had offered her the house, clinching her pride in the offer with the historic speech.

'You go for this one, Jones,' he had said. 'Go for the pick of the bunch. You're a d—d good worker ... work like a horse ... but I daresay you'll want it, all the same. I've left you a bit in my will ... left all the Joneses, in fact; but it isn't much. Can't leave you a fortune ... others ... got to be just. But you're to have the house if you want it, remember that. I can trust you not to ask for it till you feel it's your due.'

Then suddenly he had swung round and looked at her, and again the smile came into his eyes.

'All the same, I shouldn't wonder if you don't!' he had finished grimly. 'It's folks like you I build my houses for, and it's folks like you that never get 'em! You're the workers of the world ... the fighters ... the never-enders. You can't stop working because you don't know how. I sometimes think you're not allowed to know how.'

He swung back again as suddenly as he had swung forward, and took another look at the gracious view. Then he had put up his hand and pulled down the blind. 'Save the curtains!' he had remarked wisely, but with a still greater wisdom in the symbolical action than he knew. Within a month news came from his Lancashire home that he, too, had passed where he could compare these earthly efforts of his with those other houses not made with hands. . . .

CHAPTER IV

THE first excitement of recognition and discovery being now over, she was able to turn her mind to plans for the future. She had paid her debt to the dead in those few moments of revision, those thankful tears, that short sadness of regret. She was glad that she had remembered to pay it, and at the right time. She had not just hurried in and seized upon her rights, forgetting in her excitement to whose kindness she happened to owe them. She had spared the time to look back and see what it was that had made the worth of the old man's gift. Now she was free to take it and make it her own, because she had paused to join hands with the grim philanthropist of the past.

From the child, delightedly fingering and yet scarcely daring to touch, and the dreamer, going back in mind to look for those who had passed 'beyond', she became the practical housewife, busy with great affairs. She began to think about the furniture that would be coming up from the cottage, and stood, finger on lip, deciding where it should go. Also she arranged with herself when the great cleaning should begin, what room she should start in, and how long it would take. All these momentous decisions took her continually upstairs, and always, just as she got to the top, some fresh puzzle would snatch her down again. Easy as old Mr. T. had made the stairs, they still were stairs, and though she paid no attention to what her legs were saying about them just then, she was to hear them only too urgently later on.

In the House of Dreams time slipped by for Mrs.

Clapham as it actually slips in dreams, until presently, looking out of some window as she passed, she beheld Mrs. Bell in the little garden. Mrs. Bell wore the half-bold, half-furtive look of the trespasser armed with an excuse, but she also looked decidedly worried. Indeed, she stared at the house as if almost afraid of what she might see. Rather reluctantly Mrs. Clapham went out on to the step, and at once her neighbour exuded apology and relief.

'You'll excuse me coming round, I hope?' she began hastily. 'I was getting right bothered! Happen you don't know as it's four o'clock?'

'Nay, what, it can't be!' Mrs. Clapham returned, staring. 'What, it seems like as if I'd only just come!'

'Ay, it's four, right enough,' Mrs. Bell assured her. 'Tea's been ready a while. I began to get feared you weren't so well again,' she continued coldly, 'but you were so set on being alone I hardly liked to come round.'

There was still a note of reproach and hurt dignity in her voice, and Mrs. Clapham, now that her dues were paid, was quite ready to relieve it.

'Nay, you mustn't think any more about that!' she soothed her kindly. 'Folks get all sorts of silly ideas, and that happened to be one o' mine. It was right kind of you to look me up, and I'll be main glad of a cup o' tea.'

She turned as she finished, and re-entered the house, and, once in the little hall, paused a moment as if thinking. Then she went into the kitchen and pulled down the blind. . . . If she gave a half-sigh as she came out again on the step, Mrs. Bell did not hear it. The door closed against her as she set the key in the hole, and the lock fastened her out with its gentle click. . . .

'You might show me about the place a bit before I go,' she said, as they turned the corner, 'and tell me about the garden an' all. I don't know much about gardens and such-like, not having had the time.'

She slipped the key into a capacious pocket as they went along, and Mrs. Bell watched it go with a jealous thrill. It seemed to her that it might just as well have been left with her until the new tenant was really in. She was consoled, however, by the somewhat belated request to act as showman, and decided to let it stand over, at least for the moment.

'Ay, well, I'm a rare hand at gardening, myself,' she admitted loftily, 'though I don't do that much, seeing there's a paid man. But I should ha' thought you'd seen enough for one day—I should that. If you keep on at this rate you'll be fair wore out.'

'I'm just bound to see all I can!' the charwoman chuckled, still like a child that cannot be persuaded to leave its toy, but falls asleep with it in his hand. 'I'm real silly, I know, but I'll settle afore long. I'm like the folks in the sweet-shops, you'll think on; I won't give no bother as soon as I've eaten my fill!'

Arrived once more at Mrs. Bell's, she found that Mrs. Cann had been asked to meet her, a small, plump person, solemn and rather prim. Old Mrs. Bendrigg had been bedridden for the last year, but had sent a welcome and an invitation to call. Mrs. Cann, eyeing her rather stiffly, partly from shyness and partly because she had been kept waiting for her tea, delivered the greeting at the tail of her own.

'You're all very kind, I'm sure!' Mrs. Clapham managed to reach the chair which had been her salvation before; realising her renewed exhaustion as she sank into it. 'I'm main sorry I kept you from your teas. Time passed that fast, I'd no idea!' She waited politely for the request to draw up to the table, and then did so with some difficulty. 'I never looked to be tret like this,' she added happily, shining with smiles, 'and I'll be main glad to do what I can in return!'

This tactful acknowledgment met with its due reward; and the three faces, drawn together over the cups, soon began to look like the faces of old friends.

In their hearts the old inmates were decidedly of opinion that they would benefit by the new, although they had no intention of letting her know it. They knew her by reputation to be amiable, hard-working, and honest; all attributes which, in one way or another, might be turned to their own account. It was Mrs. Bendrigg who had pointed out, for instance, that a body with such a passion for cleaning wouldn't be likely to stop at her own house. Once a charwoman, always a charwoman, was Mrs. Bendrigg's summary of the situation. 'What, you'll nobbut have to step across and say you're a bit out o' sorts,' the old lady had asserted, 'and Ann Clapham'll be scrubbing your back kitchen afore you can say knife!'

'Mrs. Bell here's been telling me you were once in service with the old gent as built these spots,' Mrs. Cann began primly, opening the conversation with the usual 'pawn to king's fourth' of the highest social asset available. In her heart she would have preferred any scandal which was going about the houses in which Mrs. Clapham had chared, and hoped to lead up to it later on. But even in almshouses social observance must have its due, and old Mr. T. did nicely to open the ball. It was not long, either, before both women were listening open-mouthed to Mrs. Clapham's descriptions of the old man's Lancashire home; almost swallowing, as it were, the costly marvels which she seemed to bring into the room. Proud to have this second chance of paying him tribute, she laid stress not only upon his riches, but upon the respect in which he was held; even while she amused them by recalling his gruff ways and speech, and his habit of comprehending the universe under the name of 'Jones'. She told them, too, as she told everybody now, of how he had wished her to have the house. Only she did not tell them of how he had looked on that last day, or of that last speech of his before he pulled down the kitchen blind. . . .

The social basis having been firmly established, it was possible now to descend to charing. Mrs. Clapham's audience was pleased to discover that she was not above talking about her trade, or even discussing the houses into which that trade had happened to take her. Not that she gave them the racy bits of gossip which they would undoubtedly have liked best, but there was always the chance that she might come to those when they knew her better. But she was able to give them portraits of the families who had passed through her hands during twenty to thirty years; finishing them off with such deftness that they almost stood there before their eyes. She told them, for instance, of the numerous branches of the bewildering Bullers, who had relatives everywhere in the British Isles, and would probably have had them in the Cocos Islands, if they had been allowed. She told them how young Mr. Banbury-Wilson always insisted upon hanging his own curtains, and how old Mr. Wrench simply wouldn't wipe his feet on the mat. She told them of children, animals, and even ghosts; and of servants who were a good deal worse than any possible ghost. She told them of little kindnesses received, and little presents; and sometimes of little cheatings and slights. And over all these things she cast a glamour that was all her own, concocting a brave draught to slake the almshouse thirst for 'life'.

But she said nothing to them about the deeper things which had happened to come her way, and which even now she could scarcely remember without a rush of her ready tears. She did not mention the sorrows supposed to be dead or dumb, which yet rose up and spoke to you as soon as you went in. She told them nothing of parents and children who hated each other, or husbands and wives; of poverty borne bravely, wealth frittered, sickness carried like a jewelled cross. Least of all did she speak of the moments when she herself had risen to some crisis of fear or death; when frightened and helpless women had hung weeping about her neck, and relieved or grief-stricken men had wrung her gratefully by the hand. . . .

Even without these things, however, she had plenty to say, and all of it full of a fine human touch. It was the epic of Mrs. Clapham's life that was spoken that afternoon, even though the greater part of it was spoken only to her own soul. She was a trained talker, of course, like most women of her trade, but never before had she talked like this. It was as if the story of all the years had found its rightful moment of vent, now that the work of those years had come to its peaceful and fruitful end.

Outside, the September sun was sinking slowly towards the sea, while inside Mrs. Bell's kitchen the magic monologue went on. The heads drew closer and closer together over the table until they almost touched. The hands gripped half-emptied cups of forgotten tea, or half-finished pieces of home-made currant bun. For the time being the bent backs were unaware of the heavy burden of age, the nearly-spent lives unaware of how short a course they had to run. Life, the magician and tale-teller, was actually in the cottage itself, not merely watched through a pane of glass, passing unheeding on the road.

Breath, if not ideas, failed the lecturer at last, and they drew apart by degrees, remembering that, even in such a select company as theirs, there were such trifles to see to as 'siding' and washing-up. Mrs. Clapham, pushing back her chair and attempting to rise, found that her cotton-wool legs had suddenly changed into boards. She was accepted, however—there was no doubt about that, and physical drawbacks were details compared with that glad fact. Again she had an impression of the lavishness with which Fate gives when it gives at all, of the ease with which miracle after miracle is projected as soon as their warranted hour arrives. There was a noble sweep about the events of the day as she looked back upon them in her mind; a perfect, unwavering curve which, mounting and mounting with every hour, would drop, only when it did drop, into the falling away of happy sleep.

Yes, she was undoubtedly a success, as was evidenced by the fact that she was allowed to 'side', too; washing and wiping pots and learning their places with the intimacy of a bosom friend. It was true that, as the effect of the epic gradually wore off, each of the older tenants tried to reassert her personal value, subtly insinuating to the new arrival that, in spite of her excellent testimonials, she was, after all, only 'new'. Mrs. Clapham listened to reiterated instructions concerning wash-houses, etc., with maintained interest and respect, and had sufficiently found her footing by now to refrain from smiling at the mention of followers. With her knowledge of human nature, she was aware that they were only keeping their end up, as you might say, and she did not resent it. She *was* new— there was no doubt about that; but she would not be new long. There were ropes to learn, wherever you went, and she was willing to learn them. Nevertheless, she couldn't help smiling at the thought of Martha Jane being shown the ropes by this prim pair—Martha Jane, whose only use for ropes hitherto had been to kick her heels over them on every occasion!

Pots being sided, she was taken for a swift peep into Mrs. Cann's; only the veriest peep, however, because time was getting on, as even Mrs. Clapham, as time-lost as any creature bewitched by the fairies, realised in flashes. But she was aware that the event would not be properly rounded off without that peep, just as it demanded a visit to old Mrs. Bendrigg. So, in spite of her aching back and her stiff legs, she went cheerfully from point to point, expressing an admiration sufficiently tempered with judgment not to give the effect of fulsome praise, and climbed her last flight of stairs—unwillingly and with difficulty—to face the final ordeal of introduction. Mrs. Bendrigg, half sitting up in bed, night-capped, jacketed, wrinkled, and very old, looked up at the fine figure almost swamping the little bedroom with still-keen eyes full of satisfaction. She had never been able to get as much work as she wanted out of her other neighbours —'a poor, shiftless lot!'—but there looked a lot of excellent, skilled work to be got out of Mrs. Clapham!

The latter returned the gaze of this last of her new acquaintances with a feeling that was half pity and half repulsion. She was fond of old people, as a rule, and was always ready to do them service; but in old Mrs. Bendrigg she now realised that she saw the typical almshouse figure. The others, together with herself, were sufficiently young and able-bodied to find some interest in life, sufficient work to keep up their self-respect, sufficient movement to keep them from mouldering. But she now saw that it was for such as old Mrs. Bendrigg that almshouses were really built, broken old folk on the verge of passing away. The vision that had come to her on the day she had lost heart returned to her now with such force that she nearly broke down again. Such as old Mrs. Bendrigg she, too, would eventually become, dependent on half-willing neighbours who were neither kith nor kin. That was what almshouses really meant, when you thought it out; that was the real meaning of the House of Dreams. She stood at the end of the bed, looking down at the night-capped figure with a thoughtful eye, and for the time being felt the gift of old Mr. T. close in upon her with prison-walls.

She contrived to smile, however, as she inquired politely after the ancient's health, and listened politely to a long account of her special disease, veiled complaints about her neighbours, and a fresh list of the same instructions. 'We've always thought a deal of ourselves up here,' Mrs. Bendrigg finished, stiffening her old figure a moment in order to make an impression. ' 'Tisn't as if we was ordinary almshouse folk; we're a deal better than most. Houses is better than most, too, though I could have built 'em better myself. Ay, I've heard tell of you often, and I mind seeing you at old Mr. T.'s. You come of a good stock, and you've been decent-lived, so I'm not saying but what you'll do. Anyway, you'll keep your house like enough as houses ought to be kept—not that it'll ever be same as mine when I was able to stir. I was always that proud of my house—ay, and wi' reason an' all!—but I've no call to be proud now. I never thought as I'd come to it, but I've learned to put up wi' a deal o' dirt. Folks as has to rely on their neighbours can't have everything just so. All the same, it fair breaks my heart to see the place just slaped over same as it were a Witham slum!'

'You'll have to let me lend you a hand when I get fixed!' Mrs. Clapham laughed, trying not to notice the tossed heads and shrugged shoulders of her annoyed hosts. 'It's my job, you know,' she went on, as the old woman nodded and smiled. 'I could clean a house o' this size with nobbut the one hand!' Old Mrs. Bendrigg nodded again and chuckled and said 'Thank ye kindly!' and 'Ye can't come too soon for *me*!' and they went away, leaving her thoroughly pleased in her thrifty, grasping old soul. The hurt couple burst into loud explosion as soon as they got outside, but gradually became soothed by the cheering prospect of less to do. They were consoled, too, by the fact that the new-comer did not seem at all set up ('not to be wondered at, neither, when you thought how she'd let herself in!'). But it was not the fear of extra work that was subduing Mrs. Clapham as they made a hasty tour of the little gardens. She was quite prepared to be partially put upon, and she did not mind. It was all part of the way of the world, like the prim self-importance and the rules. What was taking her by the throat was the picture of old Mrs. Bendrigg helpless in bed; the typical almshouse figure, marring the fine grace of her House of Dreams. . . .

But she had quite recovered by the time they had finished their hasty round, and arrived, finally and fittingly, as it were, for a last pause at her own door. She ran her eye over the building in a passion of possessive pride, forgetting that only a moment ago it had seemed a possible prison. The thrill came back to her in full as she looked at the door to which she alone had the key, feeling again the glamour of one to whom the birthday of her life had come. As she stared at the house, however, she felt sorry that she had drawn the kitchen blind. She had done it half-mechanically, half as a memorial to the man who was gone, and even now she was glad that the women could not see within. She did not want them prying and peeping until the glamour had worn off. Nevertheless, remembering the last occasion upon which it had been done, she could not help wishing that she had not drawn the blind. . . .

All up the hill-side at their feet the September mist was rising and spreading, weaving its growing mesh all silent and soft as if it were the actual product of some fairy wheel. It had wound itself in great swathes around the trees in the orchard below, so that the trunks of the trees seemed to be standing on nothing at all. The slender, twisted stems, crowned with their heavy fruit, seemed to be kept in position by the mere pressure of the gentle air. All the edges of the village roofs had gone soft in the smudging light, and even the slates looked little heavier than the loose wisps of floating mist. The soft smoke, rising from the stacks, looked as if it, too, was simply the mist which was forcing a way through. Across the village there were big hollows and basins of mist up and down the park, and here and there great standard trees poised themselves also on the drifting swathes. The sun, from its low angle, still sent shafts of light into orchard and village, showing the ripe fruit to be russet and gold. Only above the sun and the sea the sky kept itself still and pure, guarding that space of opal and blue that would shrine the evening star.

This, and many an evening like it, and others, different yet all lovely, were Mrs. Clapham's heritage for the future. Even storm-nights would be wonderful, too, seen from the close haven of the House of Dreams. Somewhere, mellow, far-off voices were busy calling the cattle home, and children's voices struck up clear as the blackbird's whistle from their playground on the road. There is always healing in beauty, even though sometimes it wounds first, and the tired char-woman reached towards it with longing, still marvel-ling that the peace of the temple should be really hers.

But presently she shivered, and, turning away, announced firmly that it was time to be going. It had come to her suddenly that her beautiful day was nearly over, that it had slipped by, as beautiful days have a knack of doing, almost without her notice. It was no use lingering here until she had exhausted it to the dregs, and in any case she couldn't afford it. With her tired body, and weary, if happy, spirit, she would need all the strength she possessed to carry her safely home.

The women went with her to the gate, and once again they stood laughing and chatting, and further cementing the new acquaintance. Towards the last —'You'll have t' key, likely?' Mrs. Bell inquired jealously, assuming once more the air of Watch-Dog in Chief.

Mrs. Clapham, backing towards the road, plunged her hand in her pocket with the vim of a diver diving for pearls, and brought up the precious object with a triumphant chuckle.

'You'd best leave it with me, hadn't you?' Mrs. Bell

suggested, eyeing it greedily, but the charwoman shook her head.

'Nay, it's over precious to let out o' my sight. I just couldn't bring myself to part with it, and that's the truth!'

'What, it'll take no harm, will it, stopping another night along o' me?' The oldest tenant stiffened angrily.

'Nay, not it!' The visitor threw her an appeasing smile. 'But I can't part with it, all the same.'

'You're not thinking I'll loss it, surely?' Mrs. Bell asked in rising tones. 'Me as has had it a couple o' months back, and goodness knows how many times afore!'

A demand for apology was obviously in the air, and Mrs. Clapham hastened to satisfy it.

'As if I'd ever think o' such a thing!' she assured her amiably. 'I just like t' feel on't, that's all!' She turned it lovingly, if shamefacedly, in her fingers. 'And if I slip up first thing while morning, as I'm thinking I will, I shan't need to come knocking you out o' bed.'

'I'm up as early as most folks, I reckon!' Mrs. Bell replied swiftly, and this time, to Mrs. Clapham's alarm, in tones of active offence. But the next moment she had remembered her obligations as hostess, and pulled herself back to her former graciousness. 'Ay, well, you know what suits you best,' she hurried on, again affecting her hearer with a reminiscent shudder. 'But you're a deal more likely to go lossing it than me, taking it to a fresh spot and leaving it goodness knows where!'

'I'll not loss it, not I! I'll bare let it out o' my fingers till to-morrow morn!' The charwoman waved it exultingly, backing still farther towards the step. 'Like as not I'll sleep with it under my pillow!' she added, chuckling . . . and found herself slipped off the step and sitting heavily in the open road.

The women were about her at once, calling out and

asking her how she had done it, all in a breath; while she, gasping out anxious requests to be left alone, laughed at their futile efforts to raise her, even while tears of pain poured steadily down her face. They desisted at last, standing back in dismay, and a passing butcher, nimbly stopping his cart in its descent of the hill, left his accustomed horse to look after itself, and came to offer a helping hand.

'Nay, let me be, can't you?' Mrs. Clapham protested, still laughing and crying. 'It's queer to me how folks can't never let a tummelled body lie. They must always be heaving them up again, same as a sheep or a sack o' coals! ... I've got a bit of a shake, of course,' she informed them presently, 'and I've twisted my bad knee; but I'll be as right as a bobbin if only you'll let me be.'

'You should look where you're going, at your age, mother!' the butcher chaffed her, arms akimbo in his blue coat. 'Doesn't do to go backing down steps like a ballet-girl at your time of life, you know!'

'I'll give you ballet-girl when I'm on my feet again —see if I don't!' Mrs. Clapham gasped, chuckling through her tears, though somehow the teasing words made her feel terribly old. 'Eh, but it was a daft thing to do, and a daft sight I must look; and, eh, losh save us, what's come to yon key!'

The staring women sprang to attention at once, and, with the help of the butcher, began a search. It was Mrs. Bell who finally pounced on it where it lay, flown from the charwoman's hand in the track of the butcher's wheels.

'Happen you'll admit now as it's safest with me!' she demanded grimly, and pocketed it as the other nodded. ... 'Ay, I can't say I seem fit to be trusted with it at present!' Mrs. Clapham agreed, though with an inward sigh, and feeling as if, with the loss of the key, something vital had been taken from her. 'Now I'll be getting up again, if you'll lend me a hand.'

Crowding round her again, they hoisted her to her feet, amid fresh gaspings and chucklings and injunctions to 'let be!' 'You'd best let me give you a lift back,' the butcher suggested, seeing that she was lame; and after some more pulling and pushing she was presently seated by his side. Almost at once they had slipped away down the hill, with the houses behind them rising higher and higher. It was almost as if they were being lifted into the air, actual mansions of the blest returning rapidly into the sky. The rapping hoofs of the horse were fast dropping the charwoman into the mist in which the village was drowned, and suddenly it was over her head, and the almshouses were out of sight. The world that she knew came up about her on every side, while the world in which she had dreamed through the afternoon was gone as if it had never been. . . .

The horse paused of its own accord at the shop facing the Post Office, but was urged on again by its driver. 'I'll run you on to your own spot, if you like, missis,' he offered, breaking off a cheerful recital of all the casualties he had ever seen, and which had ended badly in every instance. Mrs. Clapham, however, would not hear of taking him out of his way, and was presently on the ground, watched, as she noticed with some amusement, by alarmed-looking faces at the Post Office window. She nodded and smiled at the faces to show that nothing was wrong; whereupon they vanished with one accord, as though pulled by a taut string. It was kind of them, she thought, to seem so troubled on her account, and then forgot them again as she turned her attention to getting home.

She was shaken, of course, and she walked lame, but she was glad to find she could get along. Her chief trouble, indeed, was that she felt sadly old, disheartened and somehow belittled by the butcher's joking speech. Then, too, she was still fretting over the loss of the key, and wishing that she had been able to fight its battle with Mrs. Bell. Even the feel of it in her hand would have helped to sustain her diminishing courage. At all events it would have been a link with the house that now seemed so hopelessly left behind.

But her spirits rose again when she found herself at the foot of her own street, opposite Mr. Baines's office and close to her own home. She would be all right in the morning after a night's rest, and when she awoke in the morning the dream would be still true. That was the important thing, after all; the great truth and the great fact. It was absurd to feel as if the loss of the key might possibly spoil her luck. Even if she lost the key every day of the week, it could not alter the fact that she had got the house.

Mrs. Tanner, she saw, was out in the street as she came up, and the sight of the birdlike figure sent her spirits even higher. Chuckling, she thought of all the wonderful things she would have to tell, hurrying along towards her as fast as her knee would allow. Mrs. James also came out as she looked, and joined Mrs. Tanner; and then, as if worked by a spring, Mrs. Airey and Mrs. Dunn. She limped faster than ever when she saw the four, feeling like some successful explorer returning to safety and kind friends.

She was able to come quite close to them before they saw her, because they were staring away from her up the hill. No doubt they were waiting for her, she thought with pride; curious, of course, and perhaps also a little anxious. They would guess she had taken the short cut across the fields, and would be looking for her from that direction. As in the early morning, they were bunched tightly together in the road, the only difference being that now they were looking uphill instead of down. A world of things had happened since that distant hour, Mrs. Clapham thought; feeling like one arrived from the Fields of Bliss, who would shortly be going back thither to stay.

The likeness between the scenes—'Morning' and

'Evening' they might have been called—was intensified by the fact that, now as then, the Chorus was busy over some object of common interest. Mrs. Tanner was turning the object over and over in her hand, now and again passing it reluctantly to one of the rest. All four were talking in low, agitated tones, and all the time they talked they threw troubled glances up the hill. They were thoroughly worried about her, Mrs. Clapham thought, just like the faces at the Post Office window. She felt pleased and proud that they should all of them trouble so much, but it was all on a par with the beautiful day. She forgot for the moment that she had been deprived of the key; feeling, as she had felt in the fields, that the world was her oyster, to open at will.

It was just at this moment, when her pleasure was at its height, her certainty most certain, and her security most secure, that the waiting group swung round and saw her. Mrs. James uttered a little cry, and Mrs. Dunn seized her sister's arm. Mrs. Clapham, amused, was preparing a lively speech and a broad smile, when Mrs. Tanner stepped quickly forward.

'Eh, but you've taken your time, Ann Clapham!' she exclaimed, approaching. 'I'd made up my mind you were stopping the night.' Then, as the smile and the speech began again to take shape, she jerked her hand towards her, with the Object in it. . . . 'This come for you while you were out.'

The charwoman stood stock still when she saw the Object, and at that moment something expired within her. The fortunate Mrs. Clapham, whose day this was, and for whom the world had been dressed anew, went out in that moment and became a ghost. The dreamer, who had dreamed of evening rest and a temple of peace, drew a last breath and died also. All that was left was the tired scrubber, returning from work, with the thought of another day's work to begin with to-morrow's dawn. . . .

Slowly she put out her hand and took the telegram from Mrs. Tanner. . . . 'Governors can't be telegraphing t' house off, surely?' she observed, by way of a joke; but nobody laughed, and even in her own ears her voice sounded dull and flat. Her fingers shook as she opened the envelope and took out the slip, and her legs changed again from unbendable boards to those limp bundles of cotton-wool. . . .

It took her some time to take in what the telegram said, and her face held no more expression when she had read it than it had done before. Perhaps she never did read it, if it came to that; not only because of her sight, but because she had no need. The women drew together again, but kept a little aloof, as if they, too, knew what was in the slip, and expressed their respect for the news before it was given out.

After the long pause, Mrs. Clapham handed the telegram back to Mrs. Tanner, saying, 'Read it, will you, Maggie?' in the same tone; and Mrs. Tanner took it from her with shaking grip. The others closed about her then, eager and tense, and presently their united voices, hastening or hanging back, spilt the news with its scent of death on the gentle September air.

'"Daughter died this morning. Can you come?" . . . And it's signed "Rawlinson",' added Mrs. Tanner.

'My daughter Tibbie,' Mrs. Clapham remarked, after the second pause; and, halting a little on her lame knee, she went into her cottage and shut the door.

PART IV

THE TRUMPET

CHAPTER I

It was the same cottage, and yet not the same; her old home, and yet a place that she hardly knew; but indeed for the first few moments she scarcely so much as saw it. All that it seemed to her just then was a shelter gathered around her in her oncoming grief. The grief had not reached her yet, but it was coming, and coming fast; feeling for her where she stood waiting in the path of its passionate sweep. She was like those who, caught on the sands by the tidal wave, found themselves fixed to the spot by the first sounds of its approach. Sooner or later, however, they always began to run; racing hither and thither, without hope and without goal. It was only she who could not begin to run. All she could do was to stand there, helpless and bound, until that deepest of tides had swung itself over her head.

The cottage was small enough, as she knew, far smaller than the House of Dreams, but it did not seem small enough to her now. It fretted her that she could not draw the walls close enough to her on every side. She wanted a place smaller still, darker and closer— more like the grave into which they would put Tibbie. From her post just inside the door she lifted her eyes for the first time, looking around her on all hands for that narrower, darker place. . . .

But even after she had begun to search, it was some time before she could find it. Her mind which, unknown to herself, she had left behind her in the House of Dreams, refused at first to visualise any other. Already it had imprinted upon itself every inch of the rooms, so that she might have inhabited them for many years. Now her eyes, resting again upon objects which, only that morning, had been more familiar to her than her face, roamed over and round them with a puzzled expression. She had seen them so long that she had learned not to see them, and now out of them beheld fresh colours suddenly springing, new contours suddenly taking shape. There was a cupboard somewhere, said her unwillingly-shifted mind, anxious to hurry away again to its happy place. She could almost feel it straining away from her like a separate thing, leaning and tugging against its leash. The cupboard was in the passage, said the impatient mind, and was firmly brought back to admit that there was no passage. It was up at the House of Dreams that there was a passage, a little hall; here there was only a cupboard under the stairs. Her eyes, focusing themselves at last, found the door to the narrow hole where coal was kept, and the broom; a broken hamper, a broken chair. . . .

Her mind gave up the struggle when she remembered the chair, bringing itself back definitely from the House of Dreams. The wrench was so fierce that for the moment it seemed almost physical; an actual body seemed to be torn away. But as soon as it was done she saw the cottage as usual, knowing it to be hers, and letting it slide back into that place where she neither consciously saw nor thought of it at all. Limping, she went direct to the dark cupboard, and, groping with accustomed hands, found and brought forth the little chair. Lifting it in her arms as if it had been the child to whom it had once belonged, she set it upon the hearth; and from that far place where the great wave of it had been held back until the signal was given, her grief broke over her, swamping her, stamping her down—rolling her, choking her, but always sweeping her on; casting her up at length on that grey beach of total exhaustion where sorrow gives up at last its simulated dead. . . .

It is always the child for whom a mother weeps

when a son or a daughter dies; not the strong man or the mature woman, but the child whom she sees through and behind them and in them all their lives. The adult may have her confidence and pride, but it is the still faintly-discerned child that holds and keeps her love. She looks up to the former, and is even a little afraid; the latter looks up to her, and sees her as God. For a mother, indeed, a child dies as soon as it ceases to be a child, though she may not weep for it then. Life, passing on inexorably, tells her that it is against nature to weep for this purely natural change. It is only when the grown man or woman, whom perhaps she can hardly recognise, is laid to rest, that she is allowed to weep. Then at last she may cry her heart out for the child who died but was never buried ever so long ago.

So it was for the child Tibbie that Mrs. Clapham wept, seated in the rocking-chair with the angry voice, her head dropped on the table on her outflung arms, and beside her the little lame chair resting lop-sidedly on the hearth. It was worm-eaten, it had lost a leg—the cane seat was ripped across; but it was still alive, as all much-used pieces of furniture are alive until they finally come to the axe. And indeed the personality of this chair was such as it seemed even the axe could hardly destroy. Low-legged, broad-seated, with a curved mahogany back, it had been a present to Tibbie from an old Colonel who lived in the place. A martyr to rheumatism himself, it had troubled him sorely to see the child sitting so often on the cottage step. 'Suffer for it—she'll suffer for it!' he used to say, stopping stiffly in front of her as he hobbled past; and after he had said it a time or two, he had sent the chair. Tibbie had simply lived in it from that time on —played in it, eaten, chattered, and fallen asleep. It had had its place by the window in summer, by the fender during the winter. It was the centre of great games played by Tibbie and others out in the street;

and she had even been seen, bound on some errand, dragging it after her on a string. It was a wonder, indeed, that it did not attend her to school. When she was older again, she had sat in it while she sewed, the centre of billows of drapery sweeping all over the floor. The last time she had sat in it was with Baby Steve in her arms, her laughing fair head leaned to his sad eyes. . . . But it was neither as the young dressmaker nor as the young mother that Mrs. Clapham could think of Tibbie just then. The years of maturity were all of them wiped out, leaving only the many pictures of the child and the little chair.

Yet it was on that very day that Tibbie had sat in it with Baby Steve, that the chair had finally, so to speak, thrown up its job. It had been a brave chair, taking things as they came; turning when required into a railway-train or a bus, a chopping-block, perhaps, or even a stand for a machine. It had been made of sound stuff by sensible, skilled hands, and it showed itself worthy to its latest hour. But, as it is with the best people, so it was with the good chair; all in a moment it had begun to grow old. Quite suddenly it began to show its scratches and dents, and to lose the last of its fine gloss. It began to creak when a hand was laid on its back, as if it had been the giver resenting a sudden touch. Presently they discovered it to be worm-eaten, and knew then that it 'wouldn't be long'. Even then, however, it had managed to hold together, until this last day when it had decided to cease. Perhaps the recent rains had got into its old bones, or else the weight of the new generation was greater than it could face. Anyhow, Tibbie had sprung to her feet, saying 'Mother! I do believe, Mother . . . the old chair's giving way!' and as they had stared at it, almost afraid, it had softly released a leg, and then laid itself down with the air of a live thing gently preparing itself for death. . . .

They had stared at it for quite a long time before

they had dared to touch it, and Tibbie had cried a little and laughed as well. It was a chair of character, she had said, and it knew its mind. It had been made for her as a child, and would serve no other, not even her own. And all the time that she had stared at the determined, absurd little chair, Stevie had stared at herself with his immutably sad eyes. . . .

But again it was not this particular Tibbie who was present to Mrs. Clapham while she sat and wept. Her mind rejected that Tibbie, just as the chair had rejected her, and as it rejected her, even now. Lopsided, battered, and old, it yet refused to evoke any picture but that of the spring flower of a child. It spoke of Tibbie as clothes speak of their wearers after they are gone; it looked like Tibbie—it *was* Tibbie, because of that picture of her which it kept alive. . . . Mrs. Clapham wept and wept, dropping her head on her arms; looked at the chair that was Tibbie and wept . . . looked away and wept . . . looked back and wept . . . and wept, and wept, and wept, *and* wept. . . .

Presently, after she had been crying for ever and ever, as it seemed, but in reality barely for half an hour, there came the same birdlike tap at the door that had startled her in the morning. Now, however, she scarcely noticed it, and that part of her brain which did chance to take it in wiped it out again instantly as some sign from a lost world. The door opened gently at last as she did not answer, and Mrs. Tanner advanced with brave if birdlike movements into the room.

She went straight to the weeping woman, and stood beside her at the table, now laying a soft little touch on a flung-out arm, now patting and soothing and smoothing the bent head. Her actions, light and neat as those of a wren, worried Mrs. Clapham no more than if they had been the hoppings of the bird itself. They gave her, indeed, something of the same feeling of friendly warmth, of unasking companionship, of brisk life that knew nothing of death; and presently, as she wept and wept, crying aloud on her dead child, turning to stare at the chair that was Tibbie, and yet emphatically was *not*—she had the impression that a bird was actually in the room. Even the little sympathetic sounds which Mrs. Tanner uttered from time to time seemed to her almost like twitters and chirps from some delicate feathered throat.

'My Tibbie! My little lass! . . .' The sleeves of the black gown were soaked through and through with tears, as well as the white front which Tibbie had fashioned with such pride.

'Poor mother—poor soul!' Mrs. Tanner, as she chirped, was gently undoing the strings of the old woman's bonnet, pulling out the pin that was supposed to be holding it in place, and setting both of them on a side-table. The bonnet would do well enough for the funeral, she was saying to herself, and so would the black gown, with a bit of *crêpe* for that touch of white. . . .

'I can't believe it. . . . 'Tisn't likely! 'Tain't true. . . . My bonny Tibbie!'

'Poor soul! Poor dear!'

'What ha' they gone and done to her? What's been wrong? What ha' they done to her when I wasn't there?'

'Poor dear! Poor soul!'

Mrs. Tanner, still giving her little chirps, hunted until she found the clean linen handkerchief with which Mrs. Clapham had completed her toilet that morning, and began to dab gently at the sleeves and the white front. She dabbed, too, at the quivering face down which the tears streamed as if all the tears that mothers have ever shed were being poured at once from that single fount. There were patches of dust, she noticed, on the charwoman's gown, and dust on her hands which her tears were turning to grime. Her skirt was pulled all awry, and her bonnet had been askew; and, remembering how she had looked in the morning, Mrs. Tanner was struck to the heart. Presently she, too, was crying as she stroked and dabbed, though with light, twittering sounds that were still rather birdlike in effect.

But the first spell of grief was nearly exhausted by now; and Mrs. Tanner's sobs, almost noiseless though they were, succeeded in bringing her neighbour's to a close. With the instinctive unselfishness of the mother who has taught herself to be always the one to weep last, Mrs. Clapham made an effort to control herself at the first signs of another's grief. Soon she was trying to sit up, dabbing for herself with the hand-kerchief, which she had taken from Mrs. Tanner, and saying—'Nay, my lass, don't cry . . . don't you grieve for me . . . you'll have trouble enough of your own'— between the great sobs which still shook her as if they actually took her by the shoulders, and the great tears that still welled and rolled and welled again after each useless dab.

'It seems that hard—and you so happy an' all!' Mrs. Tanner broke out in a little wail, hurriedly searching for a handkerchief of her own. The wail, however, put the finishing touch to the mother's effort after self-control. To be told that a thing was hard was in itself a call to her splendid courage; and, patiently scrubbing her wet cheeks with the wet linen, she presently strangled her sobs into a succession of long-drawn sighs.

'Nay, now, Maggie Tanner, don't you go saying it's hard! It's meant, likely; it's sent. . . . Tibbie would never ha' murmured and said it was hard! . . .' A large tear that had been left behind escaped boldly and followed the rest. 'Eh, but it come that sharp, didn't it?' she exclaimed wistfully. 'Never a letter to say she was ill or owt! What, she was well enough when she writ last, though it's a while now. Eh, how was it nobody thought to write and say as I'd best come!'

'It must have been right sudden,' Mrs. Tanner answered, also drying her tears. 'Happen it was her poor heart.'

'Nay, her heart was right enough, I'll swear! 'Twas always in the right place—bless her . . . bless her!' Her voice rose suddenly in a passionate wail, and she rocked sharply to and fro.

'Ay, but t' War was a great strain, you'll think on. A deal o' folks say their hearts isn't what they used to be, after that.'

'Ay, I'd forgotten t' War. . . .' So many worlds may people inhabit in one life and one world, that even a world-wide war may be shut out. . . . 'She took it hard, I know; she never said much, but she took it hard. But she was right strong, all the same, was my little lass. . . . Nay, it was never her heart.'

'It might be pewmonia, likely. That finishes folk ter'ble sharp.'

'Nay, nor her lungs, neither. They was always as sound as a bell.'

'There's other troubles, though, as anybody might have. . . .' Mrs. Tanner glibly began a list, but was waved by the bereaved mother into silence. 'Not for my Tibbie!' was Mrs. Clapham's answer to every one. 'There was nowt wrong wi' her from tip to toe.'

'Ay, well, there's always accidents and such-like,' was Mrs. Tanner's ultimate, rather helpless contribution; but Mrs. Clapham grudged even that indisputable fact. It was as if, by continuing to prove that by no possible chance could Tibbie have come to die, she would presently have succeeded in proving that she was actually still alive. . . . 'She wasn't the sort to go having accidents, wasn't my Tibbie,' she finished firmly. 'She was that light on her feet, she'd never go falling downstairs, or getting herself run over, or the likes o' that. That sharp wi' her eyes an' all—it was lile or nowt she ever missed; nigh as quick as yon fingers of hers wi' a needle and cotton!'

'Ay, she was smart, was Tibbie—right smart! Eh, and that bonny and all!' They had another weep together over the lost beauty of face and form that gives to the grave its most poignant anguish. . . . 'You'll be going to her, likely?' she ventured presently, when they were again calm. 'Telegraph said as you'd best come.'

'Ay, I'm going, of course.' Mrs. Clapham looked startled, gave her face a last scrub, and made an effort to rise to her feet. Her eyes went round to the little clock, and she gave a gasp. 'Six o'clock? Nay, it can't be! Whatever's wrong? . . . Eh, what was I doing setting and yowling here!'

She struggled up by means of the table, her voice rising until it was shrill, crying out that she must go to Tibbie, that she must be off at once, that somehow she must be with her girl before it was night. Once more the tears poured down her face as she stretched out her hands blindly across the distance that divided herself and the newly-dead. . . .

'First thing while morning!' Mrs. Tanner soothed her, also weeping again. 'It's over late now, you'll think on.'

'I'm going to my poor lass!'

'Ay, that you shall . . . you shall that!'

'I'll go, if I have to creep. . . .' She made a painful effort to reach the door, while the other twittered about her with nervous chirps.

'Nay, now, you can't do that. . . . It'll be a matter o' sixty mile! It'll do the poor thing no good, neither, now that she's dead and gone.'

The words brought her to a sudden halt, spreading their hopelessness on the evening air. She had forgotten, in her eagerness, that it was not a live Tibbie whom she went to seek. . . . 'Ay, that's so,' she admitted heavily, lifting her hand to her head. 'I'm fair moidered to-night,' she muttered at length; 'things has gone that fast . . .' and slowly, heavily, went back to the angry chair.

'Ay, sit still and rest yourself, that's it,' Mrs. Tanner coaxed. 'You must take care of yourself, think on. There'll be a deal to do at far end. I'll send them Rawlinson folk a card, saying you'll be coming by t' first train, and I'll get my Joe to ax 'em at t' "Red Cow" about the time. There'll be two or three things you'll want, likely, if you're going to stop. I'd best see about putting them up.'

Mrs. Clapham found spirit to murmur 'You're right kind!'—the identical speech that she had been making throughout the day, a sort of continual 'Selah' to recurring pæans of praise. Now it seemed as if the very words that composed it could not be quite the same; but then she herself seemed anything but the same. The silver bob of her hair had slipped from its moorings with the shock of her fall; loose hairs strayed across her cheeks, or straggled over the black gown. Her face, drained of its colour, seemed actually to have lost its shape, and wrinkles had come into being that were only the merest guesses before. Her eyes looked blind with age, with weeping, with mental and physical pain. Her hands shook as they wandered from table to chair, or came back to their miserable, fretting movement over her knees. . . . And yet even in storm and wrack she still looked wholesome and clean; fine even amid dust and tears and the crushing agony of her grief. It was chiefly the splendid buoyancy of the morning that was gone, the happy confidence, the gallant strength. Never again would she look as though she had suddenly been given the earth. Never again would she look like a ship coming homeward in full sail.

She roused herself a second time to find Mrs. Tanner hunting for something to serve as a rest. 'You'll be more comfortable-like wi' summat under your leg,' she was chirping thoughtfully. 'Whatever have you been doing to make yourself so lame?'

'Nay, I don't know, I'm sure. . . .' Again she put

up her hand and pushed wearily at her hair. It was quite true that for the moment she could not remember how the accident had occurred, so far had the events of the afternoon receded into the past. 'I fell in t' road somewhere,' she added presently, knitting her brows, and Mrs. Tanner, remembering the dust on the black gown, nodded a wise head. Still hunting for a rest, she came at last to the little chair. 'This'll do grand,' she began, picking it up, but Mrs. Clapham put out a hand.

'Nay, not that,' she said, quickly, without looking at it. 'There's summat else, likely, but—not that.'

'What, it'll do it no harm, will it?' Mrs. Tanner protested, puzzled. 'It's an old broken thing, I'm sure!'

The charwoman turned her head and gazed at it for a moment without speaking, and then—'It's—it's t' babby chair!' she managed to get out chokingly, and burst again into a storm of tears. Backwards and forwards she rocked under the fresh torrent of grief, almost tearing the good black gown with her working, sorrowful hands. 'Nay, I couldn't put foot on it whatever!' she sobbed, shaking her head so that the silver bob slipped farther and one of Tibbie's carefully-sewn hooks burst at her throat. 'It would seem near like putting my feet on the corpse of the poor lile lass herself!'

'Shove it in t' cupboard agen, will you?' she finished brokenly, turning her eyes from it at last, and Mrs. Tanner, weeping herself for the child who would sit in the little chair no more, shut it away in its dark sanctuary, as the child, too, would be shut away. . . .

The bursts of grief were growing shorter, however, as nature accepted her bitter toll. The poor mother sat quietly enough while Mrs. Tanner propped her leg with a tub, eased the strain with a cushion, and wound a wet compress about her knee; quietly, too, told her where to find pen and ink, post-card, and penny stamp.

The post-card happened to show a picture of the parish church, and, forgetting her trouble, she brightened sharply. 'Yon's where she was wed,' she began briskly; 'ay, send her that——' and then bit her lip with a deep sigh, and fell again to rubbing the black gown. . . .

Mrs. Tanner set a fire in the cold grate, put on the kettle, and began to prepare supper. 'You'll not sleep if you don't have summat to eat,' the little woman said, as she flitted about, 'and it'll be a bad job if you don't sleep. You'd best have a warm bottle in your bed an' all. I'll see about begging yon grand rubber one of hers from Mrs. James. And me or Mrs. Airey or Mrs. Dunn'll stop the night with you, if you want. I don't know as it'd be right, anyway, to go leaving you alone.'

Mrs. Clapham said again 'You're right kind—you are that,' in the same dull tone which was such a mockery of the one that had stood for ecstasy and beatification. She sat so still that she did not even turn her eyes as Mrs. Tanner flew to and fro, darting out into the road after her passing Joe, and yet again to signal to Mrs. James and to return armed with the rubber bottle. There was scarcely anybody else whom the stricken woman would not have resented at this particular moment, but it was quite impossible to resent Mrs. Tanner. Always, as she nipped in and out, quick and cheerful, yet never loud, she had the quaint, delicate charm of a hopping and flitting bird.

All the time as she worked she kept up a shower of twitters and chirps—'Eh, but our Joe is ter'ble put about on your account, Ann Clapham!' and 'My Joe says they're all crying their eyes out about Tibbie down at the "Red Cow"'—but Mrs. Clapham scarcely answered. In her state of misery and exhaustion the kindly sympathy hardly reached her. It did not seem possible that she could get to Tibbie to-morrow. Every bone in her seemed to ache, every muscle and every nerve; while the ache of her heart in the midst seemed to swallow up all the rest, yet continually sent out to them fresh weariness and fresh pain. . . .

She had tried to say to Mrs. Tanner that it was not hard, that somewhere and somehow something of which they had no definite knowledge meant it all for the best; and when the worst of the pain was over she would say it again. But, at this particular moment, although she looked so resigned, she could neither say it nor even think it. As the minutes dragged on, and Mrs. Tanner, stopping her flittings around her, suddenly flitted upstairs, she grew more and more sullenly angry and frigidly bitter. It seemed to her not only wrong but absurd that Tibbie should have died, that her beautiful day should have come to an end like this. She had been so sure of the goodness of God, and, while she was most sure, her daughter had lain dead. Her heart had gone up to Him in great chants of praise, and yet He had known that this waited for her on her very hearth. She felt so terribly put to shame that even in the dignity of her trouble she could have hidden her humbled face. Now she blushed for herself, remembering her childlike pleasure in her success. Others, too, she thought, would remember, and make mock of her love, wondering how it had been possible for her not to know. . . . For the time being even her sorrow was merged in bitter resentment at her own betrayal. Later, standing by Tibbie's coffin, self and its wrongs would be blotted out; but for the moment she could only remember that her confidence had been put to shame.

Mrs. Tanner had opened the back door during one of her many flittings, letting the last of the sun into the little cottage. Dipping through the mist in the garden, it sent a shaft of light slanting across the scullery; a sword of light, as it were, that came to rest just within the kitchen. It was as if the sun, that had come to honour the tenant in the early morning, had still another message for her before going. She had her back to it, however, sitting aching and grieving, full of deep bitterness and hard revolt. The world before her was dark beyond reach of light, even the terrible lightening of a shining sword.

She sank presently into a lethargy which was not sleep, but that dark, dreadful place where the soul no longer struggles to keep a hold on hope, but deliberately chooses for itself the eternal contemplation of woe. She sat hunched a little in the now voiceless chair, her head bent, her eyes dull, her legs stiff on the upturned tub. Her hands, which had now ceased their travellings to and fro, lay as if numb or dead on the lap of the black gown. She looked as if she had had such a severe blow that it had killed even the wish to rise—killed everything, indeed, except the power to refuse to move or to feel again. . . .

Upstairs, Mrs. Tanner's light feet drew an occasional light creak from the sensitive boards. Mrs. Clapham listened to them without hearing them; and then, suddenly raising her eyes, beheld Emma Catterall standing before her.

CHAPTER II

For a long moment she stared at her without change of expression; her brain insisting, as it had done of the cottage, that it did not know her. She belonged to her own section of this unending day, which was neither the far-off section that contained the House of Dreams, nor this present section which was wholly Tibbie's. But, each time they had met, the charwoman had been conscious of something that seemed to call to her for defence; and, presently, raising her head farther, she succeeded in bracing her tired mind.

Emma had been standing as still as a stone when she

first saw her, as if intent upon producing that apparition-like effect which seemed to be one of her pet vanities. Now, however, she came quietly forward and stood by the table, a roundabout figure with folded arms.

'This here's ter'ble bad news, Ann Clapham,' she began, in her smooth tones, her round little black eyes searching the charwoman's ravaged face.

'Ay. . . .' Mrs. Clapham's throat almost refused speech, while at the back of her mind was growing a dull wonder at the appearance of Emma in another's cottage.

'Ter'ble bad news it is an' all. . . . I don't know as I've ever been so upset.'

'Ay.'

'I heard tell of it from Mrs. James—yon stuck-up piece from over the road. I see her running with a rubber bottle, and handing it in here. . . . Eh, but I should think I cried for t' best part of an hour!'

Captured in spite of herself by this unexpected remark, Mrs. Clapham lifted her glance to the hard little face. Emma's eyes were certainly bright, and her cheeks flushed, but she hardly looked as if she had been giving way to turbulent grief.

'Of course, you might say it was a deal worse for me when my poor lad was killed in France, but there was things to make up for it, all the same. There was glory, and folks taking off their hats, and all such-like, as his lordship said. But there isn't anything cheering o' that sort when folks die same as Stephen's wife.'

The thing that Mrs. Clapham had heard crying vaguely for help aroused her now with a sharp tug. That claim upon Tibbie, which had frightened her earlier on, hurried her now into active offence.

'I'll thank you not to go calling my lass "Stephen's wife" to-night!' she burst out, so sharply and fluently that Emma actually jumped. Mrs. Clapham had raised herself even farther, and a faint ring had come

back to her dull voice. 'She married your Stephen
right enough, and right fond she was of him, too. But
she isn't your Stephen's wife, nor his widow, neither,
to-night. She's just my Tibbie and nowt else!'

Emma's flush deepened, and one of her hands
dropped from her waist to rest on the table; but before
she could answer, Mrs. Clapham had raced on.

'As for taking off hats and such-like, I don't know as
it makes that much odds. It won't give you back the
folks as loved you and held your hand. . . . I'm not
saying owt agen your poor lad as went down in France;
but do you think all they folks as knew my Tibbie
won't be lifting their hats to her in their hearts?'

Emma's mouth opened determinedly once or twice,
but each time she shut it firmly. She seemed to be
struggling equally with a desire to keep something in,
and an urgently-pressing desire to get something out.
The plump hand on the table twitched a little, and so
did the hand at her waist. . . . While she fought with
herself she kept her eyes fixed on the other's face, as if
willing her by that glance not to notice that she
twitched and fought. . . .

When finally, however, she did speak again, there
was a marked difference in her manner; so marked,
indeed, that its first effect was to make Mrs. Clapham
more uneasy than ever. She had allowed herself that
one hit at Tibbie's mother, that one scratch, so to
speak, at Tibbie's corpse; but when once that funda-
mental demand of her queer nature had had its way,
her whole procedure altered subtly. Her hands
ceased to twitch as if she were being torn in twain by
some inward strife. Even her colour faded a little, that
pronounced flush which seemed to speak of triumph
rather than grief; and into her black eyes came an
expression which was obviously meant to convey pity.

'Nay, now, you can't think I meant anything
against the poor lass!' she returned smoothly. 'She
was thought a deal of, was your Tibbie. A real

favourite she was, up and down t' village; and I reckon they thought a deal of her where she's been an' all.'

'What, she'd as many friends there as she had here!' the bereaved mother broke out feverishly. It was impossible not to talk of the dead, even to such as Emma. . . . 'She did a lot in the place—taught Sunday School, and a dress-making class, and she'd summat to do wi' Girl Guides. Parson was fit to put her in his pocket. As for the folks next door—Rawlinson's their name—them as sent telegraph, you've likely heard— they couldn't do enough for my Tibbie. Ay, and there's t' folks she sewed for an' all; they thought a deal on her, too. Nay, I reckon there won't be room enough for t' wreaths when it comes to putting 'em on t' coffin!'

'Mr. Wrench'll be rarely troubled when he hears t' news,' Emma said; 'ay, and t' parson's wife an' all. They always made out to think the world o' your Tibbie when she was here. It'll put 'em about to hear as it's happened while they've been off at the wedding.'

'She made Miss Marigold a pale blue *crêpe de chine*,' Mrs. Clapham said, and suddenly she began the eternal rubbing at her poor knees. A tear from the fount which she had thought dry welled swiftly, and ran down her stiff cheek. 'And nowt for herself, my bonny lass, but a linen shroud!'

She wept for a little while, passionately, but quietly. Even under Emma's eyes she could not help but weep, thinking of the girls who were exactly the same age, yet whom Fate had treated so differently, and who went so differently-robed that day. . . .

Emma watched her for a time with an immobility that might have indicated either sympathy or its suppressed opposite. 'Mrs. James said you hadn't a notion what took her off,' she observed presently.

'Nay, I can't think.'

'Seems to me there's something strange about that. She was always so strong.'

'Ay. Strong and sound all through!'

'Of course, if it was pneumonia, or one o' them such-like quick jobs. . . .' Emma, like Mrs. Tanner, had a score of suggestions to offer, but found them equally rebutted. Death was undeniable, and had a dignity of its own, but the sorrowing mother could not tolerate any hint of preceding weakness on the part of her lost darling. 'You'll be going to t' burying, likely?' Emma turned the subject at last, tacitly agreeing to leave it that Tibbie had not so much died as 'ceased upon the midnight with no pain,' and then, as the other nodded, she finished hurriedly—'I thought happen you'd like me to come an' all.'

'To t' funeral?' There came a sharp pause in the wearisome rubbing which was the outward expression of the fretting brain. Leaning forward with arms outstretched, she turned to stare into Emma's face. 'To t' funeral, d'ye mean?' she repeated in vague tones.

'That's what I thought.'

'Nay . . . nay, I never . . . nay, you mustn't think o' such a thing!' The colour flashed into Mrs. Clapham's face, and she stammered helplessly, looking away. It had never occurred to her that Emma might wish to be present, and the very thought of it was abhorrent. Yet what could seem more natural than that they should go together—the two mothers—the two grandmothers? . . . Nevertheless, it was simply not to be thought of, that Emma should stand beside Tibbie's grave. . . .

'Nay, you'd best bide at home,' she answered her firmly, though very uncomfortably. 'It's a longish way, you'll think on, and funerals is always a trying business for folks as is getting old.'

'It'll be a deal more trying for you than it will for me,' Emma disputed, though quite gently. 'And you're older than me, come to that.'

'Ay, but I've *got* to go, you see!' Mrs. Clapham put

up a desperate struggle. 'She was my lass. It's different for you.'

'She was Stephen's wife, as well,' Emma broke out sharply, her mouth tightening, and then checked herself equally quickly. 'Ay, but I was real fond of your poor Tibbie.'

'It's nice of you to feel that way, I'm sure. . . .' Mrs. Clapham's tone was more uncomfortable than ever, and the rubbing that began again was now not so much from emotion as to assist the processes of her mind. The something that kept calling to her for help was getting louder and louder with every minute. On no account must Emma attend the funeral, the something said, but for the life of her she could not tell what the impediment was to be.

'You're not so well, neither—not fit to go alone. Mrs. James said you'd twisted your knee.'

'A bit of a wrench, happen,' was the unwilling admission. 'I'll be right enough soon.'

'Anyway, I could help a bit if I came along,' Emma persisted. 'There's always a deal to do at a burying; always a sight o' work. There'll be the children to bring back an' all.'

'The children?' Mrs. Clapham sat up straight as a dart at that, her eyes nearly as bright as Emma's. It was plain enough now what the something was trying to say, calling and crying and clamouring at her ear. With a reeling mind, she fixed her eyes fiercely on Emma's face, but Emma's face never changed. Only the hand on the table twitched, and then the hand at her waist; and then the hand on the table again, and then the hand at her waist. . . .

'Ay, the children,' she repeated quietly, composedly meeting the other's gaze. 'You've never forgotten the poor things?'

But that, incredible as it seemed, was precisely what had happened. Mrs. Clapham's mind, which, only that afternoon, had accomplished with ease a backward leap of at least forty years, had, on returning, fallen short of the present. Like the chair, it had put its stopping-point at the new generation. Tibbie's death had brought back to her almost all that Tibbie had meant, but it had not succeeded in bringing her more than Tibbie. The child, indeed, had been with her, but not the girl with her scissors and silks; still less had she visioned the soldier's widow, with Emma's grand-children in her arms!

'I thought I'd best be on t' spot,' Emma continued, after the pause, 'seeing as the poor lile things'll likely be coming to me.'

The quiet words, falling so gently yet indisputably on her ear, acted upon Mrs. Clapham like a galvanic battery. In a moment she was stirred finally out of her dull pose, ready for battle, ardently on her defence. Scorn stiffened her backbone and put fresh energy into her frame. But for her knee she would have been on her feet in the first instant. Erect in her chair, she stared at the speaker with such mockery that the latter quivered.

'Coming to you? . . .' She repeated the words slowly, as if the mere sound of them in another's mouth was sufficient in itself to convey the fact of their arrant folly. 'My Tibbie's barns coming to *you*?'

'They're Stephen's barns an' all——' Emma began on a heightened note, and then checked herself, as before. 'Ay, well, they do seem to belong more to your lass,' she went on, with suspicious meekness, 'especially since my poor lad went down in t' War. . . . But somebody'll have to take and do for 'em, you'll think on.'

'I'll be fetching 'em here, of course!' Mrs. Clapham announced arrogantly, defying her with her eyes, her whole soul bent on concealing the fact that she had forgotten the children's existence. It was incredible, of course, so incredible that it frightened her, but it had happened, nevertheless. Also it made her ashamed, convicting her of selfish preoccupation in another's need. That, however, could be atoned for, later. The one thing that mattered at the moment was that Emma should guess nothing.

'They're Tibbie's barns, right enough, Emma Catterall!' she continued fiercely, glaring at her across the table. 'Don't you make no mistake about that! She always said as they was to come to me if by any chance she was took—not that we either on us thought as she ever would. But I've letters upstairs as is plain enough evidence what the poor thing wished. No lawyer'd go past 'em, and that's flat. And if it's plain speaking you're happen wanting as well, she couldn't abide you, nor the children, neither!'

Emma quivered again like a tightened fiddle-string, and then quietened.

'That's not very kind, Ann Clapham,' she responded patiently, 'and me with my poor lad gone down in t' War! . . . Seems as if you and me ought to draw a bit nearer together at a time like this.' She paused a moment, as if to allow her time to wince at the accusation of lack of feeling. . . . 'So you'll be bringing the poor things back here, will you?' she concluded gently. 'Ay, well, of course you know your own business best. . . .'

'Ay, I do that!' Mrs. Clapham eyed her hardly, refusing to be intimidated.

'That'll do well enough at first, likely, but what about later on? What'll become of 'em when you move to your new spot?'

It was out now—the thing to which Emma had been working ever since she came in, and in fear and defiance of which the dead had been clamouring in her mother's ear. Here again the incredible had happened, which was yet so perfectly natural in the overwrought state of the charwoman's brain. It was hardly surprising that it should have ceased to link cause with effect, half-paralysed as it was by shock,

and bewildered in any case by the events of the day.
Those last words, however, clarified it as a landscape
is clarified by lightning, while at the same time they
extinguished her temporary vitality like a blown
candle. There was no sense now in trying to conceal
the position from Emma, no use now in trying to hide
this last hiatus of a mother's mind. Slowly her body
sank down upon itself, as before, her head dropped,
her hands numbed. Her eyes returned to their vacant
staring at the floor. 'Nay, I'd clean forgotten about
t' house,' she muttered at last, in a voice that, along
with the rest of her, had grown terribly old. . . .

Nevertheless, in spite of her collapse, she was calling
upon her mind to make one further effort; that weary,
outraged mind which, during the last few hours, had
been torn so often from one point of view to another.
Given her own way, she would have sunk back into
black woe, but neither Tibbie nor Emma meant to
allow that. One on each side of her they seemed to
stand, fighting across her, besieging her dull ear.
Tibbie, at least, had a claim that she couldn't deny,
and least of all on her dying day. Emma, too, knew
what she was about, to come tempting her at her
weakest hour, even though she would go back with
her head in her hands and some searching criticism
for her pains.

For, after all, the decision was already made, and it
was sheer waste of time to ask her even to state it. As
if it was possible even to think of letting those poor
children go to Emma! Even in her grief she could
have laughed aloud at the very suggestion. It was
true that they still seemed a long way off—the poor
little pale mites who were so like Stephen—and so like
Emma! It was true, too, that at that moment the tie
that bound her was not of love nor even of blood;
nothing more noble, indeed, than jealous pride of
possession. But no matter what the motive that
constrained her, there could be no difference in the

result. Never in any circumstances could she hand
the children over to Emma.

She had forgotten the almshouse, as she had said,
but now, with the mention of it, it was coming back.
She had forgotten it as people in pain forget the sweet
time when they ran and leaped, as the long-crippled
forget what it meant to hunt, and the long-married forget what it was to love. Yet with her, as with all the
rest, it was there in her darkened mind; a far, shining
country at the back of beyond, a clear, golden country
at the edge of the coloured sea. And suddenly there
rose up in her a great longing and a great cry—the
passionate, anguished cry of her vanishing, life-long
dream.

She had been utterly wrong, then, so she said to
herself, from start to finish, from beginning to end.
There was no reward, after all, for honest toil, and
still less for childlike, trusting faith. God, or whoever
looked after things up above—or who didn't look after
them, as seemed much more likely—allowed you to
work and believe and hope for forty years, and then at
the end of them cancelled your heart's desire. Even with
a perfectly-justified heart's desire it was just the same,
a natural, praiseworthy heart's desire that couldn't do
any one any harm. Suddenly He demolished your
castle in the air, and as He demolished it He also
laughed. Mrs. Clapham felt that laugh thrill through
her in every nerve, as if it had been through the
medium of Emma He had chosen to laugh. Yet
Emma herself did not look like laughing at the
moment; was not so much as wearing her Gioconda
smile. Her attitude was her usual one of repression
and watchful calm; but behind it was a suggestion of
unusual fear and strain.

Mrs. Clapham, however, was engaged with another
problem than that of Emma's expression. Her
imagination, once more released upon the joyous
venture from which it had been dragged, was living

again through the wonderful morning and afternoon. Once more she felt the breathless rapture of expectation, followed by the more tranquil rapture of the accomplished fact; and once again journeyed on that voyage of discovery which came to an end on Hermitage Hill. She thought of the women with whom she had made friends; the tea-party, the butcher, and always, always of the house. They—by 'they' she meant the Almighty and Emma, somehow intermixed in her mind—had allowed her to have all that. They had given her the cup of those hours, pressed down and running over, and then they had emptied the cup and laughed. It was either muddle or mockery, however you looked at it, and to one of Mrs. Clapham's simple, orderly spirit it was hard to say which was worse. And suddenly she felt that, muddle or mockery, she wasn't able to bear it. The child in her, which had played with the toys of old Mr. T., rose and clung stubbornly to the House of Dreams.

Emma was talking again, she found, still standing there, still filling her with that hatred of God and her roundabout self.

'They don't take children in almshouses, so I'm told. They don't want 'em; it wouldn't do. Folks as is ready for almshouses is ready for rest, and there wouldn't be that much rest, wi' children always about. I don't know as it would be good for the children, neither, come to that. Almshouses is places where folks is sort of put away. I don't know as they'd be much of a home for them as is starting out.'

That 'put away' was a bad strategical error from Emma's point of view, and she realised it as soon as she had made it. It brought back a picture of old Mrs. Bendrigg to Mrs. Clapham—that bedridden, night-capped, wizened Old Woman of the Sea. . . . She turned her head slowly to glare at Emma and the Laughter behind her that was God, and Emma's hands twitched as she hurried on.

'Not that I'm meaning anything against them alms-houses, I'm sure! I've always heard tell they was fit for a king. What, yon time I was telling you of as his lordship come to see me about poor Stephen, he said as he'd like to live in one o' them himself. It all depends wi' almshouses and such-like who it is as builds 'em; but old Mr. T. wasn't the sort to go pinching the poor.'

The word 'poor', however, was a mistake, too, and Emma dashed on again to mend it.

'An honour, that's what it's always been, to have one o' them spots. That's why I was a bit down-like on Martha Jane—the likes of her to go setting up! It's folks like you them houses is meant for; folks as has lived a respectable life. Ay, well, you've got one on 'em now, and the best of the lot. Right set you've been on it all these years, and you've got it at last.'

Mrs. Clapham spoke at the end of all this as if she had not heard a single sentence. 'Them children'll come to me,' she said in a voice that was determined, if toneless and sullen.

Emma drew a long breath.

'Surely to goodness you don't mean as you'll let it slide! You can't go taking children to almshouses, as I said before.'

'I know that right well.'

'You'll send committee back word, after all?'

'Ay.'

'Let the house slip? Let yon Martha Jane——!'

'Ay!' It was almost with a cry that Mrs. Clapham cut through that last sentence.

'Well, I don't know what they'll say about it, I'm sure!' Emma's tone was still quiet, but she allowed herself a little righteous indignation. 'You've put 'em to a deal o' trouble and all that, and now it'll all be to settle again. I'm not sure as you've any right to send 'em back word, come to that. I'm not sure as they can't sue you. Anyway, it'll be queer if they ever give you another chance.'

'Time enough to think o' that!' The charwoman clung doggedly to her determination, even though the prospect of renewed waiting drew from her a heavy sigh. The sigh had a distinctly-cheering effect upon Emma.

'It'll mean you turning out to work again, won't it?' she inquired kindly. 'The children'll have their bit o' pension-money, likely; but I doubt you'll have to work for 'em, all the same.'

'Likely I shall.'

'Eh, but it's a shame, though, that it is—and you wi' your lame leg an' all! Not so young as you was, neither.' She was careful, however, not to lay too much stress upon age. 'You've a right to your rest.'

'I can work till I drop. . . .'

There was a pause, and then Emma changed her tactics again, or, rather, intensified them. Coming slightly nearer, she inclined her stiff little figure—the nearest approach that she had ever been known to make to an actual bend.

'Hark ye, Ann Clapham!' she began rather breath-lessly, and in a voice that actually shook. 'Let's talk this matter over reasonable-like; let's thrash it out, you and me. I don't mind telling you right off the reel as I'm right set on having them barns. You mustn't take it amiss if I mention for once as they're my grand-children as well as yours. When all's said and done, they're the barns o' my poor lad as went down in t' War. They're that like him an' all; it's only in nature I should want to have 'em. Likely they don't think much of me, as you say, but I could soon learn 'em. Children often take queer-like fancies agen the people as likes 'em best.'

Again Mrs. Clapham's face came slowly round towards the one that was almost bending over her. 'What was it you did to Poor Stephen?' she inquired dully.

Emma reddened in spite of herself, a dark-red flush

very different from the glow of excitement with which she had come in. As Mrs. Clapham looked, something seemed to rise up in her that would no longer be repressed, something that rose and rose as if determined to break into speech, but was finally beaten at the door of her open mouth. You saw it yield, as it were, sink, die down, fall and fade away, thrust back on its chain into the place from which it had come. . . .

'Nay, now, you're never going to rake that up again, surely!' she demanded, though quite gently. 'I never see such a clattin' spot as this here village! They'll never let owt die. I did think they'd put a string to their tongues when Stephen went down in t' War, but seemingly I was wrong. Of course I've known all along as they thought I didn't do right by my poor lad. A ter'ble grief it's been to me an' all, though I never let on. I shouldn't be speaking of it now if it was to anybody but you!'

She gave a deep sigh, crossed her arms and uncrossed them again, and it seemed to Mrs. Clapham that her lips actually trembled.

'That's all very well, Emma Catterall,' she replied presently, in the same dull tone of condemnation, 'but there's no getting past the fact you were right bad to Poor Stephen. You know best what you did to the poor lad; I won't say how I know it, too. But all the lot on us who was living here then know he was half-clemmed and nearly daft.'

'Stephen told you I was bad to him, I reckon?' Emma's tone was injured but patient. 'Stephen told your Tibbie, and your Tibbie told you?'

Tibbie's mother looked a trifle abashed. 'Nay, what, haven't I said we could all on us see it at the time?'

'Ay, but summat's been said—summat from inside,' Emma persisted gently, and Mrs. Clapham stirred uncomfortably.

'Ay, well, what if it has?'

Emma nodded sorrowfully, grief-stricken, but for-giving. 'Ay, well, it's only what I've suspected all along. There was I, fair breaking my heart over my lad while he was in France, and he miscalling me all the time behind my back!'

'He said nowt but the truth!' Mrs. Clapham flung at her brutally; all the more brutal because she was beginning to have her doubts.

'What he took for the truth, I don't doubt,' Emma corrected her sweetly. 'It was like this, d'ye see, Ann Clapham—it was Jemmy as couldn't abide Stephen. Jemmy wasn't much of a man himself, you'll think on, and it made him right wild that Stephen should be so weakly. It's the big men, you'll have noticed, likely, as is kind to cripples and the like; them as is weaklings themselves want their barns to be big and broad. Jemmy always had it Stephen was daft from the time he was born, but anyway, if he wasn't, he did his best to make him. Eh, but the rows we've had over the poor lad, and not stopping at words, neither! But he was my man, after all, Ann Clapham, and so I couldn't say much about it. We're both on us married folk, you and me, so you don't need telling you've to stand by your man. Eh, but it goes agen the grain with me, it does that, even to be speaking hardly about him to-day!'

Plausible as this explanation undoubtedly was, it seemed to have no effect upon Mrs. Clapham. Her expression was one of such pure contempt that in spite of herself Emma flinched. Her arms crossed and un-crossed with the regularity of some dull machine. The breath that she drew now was not a pretended sigh, but an urgent relief in a moment of fierce strain.

'Nay, now, Emma, yon tale won't wash!' Mrs. Clapham pronounced firmly. 'Jemmy was a wastrel—a real nowt—I'll give you that; but it was you and not him as played Old Harry with Poor Stephen.'

'Ay, I know that's what folks said . . . what poor
Stephen said an' all. It's right hard to have it thrown
up agen you when your poor lad's dead in France! . . .
You're a mother yourself, Ann Clapham,' she went on,
warming to an impassioned tone, 'so you won't need
telling what it's been like! But it was Jemmy as set
him agen me, as I said before; tellt him I couldn't
abide him, spied on him and a deal more—'

She broke off, then, however; even her amazing
armour not being proof against the other's stare of
superb scorn. Flushing, stammering, and choking, she
checked like a brazen bell into harsh silence. . . .

'Them's all lies, Emma Catterall, and you know it!'
was the terse comment of Mrs. Clapham. 'I don't say
Jemmy didn't do his share in harming the poor lad,
but none of us need telling it was you as did most.
Anyway, you could have fed him and darned him,
and seen to his poor wants. I'm a mother myself, as
you very rightly say, and I don't need telling *that*.'

'Ay, but it *was* Jemmy set him agen me——!'
Emma began again, losing her head completely, and
again choking and stammering into silence. There
was a moment's pause, while she stared at Mrs.
Clapham with the flush deep on her round face, and
then she flung her apron over her head with a sudden
sweep and a sharp wail.

'Eh, but you're cruel—cruel!' she sobbed on a high
note, her voice stabbing like a thin knife through the
draped folds of the coarse stuff. The charwoman,
twisted violently in her chair, gazed at her silently in
open alarm. It was as if a gargoyle on some church
had become a Niobe bathed in tears, or a cat worshipped by ancient Egyptians had opened its mouth
and mewed for milk. . . . It was terrible and grotesque,
and disturbed her beyond words; the more so that it
helped to confirm her recently-stirred doubts. . . .

'*That* cruel!' Emma continued to wail from behind
her screen. 'Supposing I *did* treat the poor lad as I

hadn't ought, d'ye think I haven't repented it long since? D'you think I wasn't haunted by it, waking and sleeping, all yon time he was out at t' War? It's easy to judge other folk, Ann Clapham, but there's a deal o' things hidden away as outsiders don't see. Folks as don't think a deal o' their husbands don't always care for their children, neither. You've seen a bit o' human nature in your time, and you know that as well as me. Happen I didn't treat Stephen right, but I've paid for it ever since. But there—what's the use o' turning your heart out to people as hard as you!'

Mrs. Clapham's mouth shut slowly as the passionate speech proceeded, and a shocked, almost humbled expression came over her face. The sullen resentment went out of it for the time being, leaving it normally human and kind.

'Don't take on, Emma!' she said at last, with a shake in her own voice. 'Likely I've been hard, as you say. . . . Fetch t' chair out o' yon corner, will you?' she added quietly, after a moment, 'and set yourself down afore we talk any more.'

There was a pause while Emma, still hidden behind the apron, apparently struggled for self-control; and then, with a long breath, she emerged slowly. As she seated herself opposite Mrs. Clapham, the latter saw that her eyelids were slightly reddened, and that the hard, round face looked haggard and strained. The growing doubt that was in her mind grew still farther as she looked, telling herself that unmistakably here before her were genuine sorrow and sincere desire. . . .

'Nay, I didn't care for him as a lad, and that's the truth!' Emma broke out again presently, still speaking a little unevenly. 'Happen things wasn't as bad as you think, but I don't know as that matters. I know well enough I didn't do by him as a mother should, and now that he's dead and gone, it fair kills me to think on. It wasn't till he was out in France that I found out what he meant; and eh! though I was right proud,

I was right shamed o' myself an' all! Ay, well, he'll not come back no more, and I can't make up to him as I'd like; but if so be as I'm given my way, I can make it up to his poor children. Yon's what I want yon barns for, Ann Clapham—to pay what I rightly owe. I know you're set on 'em because they're your poor Tibbie's, but eh! if you only knew how I wanted them that bad! Little Stevie now, wi' his black eyes and his white face—what, it would be near like having his father over again! Ay, and the lass an' all; I've always wanted a little lass. I'd be that good to 'em; I would that. I'd cocker 'em to their heart's content. There's nowt wouldn't be too good to make up for my badness to Poor Stephen. I'm young enough and I'm right strong, and I've managed to save a goodish bit o' brass. Likely I'd be able to send the pair on 'em to a good school. If you take 'em, you'll have to go back to work, give up your grand house, and start all over afresh. What, it'd be a real shame—you with your bad leg, and that tired out an' all, as anybody might see! Tibbie'd be put about if she knew she was doing you out of your rest. I doubt you won't find it so easy going back, neither. It'll be a deal harder, you'll see, than if you'd never thought o' stopping at all. What, it's only common sense, that's what it is, when everything's said and done! There's you with your plans fixed, and wanting your bit o' quiet, and me wanting summat to do, and a nice bit o' brass. There's you wi' no use, so to speak, for the poor barns, and me that sick for 'em I could break my heart! You think, likely, it wouldn't be fair to your poor Tibbie—going back on her, kind of—sort of letting her down? Ay, well, it's nat'ral enough you should feel like that; but the truth o' the matter is, it's the opposite way about. . . .'

Her voice, stammering and anxious, and growing more and more eager as she found herself allowed to proceed, died away at last into a fateful silence. Mrs. Clapham had kept her eyes fixed upon her while she talked, but as soon as she ended she turned them from her. She was saying to herself that perhaps she had been wrong in thinking that there was no possible choice. There *was* a choice, after all, and it was perhaps only fair that she should be asked to make it. In face of her new doubts as well as her new and amazing pity for Emma, she could not simply sweep her pretensions off the board. Never again would she seem to her quite the same woman as before she had disappeared under that apron. Slowly she turned the recent revelation over in her mind, weighing and sifting and making ready for judgment.

Was it possible, she thought to herself, that she had been wrong about Emma—that they had all been wrong, Stephen and Tibbie included? Nobody really knew what went on behind closed doors, and whether they spoke truth who brought stories to those without. Nobody really knew to whose account sorrows and sins would be placed at the last day. The charwoman, with the iron sunk in her soul, said to herself that she had been mistaken in God's goodness; might it not also be possible that she had been mistaken in Emma's badness? Repentance, at least, was possible, even for the worst, and in Emma's passionate outburst she had seemed to discern the ring of truth. Perhaps she really did think that she could make atonement through the children, and was full of a hunger and ache to pay her debt. Deep as was Mrs. Clapham's yearning towards them because they were Tibbie's, she knew that the loss of them would not break her heart. Undoubtedly, it was Emma who had the right to them, if she was speaking the truth; but who was prepared to say that Emma was speaking the truth!

It was at this point that she extended her bitter resentment to old Mr. T.—old Mr. T., who, only a few hours before, had seemed like an angel out of the past. While she was in his house she had been so grateful to him that she had cried, admiring and loving him for his kindly thought. Now she suddenly felt that he was only a stupid old man, after all. He had seemed at the time to be making her a splendid gift, while all that he was really doing for her was to tie her hands. He had been silly enough to imagine that, by making that rule, he was ensuring his old folks' comfort and peace, whereas all that he had ensured for this one at least was her total exclusion from Heaven. Old Mr. T. went the way of all her other ideals which had been intact only that very morning. God had failed her at one blow, and the glamour for which He stood; and along with God and the beauty of life went foolish old Mr. T. . . .

They sat there—the two bereaved mothers, the two grandmothers—with, as it were, the bodies of the children waiting decision between them. Stiffly erect, with arms folded at her waist, Emma's attitude in sitting was much the same as when she was on her feet. She kept her beady black eyes upon the battle-ground of Mrs. Clapham's face, reading the struggle that was going on in the big woman's tired soul. Over their heads Mrs. Tanner's light step drew an occasional creak from an old board, and behind their backs the light that was like a sword brightened and faded but always brightened again. . . .

They sat almost knee to knee, with the silence stretching between them that the one could not and the other dared not break, until at last it was snapped from without by the sound of a step on the stairs. The brightness of the sword dazzled Mrs. Tanner as she came to the bend, so that for the moment she could see nothing of the little kitchen. 'I've put yon few things together, Ann Clapham,' she began briskly, lifting her hand to her eyes; and then, as she hopped to the last step, her amazed glance fell upon Emma.

CHAPTER III

MRS. TANNER had to turn her back on the sword before she could finally believe her eyes. It was true, of course, that voices had reached her while she was upstairs, warning her that some other consoler had dropped in. Like enough it would be Mrs. Airey, she had said to herself, and had fully expected to see her when she came down. The sight, therefore, that actually met her gaze was simply paralysing in its effect. To find Emma Catterall inside anybody's kitchen was sufficiently staggering in itself, but to find her seated was almost beyond belief. The strangeness of it not only startled but almost terrified Mrs. Tanner, suggesting that something inherently sinister was at work. She felt, too, the ready jealousy of those who, engaged in helping others in trouble, instinctively regard them as their property for the time being. She reminded herself, however, of Emma's relationship to the dead Tibbie, and managed to stifle her feelings with an effort. Coming forward, she gave her a cool nod, which Emma acknowledged with a turn of her black eyes.

'I didn't know as you'd looked in, Mrs. Catterall. . . .' In spite of herself Mrs. Tanner could hardly keep the suspicion out of her voice. 'I hope you've said summat to comfort the poor thing.'

For the first time since her unexpected entry into the cottage, a hint of her famous smile played about Emma's lips.

'Ay, I think I've been able to say a word,' she returned gently. 'Not much, I doubt, but still— summat.'

Mrs. Tanner felt her suspicions intensify farther to the point of fear. Removing her gaze from Emma with almost obvious distaste she turned it upon the still figure sitting opposite. It could not be said that Mrs. Clapham looked any more cheerful, she thought to

herself, but it was certainly true that she looked
different. Before, she had looked broken and stunned,
sadly bewildered, deeply pathetic; but now, after
some mysterious fashion, the pathos was all gone.
There was something stronger about her, indeed, but
it was not a pleasant strength; not the glad, gallant
strength which had ennobled her in the morning. The
dignity of her grief had vanished, leaving her sullen
and bitter. Never once since Mrs. Tanner re-entered
the room had she as much as lifted her eyes. Mrs.
Tanner said to herself that she did not like the look of
things at all.

'I'm glad to hear it, I'm sure!' she made shift, however, to answer Emma with spurious heartiness.
('I'll be getting your bit o' supper now, shall I, Ann
Clapham?') 'Ay, it'll be a grand thing if you've helped
her along the road.'

'It's a sad business, of course; there's no getting
past that'—Emma drew herself up, and took in a big
breath—'but she's been fretting herself a deal more
than she need. It's bad enough, I'm sure, to have
gone and lost the poor lass, without fretting herself as
she'll have to loss almshouse an' all.'

'Eh?' Mrs. Tanner's mouth opened, and she stood,
gaping. 'Loss t' almshouse, did you say?' Emma
inclined her head.... 'What, but there's no need——'
she began again, and came to a sharp stop. She, too,
had suddenly remembered the children.

'Yon's exactly what I've been telling her,' Emma
took her up smoothly, precisely as if she had finished
her clipped sentence. 'Yon children o' poor Tibbie's'll
be wanting a home, if you'll think on, and she's been
thinking she'd have to take 'em and go back to her job.
But there isn't no need for anything o' the sort, as I've
pointed out. She can have her house as was fixed, and
the children can come to me.'

'To you?' Mrs. Tanner's eyes flew round to her
again as if pulled by a string, and her birdlike pipe

rose to a scream. It was as if something tiny and feathered and flitting had descried the appearance of an enormous cat. 'Nay, then . . . you can't mean it . . . they'll never be coming to you!'

'Ay, but I reckon they will,' Emma replied calmly, though her colour deepened. 'Mrs. Clapham and me have just finished fixing it up.'

Mrs. Tanner exploded without giving herself time to think. 'Nay, then, I don't believe it!' she exclaimed sharply. 'You've made a mistake somewheres, Emma Catterall, and that's flat!'

'I don't reckon I have.'

'What, she'd never think o' such a thing! It'd near finish her . . . she'd never dream . . .' Mrs. Tanner twittered, looking helplessly from one to the other, and then, as Emma's smile began to glimmer afresh, she turned desperately to Mrs. Clapham. 'What's she after, Ann?' she inquired miserably. 'You're never letting her have them barns?'

Mrs. Clapham stared at the floor.

'Ay, but I am.'

'Let her have Tibbie's barns?' Mrs. Tanner almost shrieked.

'Ay.'

'Her as her own lad——!'

'I've tellt you ay.'

There was a pause after that, during which none of them moved, while behind them the sword grew smaller and shivered and dimmed. Mrs. Tanner's lips trembled, and her eyes filled with her ready tears. She felt the presence of something between the two women that she could not fathom; something that, for the moment at least, it was no use trying to attack. She consoled herself with the thought that her poor friend would probably look at things differently to-morrow, especially after she had seen the forlorn little orphans—and Tibbie. But the new development had made her feel awkward and tongue-tied as well as afraid, and she was thankful when young Mrs. James appeared, cautiously peeping in.

'I just wanted to say about filling that bottle!' she began in a powerful whisper, too dazzled at first by the sword to see anybody but Mrs. Tanner. 'Don't fill it too full, you'll think on, or it'll likely burst. . . .' Her eyes discovered the two by the table, and she gave a gasp. 'Eh, Mrs. Catterall, yon's never you?'

Emma said 'Ay, it's me,' in her usual smooth tones, but Mrs. Clapham said nothing; and the owner of the bottle, feeling uncomfortable and abashed, was on the point of backing out again when Mrs. Tanner stopped her. With a jerk of her thumb towards the two by the hearth, she indicated that something was wrong, and that Mrs. James must help to amend it. The latter gaped and gasped a second time, and then stopped backing and edged in; and directly afterwards Mrs. Airey and Mrs. Dunn appeared at the door. They, too, however, when they had recovered from the spectacle of a seated Emma, became conscious of the tenseness in the room and prepared to depart; but they also were glued to the spot by Mrs. Tanner's urgently raised eyebrows and meaningly-jerked thumb.

'Ay, I tellt her one of us would be right glad to stop the night with her, if she felt that way inclined,' she began to flow forth suddenly in determined torrents of talk. 'She's ter'ble down now, poor soul—ay, ter'ble bothered and down! She'll feel a deal better while morning, likely, and a deal better after the funeral. There's summat comforting like, I always think, in seeing folks properly finished off. . . . Let's see now—I'll get her her bit o' supper and see her to bed, and the three on you can settle amongst you which on you'll stop the night. I'd stop myself, for the matter o' that (ay, and glad to do it an' all), but as I'll be going with her to-morrow, I'll be wanting a bit o' rest.'

Emma's voice fell smooth as an oiled hand across her passionate twitters and chirps. 'No need for you to put yourself about over that, Mrs. Tanner,' she observed quietly. 'I'll be going with her myself, seeing the children is coming to me.'

The information conveyed nothing to her hearers at first, and then slowly into their faces came wonder, followed sharply by terror. Into Mrs. Dunn's, indeed, there came naked horror—Mrs. Dunn, who knew only too well what it was like to deliver a loved one into alien arms.

'Coming to her?' Mrs. Airey demanded fiercely, her motherly face suddenly peaked and sharp; and 'Nay, now, she never means——!' shrilled Mrs. Dunn, in the voice that usually was so tired and flat.

Mrs. Tanner nodded a portentous head.

'Ay, but that's just what she does mean, and no mistake about it!' she explained loudly. She spoke roughly, fiercely almost—almost in a shout, as if the words were clubs with which she battered at Mrs. Clapham. 'She sticks to it Ann's agreed to let her have Tibbie's barns.'

'Nay, now . . . nay, never now! . . . she mustn't then . . . she just can't! . . .' The words seemed to come helter-skelter out of any mouth that opened to fling them first, an almost unintelligible chorus which yet managed to convey volumes. The women actually huddled against the wall, like sheep huddled before some dog. And then, just as the outcry seemed to be dying away, they began again—'Nay, now . . . nay, never now . . . she mustn't then . . . she just can't!'

This distinctly uncomplimentary outburst seemed, however, to have no effect upon Emma.

'Mrs. Clapham can't take 'em herself,' she condescended to explain, the calmness of her attitude making, as it were, an impertinence of the scene before. 'There's yon almshouse, you'll think on—she can't go taking the children there; so what wi' one thing and another, they'll be bound to come to me. . . . That's the way of it, isn't it, Ann Clapham?' she finished, turning to Tibbie's mother; and Tibbie's mother said 'Ay', staring immovably at the floor.

This final vindication, this triumph in the teeth of those whom she knew for her sworn foes, was perhaps a little too much for the careful Emma. Loosing her hold on her caution by ever so little, she allowed herself what proved to be a mistaken pleasure. 'Likely you've summat agen it?' she inquired of the women, her eyes shining with unmistakable malice.

More than one person present had plenty against it, as she knew, but she counted upon their lack of courage to take up the challenge. It was true that they had cried out, had given her plainly to understand what it was they felt, but she guessed that they would flinch when it came to stating their reasons. Until to-night there had been only one person who had ever openly flung her the truth, and that person was luckily absent. She was congratulating herself upon this particular fact when the unlatched door suddenly swung wide, and somebody who had obviously been listening in the porch almost tumbled into the room. She looked about her a moment in order to gather her scattered wits, and then—'I've summat agen it, for one!' proclaimed Martha Jane Fell.

The whole company gave a nervous jump when she tumbled into the room, as usual keeping up her unwarranted *rôle* of village clown. The effect, indeed, was almost as if she had entered it head over heels. Even Mrs. Clapham lifted her head to look at this latest comer. But Emma Catterall did more than jump. She had remained seated hitherto, as if conscious that no more intimidating spectacle could be presented to the crowd; but on Martha Jane's entrance she rose to her feet. Standing beside the table, she looked like a stout little pillar-box which had missed its allowance of Government red. Her eyes which, during that moment of triumph, had looked beady and bright, suddenly changed in expression, and became beady and dull. Her arms, which had remained still so long that it seemed they must have been clamped, released themselves now to their wonted mechanical act.

Martha Jane closed the door behind her by the simple expedient of kicking it to with an agile foot. There was something about her which nobody present could attempt to define, chiefly because she had never looked like that, or anything near it, before. She looked like somebody who had cried a great deal, and then laughed, and while she was about it had done the one as thoroughly as the other. Her face was haggard and drawn, so that from one angle she looked old; but she was also excited and flushed, so that from another she looked almost young. Her dress and her hair were both of them out of control, and she still smelt obviously of doubtful gin. Indeed, the whole effect of her was that she was still decidedly over the line, although more from some sudden astonishment than actual drink. There was a curious irony in the fact that such a respectable happening as an alms-house election should have produced these two—the wild, Bacchanalian figure that was Martha Jane, and the crippled charwoman, with her leg on a tub. . . .

'I've a deal agen it, and that's flat!' announced Martha Jane . . . and the shaft from the sun, which had almost departed, illumined her with an access of light. . . . 'Ay, and so will you all, when you've heard what I've got to say!'

It was Emma who answered her without pause, taking up the gage instantly, and smoothing her own voice still farther in order to heighten the contrast with the strident tones.

'Eh, now, Martha Jane Fell, you shouldn't come bursting in like that! 'Tisn't nice, when folks is in trouble, to come making a stir; and Mrs. Clapham's heart not what it should be—not by a deal.'

Martha Jane tossed her head.

'She'll thank me right enough, bursting or creeping, when she hears what I've got to tell!'

Emma's slow-growing smile conveyed a pitying patronage to the untutored savage. . . . 'Ay, well, you know your own business best, of course,' she rebuked her kindly, 'but I can't see how you know much about ours unless you were listening at t' house door!'

The hit was a failure, however, and Martha Jane only laughed. She did not mind being accused of a thing like that. Turning her shoulder upon her with a contemptuous shrug, she addressed herself pointedly to Mrs. Clapham.

'I'd like to say, first of all,' she began clearly, 'as I'm right sorry about poor Tibbie! I was that done when I heard t' news, I didn't know where to turn. I thought a deal o' the poor lass, though I don't know as we'd much to do wi' each other, her and me.'

Now it was Emma's turn to laugh, although in a perfectly ladylike manner. Martha Jane winced, but her head and her voice went defiantly higher.

'She was right decent, was Tibbie—eh, and that bonny an' all! Seems to me, looking back, she was much the same as I was myself . . . I don't set much by other folks' barns, as a general rule, but if ever I'd had a lass, I'd have liked her to be like yours.'

Again Emma laughed her ladylike laugh, and again Martha Jane flushed and winced. Mrs. Clapham's eyes climbed slowly and dully until they reached the intruder's face.

'You mean kindly, I don't doubt,' she said in that hard, sullen voice which seemed so strange from her kindly mouth, 'but I don't know as I'm wanting your sympathy, all the same.'

Martha Jane wilted a moment at that, and then flamed in the next instant. In spite of her exhilaration, she, too, was obviously on edge. The tears came into her eyes, but she flung them out angrily with a toss of her head.

'I'm right sorry, I'm sure,' she said in an injured tone, 'to have said I was sorry where it wasn't wanted! There's some folks, all the same, as appreciates feeling when they comes across it. Yon time his lordship lost his grandmother, he was glad enough of a pleasant word.'

There was a fresh demonstration of scorn at this, though not from Emma, who merely smiled. The usual glove thrown down evoked the usual answer from Mrs. James.

'You and your lordships!' she scoffed, from the huddle against the wall. 'Seems to me you think o' nowt else! Anyway, best-looking man at his lordship's grandmother's funeral wasn't his lordship. Everybody said it was Mr. Baines.'

'Baines!' Diverted in spite of herself, Martha Jane swung round as if on a pivot. 'What, he wasn't in t' same street!'

'Like enough—seeing he was streets ahead. A perfect picture he was, wi' his buttonhole and frock-coat!'

'A barber's block, that's about it, and near about as much sense!' Martha Jane had burst into the room a Bacchanalian indeed, but at least with some laudable purpose hidden behind. Now she was nothing better than a virulent shrew. 'And a buttonhole at a burying!' she concluded, with scorn. 'Real nasty, I call that!'

Any further support that might have been forthcoming on behalf of the elegant Baines was deprived of its chance by Mrs. Clapham. 'Say what you've got to say, Martha Jane,' she commanded, 'and get it by wi'. I can't stand a deal to-night.'

With a sharp twist the pivot twirled its occupant back to her former position.

'Ay, well, it's this, then,' she began in a quieter tone. Drawing herself up, she folded her hands, and a certain dignity showed in her figure. 'I heard Emma there say as she meant having Tibbie's barns, and I come in at the risk of a snub to ask as you wouldn't let her.'

'That's it . . . that's right . . . nay, now, you mustn't let her! . . .' Encouraged by this plain speaking, the Chorus broke into fresh protest. Emma opened her lips, but before she could speak, the charwoman put up her hand for silence.

'It's Martha Jane I'm axing to speak—not nobody else. . . . Tell me if there's owt else you want to say, and then get about your business.'

Obvious hesitancy came over Martha Jane at that, and she coloured slowly and dropped her eyes. With the toe of a broken shoe she traced a series of patterns on the floor. 'I don't know as there's owt more anybody need say,' she began lamely. 'All on us know Emma's isn't the spot for kids.'

'You're that well qualified to speak, aren't you—you wi' neither husband nor child!' Emma's smile was deadly in the extreme. 'And you wi' your repitation an' all, as perhaps one hadn't ought to mention,' she added pensively.

'Never you mind my repitation!' Martha Jane flashed back at her. 'If I don't mind it, I don't see why anybody else should. . . . Folks wi' titles and such-like manage to think well of me, all the same!' (A snort from Mrs. James.) 'But what I'm here to say,' she added quickly, 'and with the whole place backing me up, is that you oughtn't to have them children of Tibbie's.'

The pivot turned her half-left now, facing her straight at Emma. Her voice steadied again as she warmed to her subject.

'D'you think any on us has forgotten what you made o' Poor Stephen?' she demanded firmly. 'He's dead and gone now, poor lad, but we remember all right. What, I can see him now, with his poor, starved-looking little face! Seems to me, looking back, it was queer he come through at all; ay, and he wouldn't ha' done, neither, but for that good lass o' Mrs. Clapham's!'

Fury was running through Emma in sharp little

quivers, but she managed to speak calmly. She had seemed almost afraid of Martha Jane when she first came in, but, whatever the cause of the fear, it seemed to have died down. 'I reckon you know you're very near accusing me of murder!' she replied quietly, though with glancing eyes.

Martha Jane acknowledged this speech with a great scornful laugh. 'Ay, well, I don't know as I'll trouble to bite my tongue off for it, if I am!'

'And me with my poor lad gone down in France! ...' Emma's lips gave a sharp tremble, and Mrs. Airey and Mrs. Dunn, who up to this point would gladly have seen her burnt at the stake, suddenly felt their own lips tremble, too.

But—'He wasn't your lad!' Martha Jane flung at her cruelly, ignoring this touching exhibition of weakness. 'He was Tibbie's lad and nobody else's— Tibbie's making and saving all through.' Emma's lips trembled again, and she laughed callously. 'Nay, you can put on yon war-widow expression as much as you please, Emma Catterall! You won't get no pity from me! ... Don't let her have 'em, Ann Clapham,' she went on swiftly, turning pleadingly to the charwoman. 'Don't now—don't. Them poor barns with their white faces and big eyes! It'd be a blasted shame!'

The sincerity of her tone seemed to put courage into the women behind, for they drew away from the wall, and came crowding about her. It was certainly a tremendous event which drew even the elegant Mrs. James to act as echo to Martha Jane. In no other cause, perhaps, would these women who disapproved of her have condescended to come to her help; but this was a matter in which all women 'as *were* women', as Mrs. Tanner trenchantly put it, were one at heart. All women as *were* women, Mrs. Tanner found pluck to say, couldn't abide the thought of the children going to Emma.

'You'd regret it before they were well inside t'

house,' urged Mrs. Airey, suddenly seeing whole armies of little children crowding drearily into Emma's, and every one of them wearing the face of her own son. . . .

' 'Tisn't everybody as is nice company for children,' was Mrs. James's typical contribution. 'Folks in charge o' the young should have really refined minds.'

'There must be some road out of it, surely!' Mrs. Dunn pommelled her flattened brain. . . . 'Happen I might see my way to taking one on' em myself.'

'Ay, what, there's such a thing as boarding 'em out!' Mrs. Airey supported her briskly. 'There's plenty o' decent folk as'd take 'em for next to nowt.'

'Of course, it's a sad pity if you've to miss yon house,' pondered Mrs. James. 'But if ever you want another, you need only ask Mr. Baines.'

'Baines has nowt to do with it!' Martha Jane snapped, again forgetting the Cause for the irresistible lure. Even at the door of heaven she would have resented this continual trailing of the inevitable Baines jacket. 'It's his lordship as matters, when it comes to a choice. Baines is nobbut a pen-pusher, to do as he's tellt what! . . . You'd get a house right enough, though,' she swung back to Mrs. Clapham. 'Only, whatever you do, don't let her have them barns!'

The charwoman had remained silent during this concerted outpouring of opinion, all the more strenuous when it came for having been held in check. But the earnestness behind it was bound to have some effect even upon her dull wrath, her rebellion against fate, her bitter and sullen determination to snatch what she could from the damaged day. After all, it was only what in ordinary circumstances she would have said herself; what, indeed, was being said to her even now by her own heart. She reminded herself, however, that the clamouring women knew nothing of Emma's desire to atone; not that it was any use trying to tell them about it in their present mood. Led by Martha Jane, they would certainly laugh it to scorn;

or, even if they did not laugh, they would refuse to believe. It took some believing, too, Mrs. Clapham was bound to admit, with Emma's round little face expressing venom in every line. But then, even if she had come to repent, you could not expect her to change all through; and, repentance once granted, it was easy to argue that, the unkinder she had been to Stephen, the kinder she would probably be to his orphaned children. It was always the converts who went to the farthest extremes; they were the swing of the pendulum, the opposite side of the shield. Nor did it follow that, because you couldn't stand Martha Jane, you wouldn't be simply an angel to every one else. Mrs. Clapham had been as good a mother as there was in the whole world, but she, too, had never been able to stand Martha Jane.

Nevertheless, there was no doubt that Emma was not being an angel at this particular moment. 'You're a nice one to go preaching to others, Martha Jane Fell,' she was saying virulently; 'you that was dead drunk the whole o' this afternoon!'

Mrs. Clapham muttered 'Nay, now, Emma—nay, now, nay!' putting up a heavy hand; but already the words had had their desired effect. The Chorus drew away from about Martha Jane like a single soul, testifying to their personal worth by exclamations and looks of disgust. (Mrs. James remarked later that she *had* noticed a smell of drink—a really refined person couldn't miss it—but there, since the War there had been so little of it about, only them as fair lived for it could believe when they happened across it!)

'Yon lordship o' yours'll be rarely set up when he hears tell about it!' Emma finished sardonically. 'A bonny specimen for an almshouse *you* are, to be sure! . . .' And from the new huddle formed by the women against the wall came the indignant supplement from Mrs. James—'And her setting herself up to be judging of Mr. Baines!'

It was a bitter blow to Martha Jane when she found herself thus suddenly left in the lurch. Those moments of support from the respectable Clapham Contingent had been some of the sweetest in her not very sweet life. Now, however, she was once again under the ban, thrust back into the part of chief village sinner, beside whose delinquencies even Emma's looked pleasantly-pale. . . .

'Ay, and if I was!' she shrilled defiantly, as much to the virtuous Chorus as to Emma herself. Flushing, she threw back her hair, looking more Bacchanalian than ever. 'That's my own business, I reckon, as you say one had ought to know best! . . . But if you're that keen on folks minding their own business and nowt else, what have you got to say about yon telegraph, Mrs. Emma?'

A fresh quiver ran the length of Emma's stout little frame, and her arms fell away to her sides, as if they were struck. Mrs. Clapham's eyes suddenly sharpened their focus as they rested on Martha Jane.

'Telegraph?' Mrs. Tanner was saying, with a bewildered air. 'What, she'd nowt to do wi' that! I took it from t' lad myself.'

'Ay, there's been overmuch taking of other folks' telegraphs and such-like to-day! . . .' Martha Jane couldn't resist the slap. 'But I'm not talking about that telegraph, thank you, Mrs. Tanner. I'm talking of yon as come this morning.'

'A deal *you* remember about this morning!' Emma sneered in a breathless tone, lifting her arms as though they were hung with weights.

'I can remember all I want to, anyway, and that'll be more than'll suit *you*! I reckon I'm not the only one as see telegraph-boy riding up about eight o'clock.'

A fresh thrill of excitement ran through the room, drawing the Chorus towards her again, in spite of their horror of drink. Subconsciously they knew what was coming, as they had known about Tibbie's death;

and Mrs. Clapham, too, guessing the truth in that instant, waited rigidly, holding her breath. . . .

'Ay, I saw him, for one!' Mrs. Tanner piped excitedly. . . . 'Ay, and me,' added Mrs. Dunn. 'And me,' finished Mrs. Clapham, speaking with stiff lips. 'I made sure it was for t' Hall!' went on Mrs. Tanner, thrilling in every nerve.

'Nay, it was not for t' Hall, not it!' Martha Jane put her in place. 'It was a deal nearer home than that. Telegraph-boy took it to Emma, but it was intended for poor Ann. And if you want to know what it said, well, it said as Tibbie was dying, and would Mrs. Clapham here be sure and come by the first train. . . .'

For the first moment after the revelation there was absolute silence. Terrible as had been the suspicion at the back of the women's minds, it was still more terrible when put into words. The huddle at the opposite wall was more like a huddle of sheep than ever. Emma's lips were pressed tightly into a straight line, and her arms worked and worked as if they would never stop. . . .

Slowly Mrs. Clapham took her leg from the tub, and with a painful effort drew herself up by the edge of the table. Her eyes fastened themselves upon Martha Jane, who met the terrible glance without flinching.

'Are you meaning to say they sent telegraph for me this morning, and I never got it?' she inquired, speaking with difficulty.

'Ay.'

'Are you meaning to say Emma kept me from my dying lass?'

'Ay!' Pity and exultation had equal share in the slattern's tone.

'Prove it!' Emma exploded breathlessly, a-shiver from top to toe, and Martha Jane gave a contemptuous laugh.

'Ay, I'll prove it right enough, don't you fret!' she answered her, with an insolent glance. 'You see, it was like this—' she turned back again to Mrs. Clapham. 'Telegraph was addressed right enough to you inside, but outside one o' them Post Office hussies had put Catterall.'

('Eh, to think o' such a thing! Did you ever now! Eh, now, did you ever!' The stunned Chorus breathed itself back into audible life.)

'Emma was in her rights opening it, you'll think on, but she'd no sort o' right to t' news as was inside. She said nowt about it, though, all the same. She never let on. She just sat tight, and kept t' message back.'

'Ay, but why?' interjected Mrs. James, forgetting in her excitement that she had intended never to speak to the creature again; and the rest of the Chorus echoed her in a puzzled tone—'Ay, that's like Emma, sure enough! That's real like her—but why?'

'I reckon it was because she wanted almshouse message to get 'livered first. She wanted Mrs. Clapham here tied down. She knew if she got wind about Tibbie she'd be off like a shot, so she made up her mind to keep telegraph back.'

'Ay, but why? (Eh, did ye ever hear the like?) But, for t' land's sake, whatever for?' repeated the extra-thick-headed at the back of the room.

'Because she was after them poor barns!' announced the triumphant Martha Jane. 'She knew Mrs. Clapham was real set on yon house, and that she wouldn't be suited having to part with it when she'd got it. Likely she thought she'd be easier to handle about the children if things was fixed. . . . But if you feel like letting her have 'em, after that,' she concluded, dropping her tone, 'you're not the sort as I've took you to be, that's all.'

Emma had almost stopped quivering by now, and seemed to have got herself firmly in hand. 'You're talking ter'ble wild, Martha Jane!' she admonished her quietly. 'I reckon you haven't got over yon beano of yours this afternoon. I don't know as it isn't lower-

ing myself to discuss the matter at all, but where's
this telegraph you make such a song about, I'd like to
know?'

'Nay, *you*'ll know best about that!' The pivoting
prosecutor was swift. 'Kitchen fire could tell, likely,
if it was nobbut axed. . . .' Sweeping her off the earth
again, she turned back to the rest, happily conscious
of now being able to hold them as long as she chose.
'The fact is, I couldn't help feeling a bit down when
news come as I'd lost the house. I don't say as perhaps Ann Clapham here hadn't the best right, but still
there was more than a few as considered it might ha'
been me.' (She paused at this point, as if to allow an
opening to Mrs. James, but the latter was too ab-
sorbed to avail herself of the chance). 'Ay, I was right
down,' Martha Jane continued, with cheerful ease,
'and badly in want of a bit o' comfort. Likely I carried
it over far, being rarely troubled, but that's nowt to do
with the present matter. It took me as long to get over
the comfort, though'—she grinned impishly—'as the
disappointment!—but as soon as I was myself again I
writ a line to his lordship.' (Here she paused a second
time, even more pointedly than before, and Mrs. James,
awakened as if by a trumpet, obligingly played up.)

'Well, I tellt his lordship what I thought about
things in general, and while I was at Post Office
getting t' stamp, t' lass and me had a bit of a chat.
"Grand news this for Mrs. Clapham," says I, con-
versational-like, and she just gawps at me like a
coffin-hole. "Grand?" says she, as bright as a dead
fish: "you call t' news as her daughter is dying
grand?" . . . "What, surely to goodness you don't say
——?" says I, looking as much like a hen at a bucket as
she did herself. "Well, anyway, that's what telegraph
said this morning," said she; and then it all come out.
I was that puzzled I left t' stamp behind me on t'
counter, and they sent telegraph-boy after me with it.
"You was up our way this morning, wasn't you?"

I axed, as quiet as you like, and he says "Ay, message for Catterall!" as pat as butter. "Nay, what, you mean Clapham," says I, but he stuck to it I was wrong. "C.A.T.—cat; and a bad 'un at that!" says he, impident-like, and went flying off; and by t' time I'd reached home it come over me how it was.'

Emma punctuated this dramatic recital with a superior laugh.

'What, yon's no proof as I can see!' she protested scornfully. 'I tell you what it is, Ann Clapham, she's making it all up! You'll not have forgotten, likely, as she's after yon house herself? If she can saddle you wi' t' children, she'll have nowt to do but sail in!'

The next moment, however, even her self-possession had quailed before the terrible Martha Jane that came swooping upon her. This was, in fact, the very same Martha Jane that had damaged the lady of Lame Lane. In the midst of her moral darkness a gem of pure feeling had shone for once, and now it was being tarnished by the touch of a mean hand.

'It's true as God's Death!' she cried in a terrible voice, and swore another great oath in the next breath, one of those Tudor corruptions of God's Name which survive in a shrivelled distortion even to-day. 'If it's proof you're wanting,' she went on, as soon as this effort had sunk in, 'they'll repeat t' message when you like; but to say as I've let wit because of yon house is a bloody lie!'

'I don't say I wasn't set on it, though,' she added, more quietly, though with a touch of bitterness in her tone. 'It meant a deal more to me than you folks think. I'd ha' been right glad of a chance for starting afresh. But all the same I'd ha' held my tongue if it hadn't been for them poor children. Things was sad enough, as it was, without owt as might make 'em worse.'

'Them's just words—!' Emma began on a vicious burst, but the other snapped the speech at the stem.

'I'll swear it on t' Book, if you like,' she flung out—
'and a deal more!' Advancing to the table, she laid her
hand on the Bible, which Mrs. Tanner, in one of her
flittings, had slipped beneath Mrs. Clapham's elbow.
'If you'll do as I ax, I'll swear I'll refuse t' house!'

For a long moment they stood facing each other
without speaking, the respectable, honest-lived
woman, and the graceless, immoral slattern. Across
the table of scrubbed deal their two hands almost
touched; Mrs. Clapham's plump fingers bent to support her weight, and Martha Jane's long, thin ones
resting on the Book. The frizzled fringe of the one
foiled the clean silver of the other's hair; her trailing
and tawdry garments flared at the other's sober gown.
At such close quarters that they almost met, each
stared in the other's face, the one ravaged but wholesome, the other fevered and flushed and hard. There
seemed no point at which they could possibly have
anything in common, not even a mutual language
which could mean anything in their ears; and yet the
spark of true feeling which burnt in the heart of
the drab reached out to the same spark in the heart
of the good woman.

The huddle against the wall watched breathlessly,
mouths open, eyes wide. Even Mrs. Tanner could not
have spoken if she had wished. Emma, unnoticed,
uncared-for, a-quiver from head to foot, was also held
in leash by some outside power. The gods had
ordained this to be Martha Jane's special moment.

Mrs. Clapham was herself again at last, her own
courageous, splendidly-sane self. She was still weary,
of course, still grieving and broken and lame, but life
was swinging back again to its true proportions.
Under Martha Jane's stimulus she roused herself a
second time to weigh the matter that was at stake.
She did not need the telegram under her eyes to know
that the woman before her was speaking the truth.
Other things, speaking just as clearly, were before her

eyes, sign-posts pointing only too plainly to the irre-
futable fact. Emma's unusual 'joining-on', her fear of
the bell and the black gown, were all details striking
resoundingly a similar note. Especially was the
problem of the 'little chat' made clear, that sinister
conversation which had puzzled her so at the time.
She needed no telling now why Emma had insisted
upon the letter to the committee, why throughout the
whole of her studied talk there had been that deliberate
exclusion of herself. The dwelling upon the Catterall
likeness, the continual harping upon her health—
what were they both but part of the same carefully-
thought-out method to the same end? Last of all she
remembered the faces pressed to the Post Office panes,
and knew now why they had vanished, stricken with
horror, at her innocent smile. . . .

It was impossible, of course, to doubt that Emma
really wanted the children, wanted them passionately,
indeed, judging by the lengths to which she was willing to go; and perhaps it was harsh to insist that, in
face of such conduct, repentance was altogether out of
the question. She would not be the first, as even Mrs.
Clapham was well aware, to have done wrong in
order that good might come. Yet it was hard to believe that she could want the children for any kindly
purpose, that her blackened soul could under any
conditions change its skin. Would any woman, for
instance, with a heart softened either by nature or
time, have schemed to keep a mother from her dying
child? A fresh wave of sorrow engulfed Mrs. Clapham
when she remembered that, but for Emma, she might
still have seen Tibbie alive. No, there could be no
question now of entrusting the children to her, after
that.

Her expression changed slowly as she looked steadily
at Martha Jane, and for the first time she seemed to re-
semble the happy Mrs. Clapham of the happy morning.

'Nay, Martha Jane,' she said quietly, 'I can believe

you without that. You're welcome enough to the house, if you've luck to get it. And now that I know the rights of the case,' she added firmly, 'I promise them children shan't go to Emma.'

'And what about your promise to me!' Emma quivered and quavered, facing her red-cheeked, with rampantly-threshing arms.

'There's promises as is best broken,' Mrs. Clapham responded, without looking at her. Never again would she willingly look at the woman who had robbed her of her adored Tibbie's last glance. 'I'd be obliged if you'd be off home, Emma Catterall,' she finished evenly. 'I don't want no truck with you any more.'

'It's yon nasty beast as has put you agen me!' Emma quivered and shrilled—'yon drunken rattle-horn as we see lying all of a heap this afternoon. Ay, well, a nice tale it'll be for his lordship and all the rest o' the fools as promised her votes! There'll be nowt for her now in the shape of a charity-house, I can promise her that!'

'You'll do nowt o' the sort!' the charwoman stopped her with raised hand. 'You'll not mention it, d'ye hear? . . . Ay, and all t' rest on you'—she addressed the huddle against the wall—'you're none o' you to go making talk. And as long as Emma keeps her tongue in her teeth you're to say nowt about telegraph, neither. They could have t' law on her, likely, if they got to know, but as long as she keeps her tongue in her head the rest on us will keep mum wi' ours.'

'Nay, but what, it's a real shame!'—Mrs. Tanner began restively, and Emma snatched the words from her open mouth.

'Ay, it's a shame, that's what it is; and me with my poor lad just dead in France! Ay, well, I hope it'll be made up to you all, I do that! As for you, Ann Clapham, you'll likely enjoy going back to your job of doing other folks' bidding and slaping over their floors! I doubt it'll not be long afore you find as you've made a mistake. What, you're wore out now, as any-body can see—wore out ... done for ... ready for church-sod——'

A perceptible shudder ran through the elder woman, but she answered bravely.

'Ay, well, I can nobbut do till I drop. I shan't be the first to die in harness, I reckon.'

'I'd get t' children then, anyway!' Emma jeered, taking, however, a step to the door. 'Likely I could get 'em now, if it comes to that. I'm their grand-mother, same as you.'

'I've them letters, you'll think on,' Mrs. Clapham replied patiently.

'Letters? Ay ... so you say——!'

It was Martha Jane who came to the rescue again, striding across to the door, and flinging it open with outstretched arm. 'Get along out wi' you!' she ordered, pointing contemptuously towards the street. 'You've done your job for to-day, without ragging the old woman. We're sick o' the sight o' you. Get out!'

Emma began a fresh flower of speech upon the evils accruing to drink, but Martha nipped it relentlessly in the bud. 'Get out, or I'll sling you out!' she com-manded coarsely, in the lingo of Lame Lane, and Emma, as if pushed, sidled sharply towards the door. There she paused again to throw a last glance round the room, viciously at the Chorus, jealously at Mrs. Clapham, and—finally—a strange, long, greedy look at the photographs of the children. For the last time she unfolded her arms and clasped them again. Then, 'Ay, well, I reckon you know your own business best!' she remarked to the meeting in general; and, doing her best to fade as far as Martha Jane would allow, sidled towards the porch, and went balefully, stealthily out. . . .

Martha Jane, with her head round the door, sur-veyed the last of her up the street. Then she turned to the company with a ribald wink. 'I'd best be after her

and see what she's up to!' she observed, grinning.
'She's fit to set the street afire, she's that wild! . . . I
never thanked you for yon currant bread, Ann Clapham,' she added impudently, suddenly turning. 'I
was that mad when I see it first, I near flung it in t'
road; but if you've any more going begging, I'd be
glad to take it along!'

Nobody spoke in reply to this, and, looking round
the disapproving faces—almost as disapproving as
they had been for the late-departed—she flamed
violently into wrath. 'Ay, well, I'll be saying good-
evening then,'—she tossed her head on the threshold
—'especially as I notice there's no thanks going for
tackling the fair Emma!'

Mrs. James, who had been almost stunned by the
terrible unrefinement of almost the whole of the foregoing scene, now started into agonised life and
shuddered audibly. Mrs. Airey coloured all over her
kindly face, and Mrs. Dunn flattened and shrank.
Mrs. Tanner emitted a sudden twittering sound from
her birdlike mouth. But it was Mrs. Clapham who
answered the unspoken appeal, as indeed was her
duty and her right.

'I thank you kindly, Martha Jane Fell,' she said in
her sorrowful-mother's voice, 'for what you've done
for my Tibbie and me, and for my poor Tibbie's
motherless barns. . . . As for my currant bread,' she
added gently, 'as you're good enough to say you'd like,
I'll be right pleased to send you a loaf out o' my baking
o' next week.'

Once again, as at the table, across the Bible, the
eyes of the two women met and locked. Once again it
seemed as if some message passed between them, some
mystical form of touch; and then without any warning
Martha Jane burst into loud sobs. Holding her arm
before her eyes, she turned and stumbled into the
porch, and the long echo of her crying came to them
faintly down the street. . . .

When it had died away, Mrs. Tanner stirred briskly. Now that the storm was over, so to speak, she began preening her feathers and strutting about.

'And now you'll just have your supper, Ann Clapham, and as sharp as may be!' she chirped smartly. 'Set down again, if you please, and put up your poor leg! . . . Now, then, which on you folks is coming to stop the night?'

'Nay, I shan't want nobody, thank ye,' Mrs. Clapham put in quickly, before the women could speak. 'It's right kind, it is that, but I'll be best alone. I'll own up I was feeling bad a while back, but I'm better now.'

For a while they protested, however, standing about and looking distressed, but Mrs. Clapham remained firm. She sat down as ordered, and put her foot on the tub, and at last the superfluous helpers drifted reluctantly towards the door.

'I'll see t' house is ready agen your coming back,' Mrs. Airey said in her kind voice, 'and I'll be glad to lend a hand wi' t' barns an' all.'

'And I'll see as there's summat to eat for you,' added Mrs. Dunn. 'I've some currant bread o' my own, though I don't say it's a patch on yours.'

'I'll bring you a grand bunch o' flowers while morning,' was the charming finish of Mrs. James. 'I always think there's summat soothing about a real smart bunch o' flowers. . . . Eh, but I'm sorry about yon almshouse, though,' she reverted, as she went out; 'and nobody'll be more put about when they hear it than Mr. Baines!'

Then at last they were all gone, with the exception of Mrs. Tanner, and there was no need to thank them or answer them any more. Mrs. Clapham sat back in her chair with a long sigh. She did not sit forward, this time, sunk upon herself, staring sullenly at the floor. She sat back easily, wearily, closing her tired eyes. . . .

CHAPTER IV

AND still it was not much more than half-past six. . . .
Mrs. Clapham, lifting her lids at last with the effort of
one to whom every inch of her body is insisting that
the business of life is distinctly over, could hardly bring
herself to believe the face of the little clock. The
whole of her world had changed twice since it was half-
past six before. It seemed impossible that so much
could have happened within the round of a little day;
just as it is sometimes incredible that so little should
happen in the tale of a lengthy year.

But the business of life, far from being over, was,
from more points of view than one, about to begin
again. That it *would* begin again, when the moment
arrived, she was now able to believe, though even now
it seemed to her that it could be only a miserable
parody at the best. Nevertheless, before long it would
be creaking and jolting again in the ancient grooves,
although with ever so many extra drags on the wheels.
Foremost among them would be the children, hard as
it seemed to call them by such a name; but, dear as
they would undoubtedly grow to be, she could describe
them as nothing else. Some day, indeed, they would
be a help instead of a drag, but that was a long way to
look ahead. Not even Libby would be able to bring
any grist to the mill for the next half-dozen years, and
somehow the three of them had to live through those
difficult years first.

There was also the undoubted fact of her gradually
failing health, that terrible drag on the wheel of which
all with their living to earn go in constant dread. She
was not worn-out, as Emma had cruelly said, but it
was certainly cruelly true that she was worn. Weariness at least was in front of her, if nothing worse ; stiff
limbs and aching joints that would not allow her to
sleep. When the present strain had relaxed a little she
would be better than she was now ; but, however much

better she was, she would never be quite better. Never, whatever happened, would she be the same woman again. She would never be even the woman who had awakened so happily that morning. Both beauty and bitterness had taken their toll of her since then, and made her pay too dear.

The third and perhaps the worst drag on the wheel would be the inward reluctance of her own heart. Again, as Emma had so meanly and cleverly said, she would find it harder to go on now than if she had never stopped. She had taken her hand from the plough, and it would be a bitter business forcing it back. All through the hours of work, and the aching, wearisome nights, her heart would go stealing in spite of her to the House of Dreams.

Yet somehow or other this new fight that had been thrust upon her would have to be fought bravely and fought through. No matter what happened to lie before her, she must contrive to hold on until the children were old enough to fend for themselves. Her only consolation lay in the fact that every year that passed would be so much won by her in their favour. Even if the worst came to the worst, and her body gave out before her spirit—even then the struggle would not have been quite wasted. With each year that passed they would be not only older but braver and stronger, more and more able to cope with Emma should they fall to her banner in the end.

Thinking of Emma, she was again driven to wonder whether in all that tangle of plotting and planning there had lurked so much as a seed of sound, selfless, and honest love. Nobody who had known her of old would condescend to believe in it for a moment, and indeed the feat would seem just as unlikely to those who happened to know her now. Yet who could really say that beneath that growth of lies there might not be springing somewhere the tender sprout? Who could really say that a new Emma might not be quickening into being, brought to new life and growth by the strong forcing-house of the War?

That question, she knew, would be a further drag on the wheel, returning from time to time in order to give her pause. Again and again she would be tempted to go back on her word, to take her hand from the plough and forswear herself, even then. Always it would be in the background, ready to harry her at her weakest moments. Yet it was true that its antidote also would be always at hand—the memory of the inconceivable thing which Emma had done that day. The consideration of her possible motives went under again in an eddy of grief. If by any chance Tibbie had asked for her mother, and thought that she would not come!

Mrs. Tanner found her with the slow tears again stealing down her face, but she sat up at once and tried to stem them. Getting up, she limped to the glass, and began to smooth her hair with a comb taken from a near drawer. She also produced a clothes-brush, and allowed Mrs. Tanner to ply it; afterwards tying herself into one of her best aprons. She came back to the table looking a totally different creature, and addressed herself to the task of eating her supper like a tearful but plucky child.

They began, after a while, to talk of what was in front of them to-morrow, awkward, disconnected talk that became clearer and smoother as the situation grew easier. The food took the extreme edge from the charwoman's weariness, and the tea stimulated her nerves and heart. Mrs. Tanner noticed with satisfaction that she looked more and more like herself as the meal proceeded. Even the colour began to steal back fitfully into her white cheeks. It was a pity Emma could not see her now, Mrs. Tanner thought scornfully to herself—Emma, with her talk of 'finished' and 'wore-out', and unpleasant reminders of 't' church-sod!'

And still plunged through the scullery-door there

stayed a shaft of light that was like a sword, though it was getting paler and paler, and quivered from time to time as if it were urged away. Still it stayed, slanting to rest on the kitchen floor, still keeping its effect of a sword with its point transiently dropped to earth. . . .

'Miss Marigold's wedding-day's near about over,' Mrs. Tanner remarked suddenly, as they lingered over the meal.

'Ay.' The charwoman's lips trembled on the lip of the cup. . . . 'My poor lass made her a pale-blue *crêpe de chine*,' she said presently, as she had said to Emma, setting the cup down shakily on the edge of the saucer.

'She was a rare hand with a needle, was your Tibbie!' Mrs. Tanner nodded. 'I reckon them barns'll have everything just so.'

'Right as a trivet they'll be from top to toe!' A touch of possessive pride came into the grandmother's voice. 'I'll have my work cut out to keep 'em near as smart.'

'Ay, well, it's to be hoped they'll take after their mother when it comes to brains. Not but what they said Poor Stephen was smart enough when he was in t' Army.'

'They're sharp enough—as barns go,' Mrs. Clapham answered carelessly, but with the same underlying suggestion of pride. Mrs. Tanner's words had called up a vision of coloured prizes and shining medals, of quality applauding her grandchildren with elegant white-gloved hands. . . .

'Folks never repent it afterwards as does the right thing,' Mrs. Tanner asserted cheerfully, if with an unconscious lack of truth. 'They'll live to be a comfort to you, you'll see.'

'Happen they will.'

'It's right queer your Tibbie should ha' died on Miss Marigold's wedding-day,' Mrs. Tanner mused. 'Are you thinking o' going to t' Vicarage next week as afore?'

'I reckon I shall.'

'There's that knee of yours, think on.'

'It'll be better by then.'

'Ay, well, you'll not do that much work, I'll be bound!' Mrs. Tanner laughed. 'Parson's wife'll be that throng telling you about t' wedding!'

Mrs. Clapham said nothing in reply to that, but suddenly she felt as if she would not be able to endure hearing about the wedding. Indeed, at that moment she felt as if she would not be able to endure going to the Vicarage at all. Suddenly she had remembered the conversation of the evening before, and how in the midst of her own excitement the Vicar's wife had never once remembered the charwoman's hopes. It was almost as if, after some mysterious fashion, she had known what was going to happen. 'Next week, as usual, please!' she had said, as she went away; and in spite of the new life coming so near that she had actually touched it with a hand, it was going to be 'next week as usual, please,' for Mrs. Clapham, after all.

Mrs. Tanner, in the meantime, had passed on to another subject. 'Yon Emma's a real bad sort!' she shot out suddenly, and so fiercely that Mrs. Clapham felt as if she had received an actual peck. 'Eh, but what an escape it's been for them poor barns!'

'Ay ... and yet I can't help wondering, though, all the same. ...' Mrs. Clapham was still searching for that hypothetical sprout.

'Wonder all t' same what?'

'Whether she mightn't ha' treated 'em decently, after all?'

'Nay, now—you're never thinking o' going back on your word!' Mrs. Tanner pushed back her chair so sharply that it shrieked on the flag.

'Nay—not me! That's all settled and by with,' Mrs. Clapham assured her quickly. 'I—I'm beginning to want 'em, and that's a fact! All the same, I can't help wondering,' she added thoughtfully, 'whether she wouldn't ha' done by 'em all right.'

'Don't you get wondering owt o' the sort!' Mrs. Tanner responded vehemently, as she got to her feet. Her hands actually shook a little as she gathered the pots. 'There's only one thing she wanted 'em for, I doubt, and it won't bide putting into human words. I've not forgotten, if you have, how yon lad of hers used to look, a-creeping back to that devil's spot of a winter's night!'

'Nay, I've not forgotten, not I!' Mrs. Clapham said hastily, feeling rather ashamed, and for the fourth time that day seeing the vision of the little boy reluctantly climbing the dark stair. Looking out into the street, which was now full of September mist, she saw in imagination Libby and Stevie come creeping up. Hand in hand they came, clasping each other close, and with every step that they took growing slower and more afraid. Doors opened and voices called to them, but they never as much as glanced aside. Always they crept on, their mournful eyes fixed on their pilgrimage's dreadful end; making their sad way to the ancient slaughter-house which was Emma Catterall's suitable home. . . .

She almost put out her hands to clutch them when she saw them thus passing by, and, turning with a sharp start, caught her elbow against her cup and tilted it over. 'Eh, now, but that's a daft-like trick!' she exclaimed, pushing back quickly as the tea came pouring on to the floor.

'You're a bit jumpy—that's what it is,' Mrs. Tanner commented soothingly. 'Nerves a bit out of order, and no wonder, neither! It hasn't catched your gown, has it?—nay, it's nobbut the floor. Ay, well, I'll take a clout to it as soon as I'm through wi' my job.'

She went away with the pots into the back kitchen, and Mrs. Clapham, instead of sitting down again, began to wander about the room. She was still lame, of course, but the compress had eased her knee, and the stimulant of the tea had eased the ache of her tired bones. She stood for some time looking at Tibbie's picture, and wept again as she looked ; presently lifting a pitiful finger to the photographs of the children. Afterwards, staring about, she tried to imagine the house with the children in it, sitting or playing or running from room to room. Already their little coats and hats seemed to have taken their natural place on the bracket behind the door. She found herself wondering whether it would be possible to have the old chair mended for them, and then decided that it was too old. There were other things, too, that could no more be mended than the chair, things like the loss of youth and good health, and the terrible break of death. She was looking forward again now, patiently trying to believe that there was happiness still ahead ; but there was no disguising the fact that it could be only second-hand happiness at the best.

The pool of tea on the floor kept catching her eye as she stirred about ; the stain of it on the flags offending her charwoman's pride. It seemed to her it was the sort of thing you would expect in an old woman's house, an idle old woman who had grown too ancient to care. Each time that she came across it she stopped to mutter and frown. For the time being she allowed Mrs. Tanner's kindness to slip utterly out of her mind, choosing only to remember that she had forgotten the promised clout.

There came a moment at last when she could bear it no longer, and, finding the back kitchen empty, she stealthily limped in. Presently she emerged with brush, pail, and mat, and an expression of furtive excitement upon her face. Getting painfully on to her knees, she began to scrub, and almost at once found happiness coming back to her as if by magic. She was no longer afraid of life, now that she was at her job, nor of her own ability to cope with what the future might choose to send. Again, as in the morning, she turned instinctively to it for strength, and again found that it brought her courage, and that the touch of her tools brought her peace.

She scrubbed the stained patch over and over again long after it was clean, and felt her spirits revive with every scrunch of the brush. As she wiped off the soap only to put it on, for the second time that day she remembered the last words of old Mr. T. He had said that she was one of the fighters of life—a non-finisher, a never-ender. With a grim humour she told herself that he would certainly say so if he could see her now! She no longer felt bitter against the well-intentioned old man, and, indeed, in those last words found a distinct solace to her pride. God was put back in His heaven again as soon as she began to scrub; and along with her forgiveness of God went forgiveness of Mr. T.

Forgiveness seemed more possible than ever when her mind, without any obvious reason, returned suddenly to Mrs. Bendrigg. At least she would never see the heart fade out of her dream as she turned slowly but certainly into *that*! The truth was, she told herself sturdily, stopping to draw her breath, that she should never have asked for the almshouse at all. She could almost have blushed for herself for having descended to such weakness. Work seemed the only thing worth having as she lathered and scrubbed, and Tibbie's children no more than a feather-weight on her broad back. . . .

She had, later, one terrible moment when she remembered her promise to Martha Jane. The scrubbing brought to a stop with a sharp jerk, she sat regarding the prospect with acute dismay. Pride apart—and emphatically it would hurt her pride—it seemed impossible that she could ever go back again to the House of Dreams. She could shirk the promise, of course; there was nothing to bind her unless she chose; and just for the moment she felt that the only thing possible was to shirk. But her newly-restored judgment warned her that to weaken at any point was in all likelihood never to get through at all; and so, ratifying the bond with distinct ruefulness in her own mind, she put its obligations on one side for the time being, and went back again, though rather more dismally, to her work.

It occurred to her presently, however, that there was one side at least of the trying position which she had overlooked. Undoubtedly there would be some slight compensation in observing how the almshouses tackled the problem of Martha Jane! The thought of that self-satisfied *côterie* faced with Miss Fell as a neighbour tickled the charwoman even now. Indeed, it tickled her so much, combined with her own ex-periences of the afternoon, that she found herself, quite without meaning it, breaking into a laugh.

Mrs. Tanner, returning, could hardly believe her eyes when she beheld her upon her knees, and still less could she believe that laugh. 'Poor thing—she's a bit touched!' she said to herself, as she hurried in; and then, rounding the table, met the upturned face, tear-stained but normal, and wreathed with a joyful smile.

'Land's sake—and you wi' your bad knee!' she exclaimed anxiously. 'Why in the name o' goodness didn't you wait o' me?'

'Because it's my job,' Mrs. Clapham answered, sitting back on her stout heels. Her voice rang and her eye brightened. 'It's my job, and no doubt about it! I tell you what it is, Maggie Tanner; I doubt I'd ha' found yon almshouse parlish dull!'

.   .   .   .   .

There was still another task which she felt con-strained to fulfil before she would allow Mrs. Tanner to hustle her off to bed. The latter remonstrated when she heard her intention of writing at once to the com-mittee, but her protests had no effect upon Mrs. Clapham. 'If I don't write, I shan't sleep,' was all she would say, searching out paper and pen, and seating herself at the table for the last time. There had returned to her suddenly Emma's unpleasant remarks about her manners, arousing her obstinacy and her pride. Moreover, though she would not for worlds have admitted it to Mrs. Tanner, she was afraid for her strength of mind. In spite of the new courage that had come to her with her work, she could not trust herself to stick to her bargain unless she wrote the letter that same night.

It was a hard task, though, harder even than she had expected, and her spirits sank again as she wrestled with it. It was impossible not to remember, in framing it, what a different letter should have gone, by rights! Instantly, too, as she wrote, she was back again in the House of Dreams, living through, minute by minute, those wonderful hours. In spite of herself her mind insisted upon the treasures that it contained, pictured the furniture and the flowering currant, and painted the long view over the sea. She forgot the neighbours and their trying ways; forgot even old Mrs. Bendrigg in her bed. Once more she was safe enclosed in the temple of peace, tasting that exquisite bliss which is not meant for us outside Heaven. . . .

'i'm rite sorry i cant exept, and i hope as youll see and give it to Martha Jane——'

She dropped her head on her arms. For a long moment she sat and wept. Then again she took up her pen. . . .

And behind her, as if it were something else that she had taken up, as if a hand had suddenly lifted it from the floor and belted it to a brave side, the shaft of light that was like a sword vanished out of the kitchen, leaving it gentle and dusky with the coming night. . . .

5.49